THERE IS A SEASON

Also by Alice Ross Colver

THE MEASURE OF THE YEARS

THE PARSON

KINGSRIDGE

DREAM WITHIN HER HAND *(biography)*

UNCERTAIN HEART

THE MERRIVALES

HOMECOMING

FOURWAYS

and others

THERE IS A SEASON

ALICE ROSS COLVER

DODD, MEAD & COMPANY
NEW YORK

Library of Congress Catalog Card Number: 56-6830

Printed in the United States of America

This book is for my two very small grandsons

Stephen Dean Colver

and

Brandon Ross Colver

who may never read it or care if they do
but who, at a time of great difficulty for me,
played a most sustaining and joyous part in my life

CONTENTS

To everything there is a season, and a time to every purpose under the heaven . . . a time to break down and a time to build up . . . a time to mourn and a time to dance . . . a time to love and a time to hate; a time of war and a time of peace.

—Ecclesiastes III, 1–8

PART ONE

June 1756–August 1757

Chapter 1

PRUDENCE CLOSED THE TRUNK she had been helping her sister to pack, and, rising from her knees, moved to the window. Outside tall trees had laid black shadows on the emerald lawn beyond which a field of hay gleamed dull gold in the summer sun. The sweet dusty scent of it was wafted to her now on the light breeze, while her ears, attuned to listen, could clearly hear the bumbling of bees in the flower bed below, the tiny clacking of the twirling leaves of the poplar trees at the road's edge, the flutter of wings in dark secret places under the eaves. Following with her eyes the straight ribbon of road to where it dropped out of sight down by the rock quarry, she raised her glance to the curving line of surrounding low-lying hills in the near distance. They were so beautiful! No matter what the season, they were always beautiful. How could Mary bear to go away and leave them—leave any of this?

For this was home. It had been carved out of the wilderness by Pa when he had retired from the sea sixteen years earlier. He had built first a log cabin on the wide, windy hilltop, and then this cool and spacious house. With his own hands he had cleared the fields of the surrounding forests. He had put up his barns and started a young orchard across the way, and bought his livestock so that, come what may, the Martins would never be in want.

Here Ma had died. From here Andy, the student of the family, had gone away to the College of New Jersey. From here, too, Matt had run off to sea, leaving behind an Indian girl who was to die bearing a son he hadn't even known about. The slow tears crowded up as memory followed memory, but Prue blinked them back. For though the house had known sadness and a tragedy that would never be forgotten, it had known, also, great happiness. Had not David returned to her here after her long years of waiting? And had he not given her two darling children? Oh! She—Prue—was built into Martin Manor as much as its great chimneys and never would she want to leave it. But Mary, of course, was different.

A sound behind her made her turn. Mary, dressed in her full-skirted bombazine with its matching high-crowned bonnet, had given up trying to view herself whole in the small square mirror that hung on the wall and had turned from it finally in quick impatience.

"I can't half see!" she cried, her voice at once hopeful and despairing. "Tell me! How do I look?"

Prue's blue eyes surveyed the young, girlish figure before her with a glance that held in it a mingling of love, misgiving, tolerance, and pain. But love predominated. Before she could speak, however, Mary rushed on. "This ugly, muddy brown!" And her hand swept her skirt disdainfully.

Prue said gently, "It just matches the chestnut of your hair, Mary. I think it becomes you well. And you've brightened it wondrously with those little goldy buttons down the front." She came closer to adjust the small cluster of cherries nodding on the brim of the bonnet that framed Mary's piquant, heart-shaped face, and then her fingers fixed into a perky bow the ribbon that tied beneath her round, determined chin. In so doing she looked deep into the restless sparkle of the other's dark eyes, seeing there, as her mother might if she were alive, all the qualities that made her sister at once a joy and a worry. But she only said, "If there'd been time we'd have made up something new for you. Still, you couldn't have anything more serviceable than this for traveling."

Mary made a little face. "Serviceable! I do hate serviceable clothes! I'll be so glad to get there and have Esther's dressmaker start to work on those lovely silks and satins Matt brought home to us." She threw her arms around Prue in suddenly remembered gratitude. "I think you gave me more than my share of the goods, Prue."

The warmth of her embrace loosed one of the corn-yellow braids that Prue wore like a coronet about her head, and she released herself to pin it fast again.

"What use have I for silks and satins here on the farm?" she asked, with a smile. "Newark is a big place, and Esther mentioned teas and concerts when she invited you. It's you who will need the finery, and I'm glad you're to have it."

Mary said slowly, "Sometimes I'm scared to go."

Prue nodded understandingly. As Jonathan Edwards' daughter, Esther had been brought up in a sternly religious atmosphere. Now she was the wife of Aaron Burr, also a minister, and Mary would be obliged to live according to a strict pattern.

"I may upset them," Mary went on.

"You'll have to try not to," Prue said. But she was thinking that Mary might, indeed, do just that. She had upset Prue more than once by her fearless curiosity, her recklessness, her willful, capricious ways. Yet surely Esther knew Mary well enough to realize what company she was getting, having lived here in Stockbridge for a number of years before she married Mr. Burr. "You must remember," she continued, "that Esther has two small children, and you must help her with them as you have helped me with Mark and Faith."

"That part doesn't trouble me. It's—it's the atmosphere."

Prue smiled. "When the New Jersey college moves from Newark to Princetown in the fall, I understand from Esther that Mr. Burr will then give up his ministry and devote all his time to being the college president. That should ease the atmosphere for you somewhat, shouldn't it?"

Mary nodded. Then, pushing aside a voluminous skirt and a small coat for which there had been no room in the trunk, she changed the subject abruptly. "Prue, will you be sure to let me know if Matt ever writes you he's coming to New York?"

"Of course, Mary. Do you think to meet him there?"

"I'd like to. He's such an exciting kind of person to have around. I mean to tell everyone I've a brother who was once captain of a pirate ship. That'll make them sit up and take notice, I'll warrant!" Her eyes began to dance and she clasped her hands together against her breast and then threw them wide in an exuberant gesture. "Oh, Prue! I can hardly wait to be off! Do you know what it feels like to me—this going away? It feels like—like the very *beginning* of life." Her hands dropped to her lap. "Up to now, you know, nothing's ever happened. I've just marked time waiting for it to. Think on it! I've never been further off from this Indian Mission village than Sheffield! And that's not fifteen miles away."

Prue's blue eyes, meeting Mary's brown ones, held a complete understanding of her eager anticipation, though how they could when she, herself, never wanted to go anywhere, Mary didn't know. But that was Prue, always able to enter into the hearts of others and always willing to help them realize the secret dreams and desires she discovered there. Before such unselfishness, compunction smote the younger sister briefly.

"Prue, are you sure you don't mind my going? It leaves only Pa and the two babies to keep you company now that all the men folks have gone off to war."

"I mind, of course, but I want you to get away for this visit." Prue's face took on a soft, remembering look. "It isn't easy to feel the years slipping away when you're young, and hope slipping with them."

Prue knew. How well she knew! But it had turned out all right for her. David had come back—finally. And he would come back again whenever the British licked the French and Indians to their knees. So would Johnny, the youngest brother. But it wasn't the same for Mary, Prue said now.

"No." Mary's eyes dropped to hide a distant, secret look. "It isn't the same for me. There's no one to come back. No one at all."

Without answering, Prue rose and returned to the little leather trunk, and, lifting the lid, tucked in a pair of gloves that had rolled, unnoticed, from bed to floor. Some time ago—Prue did not know exactly when or why—Mary had made up her mind that of the few eligible males in the eighteen white families living here, there was none worth her looking at. Mere words would not change her opinion now. Well, let her go and meet others, then. Prue sincerely hoped she would. Surely in a place as large as Newark, the men would not, all of them, be serving in the militia at the same time as they were here.

Still kneeling, she said, "Write me, Mary. Write me

everything that happens. Everything you do and everything you think."

"Oh, I will! I will!"

But she wouldn't, Prue knew. She was not a good hand at letter writing the way Johnny was. She would write only when there was nothing more interesting for her to do. And she would certainly not tell Prue everything, because, for all her easy chatter and apparent guilelessness, she was one who kept her deepest thoughts to herself.

"Is there anything more to go in or shall I lock this now?" Prue asked, hearing Pa on the driveway below bringing Daisy and the wagon to a halt.

"Did you put in my bust-plumpers? And the paduasoy cape? And all my shifts? Are you sure? That's all, then. Yes, lock it, please."

Prue turned the key and gave it to Mary who dropped it into her reticule. Then Pa came stumping up the stairs, his dark, square, bearded face and his brilliant black eyes plainly showing how much he disapproved of this whole business.

A home was meant to stay in, not go gallivanting off from, he was thinking. Certainly the place contented him. Long before this it had won him entirely away from all hankering after the sea, though he had had some doubts in the beginning. He had hoped it would be a sure anchor for his children, too. But first Andy had gone off after college to settle in the west. Then Matt had run away, because he had the sea in his blood, Pa reckoned. Well, that being the way he was, you couldn't rightly blame him. (Matt had come back, though, and might have stayed if the Schagiticokes hadn't carried off his half-breed son.) And of course Johnny and David had had to go to war, so there was no blame to anybody there, either.

But now to have one of his two daughters flinging out

into the world—he did not hold with it even if it was only for a visit. Who would tell what it would come to, Mary being what she was, flighty-like and undependable? No, he did not hold with it. But he had had his say, and Prue, who had been the mother here for so long, thought Mary ought to have a change. And he never disputed Prue. Not any more. Not since that night she had been so bold as to bring Matt's newborn son home here and say she was going to raise him like a Martin. He had lost out then and had never faced up against her since.

All these thoughts went through Pa's head, as, scorning to pamper his stiffened right arm, he hoisted Mary's trunk onto his broad back and carried it, unaided, down to the wagon. Took more than a bad break badly mended and the gouge of a deer's antler in his shoulder to keep him from doing what he'd a mind to do.

The girls followed. Downstairs six-year-old Mark and three-year-old Faith ran out from the kitchen where they had been in the care of old Zeke and young Becky—the only slaves who were willing to remain on this lonely hilltop during these troubled days. Mary stooped to kiss both children and then turned again to Prue on the porch.

"Good-by, Prue," she whispered, a sob catching in her throat, to her considerable surprise. "I'll miss you. Don't —don't miss me too much."

Prue's smile held steady as did her voice, though Mary's departure would leave her bereft, indeed. She said, "I'll try not. I'll live for your letters, though. You will surely write often, won't you?"

Pa broke in gruffly.

"You think that stage wagon is a-goin' to wait on your special pleasure down at the store? You think it's runnin' jest particular to carry you from here to Albany? It's two mile to the village, remember. Esther'll likely go off without you if you ain't there."

"Oh, Pa!" Mary broke away laughing, and climbed up beside him. Once again she was all joyousness. "Good-by! Good-by!" she called, waving and blowing kisses to the little group on the steps. Then—"Wait a minute, Pa! I forgot something." She turned towards her sister. "How long do you reckon I should stay, Prue?"

Prue came close to the wagon.

"You don't want to outstay your welcome, Mary. But Esther did say something about being glad to have you there when she moves to Princetown. That would be in the fall. It would be a nice way to return her hospitality to lend her a hand then."

"All summer! And till after she moves? That's four or five months, Prue! Are you sure?"

"She's sure. She's always sure an' 'most always right. Set down, Mary. Gedap, Daisy."

They rode in silence for a while. Mary was thinking that though Pa had seemed to feel they ought to hurry, he was letting the old mare set her own pace as he always did. She could remember only one time when Daisy had been made to gallop. That had been three years ago. Would she ever forget that day?

There they'd been, the whole congregation sitting quiet as scared mice under the usual terrifying threat of Mr. Jonathan Edwards' sermon, when a strange man burst in through the front door, crying out in a hoarse and breathless fright—"Injuns!"

Not even Mr. Edwards had been able to control the instant pandemonium as men and women surged to their feet and crowded out into the aisle to surround the stranger and discover how close the danger lay.

After that it was all a blur in Mary's mind. She could

remember only a few things clearly. David's demanding voice saying over and over, "Which farm?" And Matt's huge figure literally shaking the answer out of the frenzied man. And Prue's white-faced look of agony when she heard the fateful words: "I'm tellin' ye! 'Twas the first farm as I come outa the woods."

Martin Manor. Their own place. It was their house that had been attacked, Prue's baby girl, Esther, killed and Aaron, Matt's boy, kidnapped. Mam Beck, the faithful Negress, had been struck down, too, but not before she had hidden Mark, Prue's oldest child, under a feather bed.

So Mark had been saved. And Prue had somehow lived through the premature birthing of little Faith in the very room where Esther had met her death.

It had been that day that Daisy had known the whip. Even now Mary could see her as she had gone racing out of the church grounds. And it had been because of that day that she, ever since, had tried by faithful and unselfish devotion to make up to Prue for all she had been through. It had not been easy, and Prue knew it. For that reason Prue had been quick to seize this first chance of both releasing and rewarding her sister.

The opportunity had presented itself when Esther Burr came to visit her father in Stockbridge. On an afternoon with Prue and Mary, the talk, naturally, had centered about the war and the threat under which this small village, remote from civilization, close to the wilderness and depleted of man power, constantly lived. Indeed, at this time there was only one young able-bodied private to protect them all.

"How do you stand it?" Esther asked with a shudder. "I've hardly slept at night since I've been here. How do you stand it, Prue, when you've already been through so much?"

Prue began to answer in her quiet way, when Mary broke in.

"It's horrible! We don't ever dare do a thing! Or go anywhere! We just sit and wait and wait and wait for something dreadful to happen. I'm like to *die* waiting!"

She knew, as Prue knew, that her outburst was caused as much by the dread thought that here she was nigh twenty-one—practically an old maid—with no romance you could call a romance behind her and little enough prospect of any ahead, since this war seemed likely to go on and on forever. Her desperation had sounded clearly in her voice, and Esther was quick in sympathy and understanding.

She said at once, "Why don't you come back to Newark with me when I go, Mary? You could meet new people and see new sights. There'd be teas and concerts and lectures, too. Could you spare her, Prue?"

Prue had assured Esther that she could, and now Mary was on her way.

At this point she was interrupted in her thoughts by Pa as he drew Daisy to a halt at the edge of the Martin property.

"Look around you," he said, in his most commanding captain's voice. "I want you to take a long look around afore you go down off this hill. Look back at the house first."

Wondering, Mary tossed a glance behind her. "I see it."

"No, you don't see it. I said *look* at it. 'Tis a noble house, my girl. 'Tis a gracious house. And 'tis a solid-built house, too, that'll stand against any storm that ever comes. Look at it close now an' remember what I'm tellin' you." He paused a moment. "Love built it," he went on abruptly. "And love lives in it the way it always has. You kin feel it like a blessin' fallin' on you the minute you go through the door an' Prue steps out with that smile o' hers to greet you. Your sister Prue's love, Mary, is as wide as this world an' as deep as the sea. And should you ever git to feelin' lonely or troubled by aught whilst you're gone, jest you stop and remember that Prue's love is reachin' out to you from that house." He paused again and cleared his throat noisily. "Mine, too," he finished gruffly. "Gedap, Daisy."

It was a long speech for Pa to make, and Mary was held quiet by it and by the rarely expressed emotion she felt lay behind it. She could not guess that what prompted him to speak so was the special kind of love he felt for her —and had always felt—because she was so much like her mother. It gave him a startle sometimes, for a fact. But when her mother had stepped out from her home in Boston years ago to join her life to his, she had had him —Mark Martin—to steer her course for her, whereas this child of theirs didn't even have proper ballast. Suppose she ran into squally weather down there, would she know how to trim her sails so as to come through safe? Well, he had said what he could the best he could. There was only one thing more.

"And look yonder at those hills," he went on sternly. "I tell you, Mary, there's no hills anywheres can give a body the peace and calm and—and—sense o' surety that those hills do. From anywheres on our land you kin look up and see 'em, I don't care where you're workin'. It always comes to me when I fix my eyes on 'em that God's in them hills. Winter and summer, spring and fall, He's there, workin' His marvels. And that's a good thing to remember, too, if life down in that city place fashes you any."

"It won't!" Lightly Mary turned aside from this disturbing gravity.

"You're mighty sure."

"I am sure. I'm going to love it down there. I know I am! Just think. Last week—nothing in sight except the same old humdrum I've known forever. And now—the world!"

"Newark ain't the world." Pa spoke out of his remembered knowledge of the Seven Seas. "Nor New York ain't, neither."

"But all the world comes there! To New York, at least. That's what I mean, Pa!"

"Mebbe. Well, don't fergit what I told you."

Silence fell again. The road dipped down now between high woods. Behind them lay the plateau that comprised Pa's land. Not to hurt his feelings—in case she had—Mary turned and gave it a last look. Yes, there it was. The broad level sunny acres, the neat thriving orchards, the pumpkin-colored barns, the tidy fences—and the large, white house, serene and dignified against the dark green of the wilderness to the north. A bulwark of peace, she thought.

But peace was not what she needed or wanted now. Life was what she wanted. Life—gay, perhaps dangerous, too—and free. Ever since Matt had come home from the sea with his tales of far-off places, Mary had felt this way. If only he had asked her to go along with him when he left again! On the other hand, Mary reflected, Matt had headed for the western wilderness, hoping to track down his kidnapped son, and the Connecticut Reserve was not the place she wanted to go. That was even more uncivilized than Stockbridge.

This was better, anyway. For think what lay ahead of her! First—the stage wagon to Albany. Then a sailing vessel to New York. Then a shallop or periaugue to New

Jersey. And then another stage wagon to Newark. All new experiences. All new places.

Albany–New York–Newark. The world! She was right, and Pa was wrong. It was the world. At least, it was the beginning of it. And who could tell where that beginning would end?

In time to the rhythmic klop-klop of Daisy's feet, Mary named the names over again. Albany–New York–Newark–

Newark. That was where Nick lived. But Mary doubted that Prue remembered this. Or that she even remembered Nick at all. Mary, however, had never forgotten. And she touched the little gold buttons on her dress with light, loving fingers.

Chapter 2

MARY HAD FIRST met Nick when she was fifteen. She was down by the rock quarry picking berries from bushes along the roadside when she heard the light tinkle of a bell, and, looking up, she saw a strange apparition topping the rise in the road at the edge of the Martin property. At first she could not make out who or what it was. Then the apparition took on the size and shape of a man—a tall, rangy fellow—who was bearing on his back a small trunk, attached to which and sticking out from which at all angles was an odd assortment of articles. As he drew nearer she could distinguish what they were. Brush splints, woven Indian baskets, strands of cane for weaving chair seats, and a pair of beaver hats.

He must be the pedlar of whom Amy Stiles had spoken to Prue, Mary thought, the one Amy's aunt from Guilford, Connecticut, had written about to Mrs. Stiles, saying that he had a wondrous plaster which was able to crawl after a pain anywhere on the body. Mrs. Stiles, being full of pains, had requested her sister to urge the pedlar to venture as far north as Stockbridge, and Amy had promised Prue that if he came she would send him on up to Martin Manor in order that old Zeke might try a plaster, too.

So there he was, walking with a quick, light step for all

his load, tinkling his merry little bell, and singing in a full, free voice,

"Rosa, will ye be mine now, mine now, mine now?
Rosa, will ye be mine now? Oh! Rosa, sweet!"

Catching sight of Mary, he stopped before her, and sweeping off his tattered hat, he bowed low with an easy grace, his hand over his heart and a white smile flashing at her. "And are you *Rosa,* perchance?" he asked, half mocking, half serious, and somehow wholly flattering.

Right then and there Mary's heart turned a somersault within her. But instinct prompted her to conceal her reaction to him and at the same time it gave her a boldness to match his own. Tossing her head, she replied, "No, I am not! And thankful am I for it!"

"Tut, tut, little lady!"

He came close, quite unoffended, and playfully shook his finger at her. And then she saw that his eyes were a startling blue against his bronzed skin and that his black lashes had the sweep and curl of a woman's.

"What's wrong with me that a first glance puts me so to scorn?" he asked, and he cocked a dark eyebrow at her in confident amusement.

"Your hat is battered and full of holes," Mary replied instantly. "Your hair is tangled in the most slovenly fashion, as if it had never been combed. And your shirt is none too clean."

"So long as the body 'neath the shirt is clean, I do not fret about the shirt," he said with a laugh.

"And," she went on, coloring before the intimacy of his words, "you have a wicked look in your eye. If, indeed, I were *Rosa,* never would I trust a man with a look like yours!"

Whence had come such impudence? She could not guess.

It had simply bubbled up in her naturally and irrepressibly. For that was what he did to her from the very first moment. He gave her a challenge out of which might come triumph or terror—or both. He filled her with a daring, defiant desire to seize that challenge. In short, he brought her tinglingly and excitingly alive. Never had she felt so before.

The memory of the details of their walk back to the house was lost in the confusion of her mixed emotions. She could only recall now that she continued to act the role she had first chosen—that of one who found him little to her liking—while all the time she wondered desperately if playing such a part were wise. But it had become fixed on her and, indeed, his blithe indifference to her clear contempt had spurred her to a still greater show of it.

Then they reached home and Prue came out to the porch steps, and Mary could sink down on the lowest one and try to pull herself together as Prue greeted the man.

"Oh, good afternoon! You must be the pedlar Mrs. Stiles has sent to us."

"Pedlar, ma'am?" Again the hat swept off, again the low bow, again the flashing smile and the half-mocking, half-serious, wholly sweet cajolery of his voice, as he quickly saw that Prue must be won to liking before he could pursue any kind of game, serious or playful, with her younger sister. "The word scarce gives me the credit I feel I deserve. I would humbly remind you that I am, of sorts, a doctor, though I do not lay claim to being a cure-all. I am also, upon occasions and when pressed, a preacher, having more than once prayed over the dead, though I have never united the living. Moreover, in lonely and distant places when the master is ill or absent, I have been known to oblige as a family man, at which times I am by turn, a cobbler, a hooper, a tinker, a tailor. Indeed–" And his look warmed with his own fervor. "–I am of the utmost possible value as a family man. Would you, perchance, have need of such at the moment?"

Prue, unused to so great a torrent of eloquence and unsure of the character of the stranger before her (for she had heard these pedlars were all rascals) answered sedately and warningly, "I am happy to state that I have several family men at my beck and call, thank you. My father, my husband, my brothers–"

He raised a silencing hand in pained chagrin.

"My misfortune. I'd have been pleased to prove my words to you by deeds rather than by echoing phrases. But since I have no choice, I will continue." He cocked his eyebrow at her as he had at Mary and went on. "I am also, if I may say so, a prime entertainer, being a spinner of strange tales born of the strange people I have met, the strange places I have been, and the strange experiences I have had. All vouched for as gospel truth with–" And now he slanted a mischievous look down at Prue and, lifting thumb and forefinger in the gesture of one taking a pinch of snuff, finished, "–with only the merest *bit* of fancy embroidering my stories."

Had she wanted to resist further his open, genial, persuasive friendliness, Prue could not have done so. But there was no reason for wanting to; surely such a command of language indicated he was well-born and well-bred. No doubt he was using this trade to satisfy his venturesome spirit and see the world, as her own brother, Matt, had used the sea. Besides, he was entertaining. And he had a most honest countenance and a most direct blue gaze. Seeing her guard relax, he went on, but thoughtfully now and with a becoming modesty, knowing he was on solid ground.

"You might, in addition, name me a trusted carrier of

the post, since many are the missives sent from here to there that I have willingly and freely and reliably delivered."

"I am sure of that."

"And finally, to cap all my accomplishments, I am a walking newspaper, gleaning the latest account of current happenings, local or national, wherever I go and passing it on at my next stopping place. Almost, you could say if you so desire, an historian. For what more does he do than I, save to record in ink and on paper rather than by means of the tongue and the vocal cords?" He shrugged and spread his hands in a gesture at once deprecating and pleading. "Yet you call me a mere pedlar!"

There was a smile in Prue's eyes now. "I begin to believe I have greatly underestimated your calling—and you," she said.

"You have, for a fact, ma'am," he agreed cheerfully. "Especially me," he added. And now he swung his trunk to the ground at her feet and commenced working at buckles and straps even as he kept on with his light and easy talk.

"Yet if you insist upon a trade name for me—Well, you have only to view my wares to know that I am no mean pedlar of small cheap trifles. Look!" He flung open the trunk, and Mary saw it packed to the brim with all manner of things, small items fitting into neat compartments in a tray or fixed securely in the lid, the larger ones compactly and tidily folded beneath the tray which he lifted out. "Here before you," he told them proudly, "are the contents of an entire country store."

"There are, for sure," Prue admitted, while Mary continued to hug her knees on the bottom step of the porch in a dazzled, breathless marveling. He had won over Prue, too, she thought. Her sensible, cautious sister. Did he have such a powerful effect on everyone? Oh, what a man! Handsome, gay, fearless, with the grace of a courtier and a mind full of wit and knowledge. And able, too. Such a one as he would undoubtedly make his mark in the world!

"I am a dealer in all manner of merchandise," he was saying. "From Bibles to buttons. From whangs for your boots to white goods for your—by the yard, I mean. From perfumes to pot holders. Take your pick." He knelt on one knee and looked at Prue with his quizzical, gleaming glance. "Or are you still searching for a proper name to call me by? If so, permit me to suggest the title of *mind reader*—unless the word *magician* might state the case more accurately. For how else, without such an ability, would I discover how to fetch people what they want? Or how to make them want what I fetch?" He rose to his full height and bowed again. "A pedlar you called me, I think. Let us settle this once and for all, ma'am. With your approval may I present myself as an artist. An artist who has learnt by painstaking practice to shape the wishes of the heart to the contents of the trunk. My name, Nicholas Fanshaw. Nick to my customers and friends."

"Mr. Fanshaw," Prue said, her eyes on a collection of ribbons and laces he had craftily exposed to her view. "You are, indeed, an artist. You have created in me a desire for more than a sticking plaster that crawls. Are you willing to tarry a bit whilst I examine a few of your things?"

"Ma'am," he replied softly, and for the first time since he and Mary had arrived at the house, his glance now touched the younger sister. "I shall find it hard, no matter how long I stay, to tear myself away."

So had gone the first visit. To Mary, the waiting for the next one and the one after that and the one after that had been endless intervals filled with a mingling of hot hope and cold despair. What had she hoped for? She could scarcely say. A look—a laugh—were enough to start the delicious little fires running all through her. But after he was gone they were not enough. Then, regretting her haughtiness, her pretended indifference, she found herself wishing, in an anguish of vague, frustrated desire for something more. A warmer touch, perhaps, than his hand folding hers over the shiny brass buttons that she had wanted for her brown bombazine. Or more meaningful words than the song he had changed and sang so carelessly.

"Mary, will ye be mine now, mine now, mine now?
Mary, will ye be mine now? Oh! Mary, sweet!"

Amy Stiles said he sang that to her, too, using her name when he did so. Oh! His blandishments, the same to all girls, and his laughing mockery, as if he knew her misery and delighted to provoke it! They put her in a rage, while the need to be special in his eyes, to bind him to her by something more than the purchasing of his wares, grew to be a craving in her.

And then she would wonder if, perchance, he was already married. That was when the cold despair struck through her, for he had never said, and she could not ask, having adopted an attitude of complete indifference towards him.

Thus nearly three years passed. Nick made five calls at Stockbridge and Mary both knew him and did not know him at all. By that time Amy had given him up and married someone else, but Mary only turned the more obdurately from all courtship because of the storm he had raised in her heart. Finally came a never-to-be-forgotten day.

Prue was not at home when Nick arrived that time and, after Mary bought all she dared, she watched, with desperation in her heart, as he packed up his little trunk. Did she mean nothing to him that he could so cheerfully start to whistle at his departure from her for another six months? She felt she could not endure it any longer. Here she was eighteen! Old—old—*old.* Was she to die unwooed and unwed?

His whistle ended and, looking at her, he rose to his feet, fastened his trunk straps, and then, reaching out in a swift movement, pulled her to him. Putting a finger beneath her chin, he lifted her face to his and she saw, for the first time, his blue eyes without laughter but ablaze with a fierce and frightening fire.

"You're a hoity-toity wench, Mary, and you've put on a fine display of disdain for me. But you've never deceived me. From the beginning I could see through you as if you were glass, and I know your feeling for me as I know mine for you. They are the same." He stopped and she felt his heart pounding against hers and thought his arms would crack her ribs. But abruptly he released her and stepped away, almost throwing her from him. And anger came into his voice, making it rough and hard to her ears.

"But you're too proud! And I'm too proud! So neither of us would ever forget you come from a fine house and a fine family whilst I'm a mere pedlar." He paused a moment as a flame of resolution suddenly swept the anger from his face. "But listen to me, my girl! It won't always be so. This I vow! Some day I shall have my own store set up in Newark, and my own business that will cater to only the grandest in town, and when that time comes I'll be back for you. If—" And he laughed as the mocking light returned to his eyes—"if I've not forgot you in the interval." Then he sobered once more and caught her hand again and again pulled her close to him. "Meantime, were you other than you are, I'd love you, anyway. But since that is impossible, I'll give you a taste of what love could be like with the pedlar, Nicholas Fanshaw!" And he bruised her face and mouth with such kisses that the world turned dark and tipped about her. Before it cleared and righted itself and she could get her breath to speak, he had swung on his heel and was gone.

She watched him striding off down the drive and down the road, tears of fury in her eyes, her hand to her throbbing lips. She had wanted to cry out and run after him but she had been held back—by what? She did not know then, and she did not know now. Insult? For his gay whistle had drifted back to her as if he had meant nothing he had said. Injury? But where did that lie unless it was that something now unfinished—and perhaps never to be finished—stood between them? Doubt? Uncertainty? Oh, she could not say! Only today she knew that not again would she let him so easily slip away from her. For surely if ever there had been a declaration of love that had been one, however rudely made.

What a fool she had been, she told herself for the hundredth time, to stand still there all a-burn, and do nothing while he went out of her life. For soon after that the French and Indian War began and Nick had not ventured to Stockbridge since. Not for three interminable years. Doubtless he had heard of the cruel murder of Prue's baby, and Mary could not blame him if he considered the wilderness stretches around the Mission too full of danger for a white man to traverse alone.

Had he forgotten her by now, as he had almost seemed to threaten? Had he married some other woman? Or had he, perhaps, opened his store as he had boasted he would?

Was he only waiting for success before he sought her again to make her his wife?

She did not know. But she had to have the answers during her visit to Newark, for Nick had taken possession of all her thoughts and feelings. It was as if, like the magician he claimed to be, he had cast a spell over her that could only be broken by himself.

Chapter 3

THE JOURNEY TO ALBANY in the stage wagon with its narrow, hard, springless seats was tiring and uneventful. It was a disappointment to Mary that, arriving after dark, she could see nothing of the city. Her only glimpse of it was a brief one as she and Esther sailed away down the river the next morning.

Esther was ill on the water, but Mary thoroughly enjoyed the three-day trip and moved freely about, talking to everyone. For this "forwardness" she was rebuked by her friend. "This provoked me," Mary wrote Prue later, "since I am not a child, and one of my pleasures in making this visit is to meet people. I did not, however, let my feelings betray me and do not mean to do so. But I will not be swayed by Esther's advice more than suits me and, I trust, in time she will come to realize I am as adult as she is."

In New York it was learned that the next sloop for New Jersey would not be departing until the following day. Accordingly Esther and Mary went to the Shakespeare Tavern—a quaint low building of small yellow bricks—where they were able to stow themselves and their trunks in one of the three tiny rooms under the roof. Then Esther said, "Now I will show you the city."

They went out into the streets. Mercy! What a bustle

and noise and scurrying everywhere! And what sights! The Fly Market where fine gentlemen in laced shirts and silver-buttoned cloth coats and flowered green silk breeches were to be seen doing their own purchasing of meats and carrying their parcels home under their arms or in a wheelbarrow. The groups of sturdy, well-fed farmers, some in wooden shoes, all with their hair pomaded by the orange butter they used. The scattering of half-naked Indians selling their game and fish. And, in the gutters, the ragged darkies who danced for pennies or eels. Mary, her brown eyes wide, her heart hammering with excitement, thought she would never get her fill of this teeming metropolis and secretly resolved to return here at her earliest opportunity.

Esther's voice, introducing her to someone, broke into her thoughts.

"Mary, may I present Mr. William Wilcox? Miss Martin, William. She is from my home town—Stockbridge—and is to visit me in Newark for a few months."

Mary turned, her eyes dancing, her face alight, and bestowed on the pock-marked and pallid young man before her one of her warmest and most brilliant smiles. The effect was instantaneous. William attached himself to them and constituted himself their escort. With him they saw the City Hall where the new Society Library was housed, the Slave Market, the Collect where people went to get their fresh water, the Trinity Church, and the fashionable Promenade there.

"He lives in a handsome mansion that is the talk of New York," Esther managed to confide in a whisper.

But the words had no meaning for Mary who did not find the prim and cautious young man amusing. It was with relief, rather than disappointment, that she heard him regretting a business engagement which necessitated his departure, and to his earnest promise that he would see her again in the near future she nodded indifferently.

Back, then, to the inn where word was awaiting them that the sloop for Amboy would sail within the hour. Once they reached Amboy a stage wagon would take them to Woodbridge, then to Elizabethtown, and then directly to Newark. It was a long way around to their final destination but, as there were nothing but rough riding trails on the Jersey side of the Hudson inland, a crossing of the river, though possible, was out of the question for the two girls with their several trunks.

Mary's first glimpse of the flat, red-soiled country side of the New Jersey colony brought her a keen disappointment. Why! It was naught but farming land with tilled fields and browsing cattle and the lethargy of calm living, everywhere she looked! It was exactly the same as home save that it was so flat—and hot. The heat was like nothing she had ever experienced. It was clinging and sticky, and she felt as if she were enveloped in a wet blanket. If she had any choice in the matter—after she found Nick—she would go back to New York. It might be as hot there as here but there, at least, life ebbed and flowed with the tides that brought in so many different boats from so many different ports. There, for sure, was excitement.

They were met at the tavern in Elizabethtown by Esther's husband, Aaron Burr. He had been visiting Governor Jonathan Belcher on a matter pertaining to the college, and with him, as he came forward to greet his wife, was the governor himself. He insisted on their all going to his mansion for tea, after which, he promised, he would send them on to Newark in his own private coach.

This was a pleasant break in the long journey, and Mary enjoyed her glimpse of the great house which was furnished, for the most part, with dark mahogany pieces brought over from England and many silk-like rugs from the Orient—all in marked contrast to the plain pine and butternut and applewood furniture and braided cotton rugs she knew at home. There were silver pieces too, and one in particular that stood on the tea table caught her eye. It was of a shell shape divided into two compartments, one holding sugar lumps, the other containing spoon sugar.

"This is called a 'bite and stir' dish," the Governor explained, seeing her interest. "By the way, I have a remembrance of having met you years ago when I lived in Massachusetts Colony prior to coming here. At that time I was a staunch supporter of the Indian Mission and of Mr. John Sergeant. I was visiting him one day and had the pleasure of being introduced to a Captain Martin who had with him a small child called Mary. That must have been you."

"I don't remember," Mary said, with smiling frankness.

"Naturally. You were too young." He went on, then, to say how much he had enjoyed his years in the cultured atmosphere of Boston and how—save for a few men like Aaron Burr—he found most of the New Jersey inhabitants "rustical."

True to his promise, he summoned his own carriage for the last lap of their journey. It was easier riding than the stage wagons had been, having springs to the seats. Even so, Mary was not sorry when at long last they reached the fence-enclosed parsonage on Broad Street in Newark. To her eyes it was much like a three-storied New England house with its center door and small portico and end chimneys. The only difference was in the new lightning rods that had been erected at each corner of the roof. The redemptioner woman, who had cared for Esther's children during her absence, was there to greet them, proudly saying both babies had kept well the entire time. Little Sarah, aged two, looked the picture of health, but in Mary's opinion young Aaron had a fragile look with black eyes far too big for his baby face.

Mary went at once to her room to change her clothes and to rest. Perhaps, she thought, she could get a letter written to Prue before supper, but when she lay down on her bed she felt too tired to do more than think about it. One of the things she would be sure to say, she told herself, was how surprised she was to discover Mr. Burr so much older than Esther.

"I really do not understand how she could marry a man so much above her in years," she thought. "And he is small of stature to boot. Never in this world would such a one attract me. Yet his manner is more courtly than ministerial and more gracious than stern, and I suppose this had its effect. At any rate, they seem to love each other as do Prue and David."

Did she love Nick in the same way? With the question came a resurgence of that mixture of misery and happiness her thought of him always brought her, and, crossing her arms under her head, she gave herself up to planning how she could find him in this place without appearing to search for him.

It would be difficult, for Mary was not given to confidences and not even Prue knew of what had transpired between her sister and the pedlar the last time he had been in Stockbridge. If anything had been settled then, perhaps Mary might have been less secretive, but the doubts that lingered in her mind were not ones she wanted to voice. Besides, for all Prue's friendliness toward Nick, Mary knew she would not approve any serious interest in him. Nor would Esther, were Mary to divulge the secret to her.

"I must move cautiously," she decided at last. "I must

very casually visit each day one or two of the dozen or more stores that are here, until I have been in them all. After that—"

But she could not see beyond that.

* * *

In the weeks that followed Mary kept to the plan she had made. Yet nowhere did she find Nick, and nowhere did she hear mention of him. He was not to be seen strolling down the streets with his pack on his back, though she strained her ears for all faint and distant sounds, hoping to catch the familiar tinkle of his bell. The only pedlars to come into her vision were the fish monger, who intoned his offerings in a nasal whine, and the meat man who announced his presence by blowing a horn. Sometimes a farmer came through on his wagon loaded with produce. Sometimes a traveling show, consisting of an acrobat and a trained dog or pony, made Newark a stopping place between Philadelphia and New York. But there was no sign of Nick.

Finally, casting discretion aside, Mary asked Esther if a Mr. Fanshaw who lived here was known to her. Esther said he was not. "Does he attend Mr. Burr's church?" she inquired.

Mary could not say. Indeed, she could not picture him in any church, come to think of it, though not to go was an awful wickedness.

"Is he a student at the college?" Esther then queried.

Mary replied, "No. He's a—a business man."

Naturally, Esther asked next what business he was in, and Mary, sensing her growing curiosity, replied a bit shortly, "I suppose you might call him a merchant. At any rate, he told me he had a store here."

"But there is no one by that name having a store here

in Newark, Mary. You've been in them all. You know that. Perhaps you mistook him? Perhaps he said New York?"

Newark—New York—they did sound somewhat alike. At least this gave her fresh, though somewhat frail, hope. For how would she ever discover Nick in New York? And when would she ever get there again herself, it being the distance it was?

Yet perhaps he was here, after all, and had just not been able to start his store. Or perhaps he had enlisted and was serving his time with the militia. That was, truly, quite likely. All she could do in such case was to wait for his return, meanwhile being watchful—

Esther's voice broke into her thoughts.

"Who is this Mr. Fanshaw, anyway, Mary? Where did you meet him? I've not heard you mention him before."

"Oh, la, Esther! There's no need to get excited! He's nothing to me. He's just a man who came to Stockbridge a few times with some goods to sell. Amy Stiles bought her wedding silk from him, and I promised her I'd find out if he could still match a sample of something else she had from him. I'll have to write Prue to tell her I can get no trace of him and will not bother any more."

There! That should silence Esther. And, thankful heart, Amy had, for a fact, commissioned her to match a piece of cotton goods, so no lie had been told.

Except a small one. For of course Mary was not really going to mention Nick's name to Prue at all. Not yet.

Chapter 4

MARY'S FIRST LETTER reached Prue in early September. She was weeding in her flower garden when Zeke turned in at the driveway with it in his hand.

"It's from Miss Mary, Zeke!" she said happily, as he gave it to her.

"Yes'm."

He hovered respectfully near for news, while Prue read and reread the words before her. It was an interesting account, she thought, of Mary's trip and other experiences, but somehow it seemed lacking in the enthusiasm Prue had expected. Was Mary disappointed in any way? Was Esther being difficult to live with? Or was the let-down Prue felt in the letter due to the fact that Mary had not yet met any attractive men? She had mentioned only the pallid and pock-marked Mr. Wilcox. Yes, that must be it. For Prue was aware that it was romance Mary wanted as much as she wanted anything. Seeing the world was merely her own private deception about her deepest wish.

Prue sighed faintly, and Zeke spoke. "Miz Mary all right?"

"Oh, yes, Zeke, she's all right. But I guess it isn't quite as lively down there as she had hoped."

Zeke shook his grizzled head. "Miz Mary, she one want to go slam bang into eberyt'ing. She can't go slam bang, she not happy." And he made his way toward the barn.

Left to herself, Prue read the letter a third time. And now the feeling came to her that Mary was not telling her everything. Something—some unhappiness—was being withheld. Oh, what wouldn't she give to have Mary as securely and serenely established as she herself was in wedded life! If only, in Newark, Mary might find another David!

"Well, it's early," she told herself. "Mary has been there scarce six weeks as yet. I must wait."

But it was hard waiting. And long before the next letter arrived, Prue received other news of a most disturbing nature. It was given to her the day the Sewing Circle met at Martin Manor.

"What do you hear from Mary?" Amy Stiles asked at once, her china-blue eyes bright with curiosity. As Mrs. John Pixley now, married a good two years ahead of Mary, her tone held a smug pride. How smart she had been, she was thinking, to drop her interest in that pedlar who used to come to these parts, especially now that she knew what she knew about him. Mary hadn't been so smart. And Amy would hazard anything that one of the reasons Mary had gone home with Esther Burr was to find out what had happened to Nick, for he lived down that way, he had told them.

"I had a letter about a week ago," Prue answered. "Would you all like to hear it?"

"Oh, yes! Tell us what she's doing down there!"

"I have it here in my pocket. Let me see—"

Prue's glance skimmed quickly over the pages. All the Sewing Circle was here: Amy and her sister, Anna Jones, Judith and Elizabeth Williams, and Abigail Sergeant Dwight. Prue must be careful what she said, for in no time the news she gave would be spread over the whole village.

So she read of the trip down and of the sightseeing in New York, although she carefully omitted all reference to Mr. William Wilcox. She read of Esther's house and of her two children, and then she paused. "I think that's about all. Oh, no! Here's one other item. 'Esther plans something out of the ordinary for me about twice a week,'" she read. "'Last week, for instance, Mr. Burr drove both of us to Orange to visit the famous gardens of Colonel Peter Schuyler. He has a rare collection of tropical plants, citrons, limes and lemons, as well as aloes and pomegranates and balsams from Peru. In addition, he has an enclosed park where deer and moose wander in captivity.'"

There were little polite murmurs of interest. Then Amy said, "Does she mention having seen Nick yet?"

"Nick?"

"Nicholas Fanshaw. The pedlar who used to come here so much. He lives down in Newark, you know." Amy's bright eyes screwed up to small pin points of light. Prue needn't act like that. She remembered Nick, all right! She probably just didn't like to be reminded that he was there so close to Mary.

For some reason unknown to her, Prue's heart took a swift downward plunge at Amy's words.

"Mary hasn't mentioned him," she replied briefly.

Amy was annoyed. Prudence Martin always gave herself airs, keeping her family's business to herself as if she were better than the rest of them and they not fitten to know what went on. Yet she wasn't one smidgen better. Look what her brother Matt had done. Lived with a squaw and got himself a son Prudence had to raise till he was stolen. Nary a word had she ever said about that, either. Well, if there was news about Nick, Amy would pry it out of Prue. And she could, too, because of what she'd learned about that young man since Mary left.

She said now vindictively, "Well, if she ever does say she saw him, tell her not to bother about trying to match up that sample I gave her. I wouldn't buy anything more from him if I was paid to."

There was a babble of eager questioning cries, but Prue said nothing. *Nick.* Nicholas Fanshaw, the pedlar. So he lived in Newark. Probably Mary had known it. And most likely she was building dreams around him because he was undeniably charming. Or would she be so foolish? A *pedlar.* Prue tried to remember how Mary had acted with him whenever he had stopped here, and it came to her clearly that her sister had always treated him with scorn. Surely, then, she entertained no wild or silly notions about him. Yet Prue was not reassured, for it occurred to her now that Mary might show her interest by pretending scorn.

She came back to the voices about her, hearing Judith put the question all wanted answered.

"Why wouldn't you buy anything from him, Amy?"

"Because he's a thief. That's why!"

The words fell into a stunned silence. Then Prue lifted grave, reproachful eyes. "Oh, Amy! That's a dreadful thing to say about anyone."

Amy turned towards her. "It's the truth, though. When I think how near I was to being taken in by him and his ways, it fair makes me shiver."

"How do you know he's a thief?" Elizabeth Williams asked.

And Abigail Dwight added, "Yes. What makes you say that?"

"Because the last time he was in Guilford he stole one

of my aunt's silver spoons. My aunt told my mother when she was visiting there this summer."

There was another silence. Out of it came Prue's voice, quiet yet indignant. There was no need for her to defend Nick, but common decency—and a vague, secret fear—demanded that she should.

"Could your aunt prove that, Amy? Perhaps she lost it herself. Perhaps it got mixed up with the leavings from the kitchen and was thrown out. Or perhaps—"

But Amy, sensing Prue's hidden disturbance and spitefully elated by it, interrupted with a shrill positiveness.

"No! She said they were out on the table, all six of them, the day Nick called there. And she remembered distinctly how he picked them up, one by one, and admired them extravagantly. Then, after he'd left, she discovered one was missing. There's just no doubt about it. Else why hasn't he been back to Guilford since?"

"Because of the war, perhaps," Prue suggested, her voice still quiet above the growing turmoil of uneasiness which Amy's words gave her. "He hasn't been here, either. Not for three years. Yet I never missed anything from my house. And I've heard of no one else who has."

Amy tossed her head. "All that talk about his starting a store some day, too! Did it ever get started? Does Mary mention it? No, I thought not. You just couldn't believe a word he said."

"What's more," Amy's sister joined in, "our aunt isn't the only one that's missed articles since Nick was there last. She's heard of several others who have, and they can't think of anyone to blame but that pedlar!"

"I think," said Prue, deliberately changing the subject as she rose from her chair, "that we will have a cup of tea now."

She wanted to ask Amy if she had ever voiced her aunt's suspicions of Nick to Mary, but she would not. Amy was a gossip. And if she thought for a moment that Prue was worried, she would enlarge upon that worriment until—somehow—the whole village would be talking about the way Mary and Nick were seeing each other—and Nick known to be a thief, too—when actually they weren't seeing each other at all.

For she knew, quite suddenly and certainly, that Amy's jealous eyes had seen what her own had not—that Mary had taken a fancy to Nick and that it was not seeing him in Newark which accounted for the lack of enthusiasm, the vague unhappiness, she had sensed in Mary's letter.

Well, then, what should she do? Send a warning not yet needed? But if there were a grain of truth in Amy's story, Mary should have that warning sooner rather than later, for her whole future happiness might be at stake.

Prue put the problem aside until the Sewing Circle had departed. Then she faced it squarely. Ought she to pass on this ugly rumor or remain silent? For rumor was all it was so far. She was of two minds about it. Mary was safe enough at the moment, apparently. Perhaps she would remain safe. Perhaps Nick had gone off to war. Or perhaps the rumor, having no foundation in fact, would die a natural death. On the other hand, there was no guaranty that the rumor wasn't truth.

It was knowing her sister that brought Prue to a decision finally. Mary was emotional. She was loyal, too, and generous in her thinking. This story, reaching her at the wrong moment, might only send her rushing to Nick's defense, denying everything passionately. Indeed, it might stir her to such a defiance that she would run headlong into Nick's arms.

Prue would wait to hear from Mary again. If she mentioned Nick, Prue would have her opening. If she didn't —well, if she didn't, Prue would have to face that moment when it arrived.

Chapter 5

FOR MARY, meanwhile, the days fell into a pattern. Morning prayers, breakfast, household tasks, the children to feed and bathe and air, marketing, or, perhaps, preserving, then lunch. After lunch, while Sarah and the baby napped, Esther was apt to pursue her study of Latin, since Mr. Burr desired her to maintain her proficiency in that line and assigned daily lessons to her. He, himself, at that hour, retired to his study while the redemptioner woman busied herself in the kitchen. Or there might be a missionary meeting, or sewing bee, or some other church gathering.

Sometimes this routine changed. If soldiers were grouping at the Training Ground preparatory to their departure for the war, Esther and Mary would accompany Mr. Burr, who always joined the men to offer up a prayer in their behalf. It had taken a year or more before New Jersey had shown any lively interest in the threat to the country in this crisis, for most of the Indians in the Colony were peaceable and friendly, but after incursions of the savages along the upper Delaware and Susquehanna—savages who were allies of the French—and after hearing the tales of the Pennsylvanians who fled for safety into New Jersey, the inhabitants bestirred themselves and contributed money, as well as raising a number of full companies.

Even so, terror did not hang over the town as it had hung over the village of Stockbridge in the northern wilderness, and the marching off of the boys was much less grim. It might almost be called gay, in fact, with the gifts and the martial band and the kissing all around.

Barring this local excitement, Esther might plan an afternoon excursion for Mary. After the visit to the Schuyler place, the two women together (for Mr. Burr was otherwise engaged) rode horseback to a Mr. Clark's in Rutherford, where guests from New York as well as New Jersey had gathered for the day. Here everyone was invited to pick roses from the magnificent gardens and then to watch the distilling of these into rose water, a tiny bottle of which was later presented as a gift to each visitor. It was that day that Mary met the DeLanceys from New York who owned some famous race horses, and it was that day, too, that she again saw the pallid and pock-marked Mr. William Wilcox. He immediately attached himself like a cocklebur to her side. Indeed, before he left he invited Mary and Esther to a place of entertainment in the city known as Ranelagh's, the next time they should be in New York.

"Where is that?" Esther asked. "I don't think I know it. And what kind of entertainment is offered there?"

Goodness gracious! Such care and caution! Mary thought, a trifle impatiently. It must be truly terrible to be married to a minister and have to consider every move you made to be sure you were setting a good example! But Mr. Wilcox was answering.

"It is the Anthony Rutger's place near Thomas Street and Broadway. When he built there he drained the swamp at the foot of his hill where Broadway ended. Perhaps you know that area as Lispenard's Meadow. His house he left to his married daughter, and it is presently leased to a Mr. Jones. The entertainment, I assure you, is of a high class. Sometimes there are concerts or singing, violins and flutes. Sometimes there are lectures. Sometimes there's an exhibit of a strange wild animal in a cage on the lawn. And always the food is excellent and the gardens beautiful. I trust you will permit me the pleasure of escorting you both there in the near future."

"It sounds delightful, Mr. Wilcox, and we thank you for your thought of us. A visit to New York will not be possible immediately, nor, indeed, for several weeks to come. Perhaps later—"

"I shall consider that a promise and will remind you of it," he said earnestly.

With this Mary had to be content. Though not amused by Mr. Wilcox, she was yet desirous of accepting his favor for the chance of being in New York again. For in New York, perhaps, she would find Nick.

* * *

It had been July when Mary arrived in Newark, and it was September before she learned anything about Nick.

The two months had, for the most part, been hot and humid, a kind of weather that Mary found most trying after her years in the Berkshire hills. Esther took refuge from the sticky discomfort behind closed doors and shuttered windows, but Mary felt as if she would smother staying inside that way.

So she would put on her coolest dress and her broadest-brimmed bonnet as a shelter from the sun and sally forth into the streets where, by now, she had a speaking acquaintance with many church members and a nodding friendliness toward others not of Mr. Burr's congregation. Sometimes she would go to Mrs. Duncan's house where the widow, who was Esther's dressmaker, was already at work on the lovely silks and satins Mary had brought with her. Sometimes she would go to Market Street to pick up an item Esther wanted or had forgotten. But most often she would take that opportunity to venture to a new area along unknown streets where she had never been before, in the unfailing hope that there she might discover Nick.

Thus it was that one day she came upon a Dutch house set off by itself in a sparsely settled section of Newark and presenting so charming an appearance she could not help but pause before it. The first floor was built solidly of stone that had weathered to a pinkish-gray, and its long roof swept down in a lovely curve to hang over a narrow "stoep" that ran the full width of the house. Before this "stoep," and, indeed, covering the whole little plot of ground clear to the pathway where Mary stood, was the gayest, brightest garden she had ever seen. All colors danced in the hot sunlight and, above them, bees and humming birds hovered in an audible ecstasy. As she gazed, she became aware of another sound, and, looking toward the house, she saw a plump, blond Dutch girl of about her own age, with a black apron over her green dress, sitting in the shade of the "stoep" and singing a soft lullaby to the baby she was rocking in a cradle with her foot, while her hands were busy with flying needles.

"Trip a troup a tronjes,
De vaarken in de boonjes,
De koefes in de klaver–"

A little stab of envy went through Mary, and for a brief moment she deplored her own restless spirit that would not permit her to enjoy such a simple happiness but drove her to a wandering and a seeking in a big and beckoning world. Then, on an impulse, she turned into the neat walk between the flower beds and followed it up to the house. As she approached, the Dutch girl ceased her singing, and, with her finger on her lips in a warning gesture, rose.

"Will you come in?" she asked, in a whisper, her Dutch accent marked, her round rosy face beaming in friendliness. "It is so hot out there! I give you a cool drink of water. You like?" And, pushing open the lower half of the heavy front door—the top half was already swung back—she led Mary inside.

The room into which they came was the full size of the house, with great rafters showing in the ceiling overhead. Around the wide-throated fireplace opposite the front door were blue and white tiles picturing Bible scenes, while on the narrow shelf above stood a row of pewter plates, all agleam, and at one end a rack of long tobacco pipes. Two high-backed wooden settles faced each other before the open hearth, before which (and, indeed, all down the full length and breadth of the room) fresh sand had been swept into a lovely swirling pattern.

"It's a shame to walk on it!" Mary exclaimed.

"Nein! No!" her hostess laughed, and she walked, herself, to the pail and dipper that stood on a bench in a corner. "I can sweep again. 'Tis no trouble." And she waved to Mary to seat herself on one of the settles where she brought her a cup of clean cold water.

Mary nodded her thanks, her eyes on the numerous pots and skillets that were hanging neatly on their respective hooks in and around the fireplace.

"You cook here," she said.

"Cook, eat, and sleep." The girl's blue eyes twinkled as she observed Mary's puzzled gaze taking in the meager furnishings, which, besides the settles, consisted only of a table, a chest of drawers, a tall cupboard, a dry sink, and two straight chairs. "You think there is no place for sleep?

Wait! I show you!" And she moved to an end wall where a curtain of heavy blue-and-white material hung from ceiling to floor. Drawing this aside, she showed Mary how a wide bed had been built into an alcove hidden behind the curtain. In the wall at the foot of this bed and slightly above it was a smaller alcove, really a mere niche, where a second tiny bed was made up.

"For the little one," she explained.

"But why don't you use the cradle that's on the stoop?"

" 'Tis better not," the other returned. "So—this way—I reach at night without my feet getting cold."

Mary laughed. It was good to talk to someone "rustical," as Governor Belcher had expressed it, for the erudition of the Burr household was a bit oppressive at times. Soon Annetje was showing Mary her treasures—her linens and her Delft plates, heirlooms which were always a part of the Dutch dowry. Presently she learned that the Dutch girl knew she was a guest of the Presbyterian minister's wife.

"I see you many times," Annetje said, dimpling. "I see you when you walk with yourself. I think you lonely little bit, maybe. Ja?" And she peered with a bright, friendly curiosity at Mary.

"Not lonely exactly but—" Once again Mary responded to an impulse by asking Annetje suddenly if she had ever heard of a Mr. Nicholas Fanshaw.

"Fan Shaw. Fan Shaw." She made it sound like two words. "Nein," she said regretfully. Then her face brightened for a moment. "Wait. I think I hear my man, Jan, speak such a name once. What he say?" She frowned, trying to remember. Then, as it came back to her, she looked at Mary in a troubled way and shook her head. "Is not good."

Mary leaned forward in a tense eagerness. "You mean

you can't remember what your husband said about him?"

"Nein. What I mean—what he say is—Fan Shaw not good."

"Oh, he *is!*"

Annetje appeared first startled and then uncertain before Mary's swift vehemence and contradiction. "Maybe I make mistake," she said slowly. "Maybe Jan not know same one you know."

Mary hardly heard.

"Where does he live—this one you know—Jan knows, I mean?" she demanded. "Where did he see him? Tell me!" She drew a quick breath and changed her tone. "Annetje," she finished, in a soft pleading, "it means so much to me."

"Ja," Annetje nodded understandingly.

"And I'm sure you're mistaken—Jan's mistaken—about his being no good. Why! He's one of the handsomest, ablest, cleverest—" she stopped.

"You love him," Annetje said. She was thinking. Possibly her Jan did not like Fan Shaw on account of that fight they once had. And when the fight was over, Jan's money was gone. Oh! He had been angered when he got home that night with one eye shut and no money to see with the other! But she had said to him, "Well, you will go to the tavern." Yet not truly scolding, for a man must take a little drink now and then.

"Where does he live?" Mary was repeating.

"I not know."

"Oh, you do! You must!"

Annetje shook her head. "But I tell you where Jan see him. If you go by the Training Place and by the swamp on the south side Market Street and come to the Salt Meadows on edge of town, could be somewhere along there you find him. When Jan is bringing the cows home sometimes Fan Shaw is there nearby. He lives by the Salt Meadows. If not there, then–" She hesitated, the troubled look returning to her face.

"Then where? You must say, Annetje!"

"Then–at tavern. Oh, I not know! Maybe better I never tell you these things! Maybe better–"

"It's better you do tell me," Mary said. "Much better." And she rose, her eyes flashing warmly down upon her new friend. "Some day you'll be glad."

"You will come back and tell me when you find him?"

"I promise. And now, thank you from my heart–and good-by."

The Dutch girl's soft voice followed her. "Annetje Wicoff wish you good luck!"

Despite the cloying heat, Mary's feet carried her rapidly from Annetje's house toward the Training Place and beyond this in the direction of the swamp and the Salt Meadows, where cattle grazed and where she had never been before. It was an unattractive area, with only a few scattered houses dotting it and, as she noticed their impoverished aspect, Mary, for the first time, knew a small doubt. Nick–here?

She was close to a tavern at that moment. It was not the main tavern where travelers from Philadelphia to New York could find food and lodging for the night. This was more of a local meeting place and was not, she imagined, held in too good repute. Through the closed door now came the sound of rough quarrelsome voices, and Mary hesitated before venturing further. As she stood uncertainly in the shade of a spreading bush, a man emerged, and, without seeing her or giving her more than a brief side view of his face, stepped off the porch and started along the road in the direction of the Salt Meadows.

It was Nick.

Yes. Surely that was his tall, loosely knit figure. She would know it anywhere. And his tousled head of black, curly hair. And yet—and yet—there was something unfamiliar about him, too. Something unkempt and shambling.

The call that stood in her throat died as she saw him lurch once, regain his balance, and then go on his way. Oh, no! This was not Nick! It could not be! She had never seen him like that. Never!

But if not Nick, then who was it? She must find out! Until she was certain, doubt would linger.

Her hesitation gone, she picked up her skirts and hastened after him, waiting until a curve in the road took them both out of sight of the tavern behind them before she softly spoke his name.

"Nick."

The figure ahead of her stopped, shook his head as if he had not heard aright, and then moved on without a backward glance. Again she called in a louder tone.

"Nick!"

This time he turned. Oh, thankful heart! It was truly not Nick! There was a resemblance, but that was all. For though the features were the same, the face had none of the clear, lively sparkle she remembered. It was closed and sullen, the skin pallid, not bronzed, and the eyes a smoldering black. As she met them she experienced a curious, cramping feeling of fear, for the look in them held a hard, measuring craftiness.

For a moment he stared as if he could not believe what he saw. Then he came back to her.

"D'you call me?"

She nodded, withdrawing a little instinctively. "But—but you aren't Nick. I made a mistake. I'm sorry—"

He watched her stepping backward and followed her. "Why be sorry?"

They were alone on the road. The tavern was out of sight and the nearest cottage too far away to hear her cry if she should utter one. Even so, she halted, unwilling to let him guess her fright, and lifted her chin to meet his gaze. "I'm sorry because it was Nick I was looking for."

"Nick," he repeated. "So you're lookin' for him. Well, I c'n tell you about him if you want."

"Can you? Who are you? You look like him in a way, but—who are you?"

He came a step nearer and now he was close.

"I'm his brother. That's who I am. Brother Nigel."

She might have guessed. And a much younger brother he was, for all his size. Near to him like this she could see the meager growth of down on his upper lip, the whole map of his face blurred and uncertain because he had as yet not enough knowledge or experience of life to give it a definite character. About the same age as Johnny, she would think, not more than seventeen at the most. But Johnny was off helping to fight the French and Indians. Why wasn't this lad doing the same, instead of spending his time at a road tavern? A little gust of angry contempt swept her at the question. He saw it registered plainly on her face and, reaching out a hand, he seized her wrist and held it fast.

"Any woman comes runnin' after my brother better not look at me like you're lookin' at me now," he said gratingly.

Furious, she tried to shake him off, but he jerked her closer and kept her there.

"Stay still if you want me to tell you about Nick. Do ye? Or don't ye?"

"Yes!"—breathlessly. "Oh, yes, I do! Wh-where is he?"

"He's gone."

"Gone where? To fight the war?"

He gave a rough laugh. "Nah! Nick's gone to make his fortune like he's always goin' to." He drew her against him suddenly with meaningful force. "He's gone, all right. But I'm here." And his face, with his bright, cunning black eyes, came down to a level with her face until she could feel his hot fumed breath on her cheek. "I'm here. And I'm a man, too. As much as Nick." And he boldly plucked her handkerchief from the bodice of her gown where she had tucked it.

For answer she struck him a blow on the cheek with her free hand, trying to break away. But her attack only angered him and she found herself caught in his hard, close embrace. For a moment she struggled, fighting silently and fiercely, until she succeeded in seizing one of his thumbs and bending it backward. With a grunt of pain, then, he loosed his hold a trifle and in that instant she managed to tear free.

He started to follow her as she ran. She could plainly hear his plunging unsteady footsteps. But after a moment these stopped and she heard nothing. By the time she reached the bend in the road there was only silence behind her. Even so, she did not abate her speed. Disheveled, her cheeks burning, her heart hammering, she hurried on, with shame and horror and a turbulent, sickening disappointment all churning violently within her.

She skirted far around Annetje's little house, not wanting to be seen from it. Not for worlds would she go back there to tell what she had discovered. Not until she, herself, had had a chance to consider all that it might mean —or might not mean—in her life. At the moment the shock she had suffered held her in complete confusion. For Annetje—Jan—had been both right and wrong.

Picking her way the length of the quiet, dusty streets, holding her skirts with one hand so as not to let her ripped sleeve be visible, and hoping her bonnet would hold her disordered hair in place until she could reach the Parsonage, Mary hurried along. But fast as she went, and though her reason denied it, she still imagined heavy, clumsy feet following her.

How glad she was to reach the safe-fenced yard of the Burr home! And how thankful to slip, unseen, into its cool, dark interior, past Esther's bedroom and up to her own. There, with trembling fingers, she tore her dress from her, flung it in a heap in a back corner of the big wardrobe, and, in her stays and petticoats, threw herself on the bed, her hands pressed to her eyes.

Not until then did she ask herself the question that had been pressing for an answer all the way home. If that were Nick's brother, did she want to have anything more to do with Nick?

Chapter 6

IT WAS IMPOSSIBLE, of course, for Mary to put Nick out of her mind and heart. She had lived with her dreams of him too long. Anyway, what if Nigel were his brother? Matt had been Prue's brother, too, and David had not turned from Prue because Matt had been wild in his teens. Indeed, should not Nigel's very youth make Mary forgiving of him, as Prue had been forgiving of Matt? Mary could not remember ever having heard Prue sit in judgment on Matt despite his moods and tempers and uncontrollable passions. She had been tolerant even when he had brought what Pa called disgrace on the family. And Matt had, finally, turned out all right. He had come back rich and successful and had, without shame, claimed his half-breed son for his own. No, Mary would certainly not cut Nick out of her life because of Nigel.

Yet the memory of the threat he had been to her persisted and kept her in fear of meeting him again. For that reason she never walked alone any more. She did not return to Annetje's, which was some distance out of town. And she went only to church or to Mrs. Duncan's or to market if she were not with Esther.

So passed September, and in October the concerts and lectures for the college students began and Mary was able to wear some of her new dresses. In November the Burr family moved from Newark to Princetown. The move was made without Mary's knowing the answer to the question —Where had Nick gone to make his fortune? All she did know for certain was that he was not in Newark.

It took three wagons to hold Esther's household goods, and with the roads so terrible it seemed as if everything would get shaken to bits before ever they reached their destination. It was not an easy journey. The children were fretful and the cold rain came down and made a dreadful mire, so one wagon was stuck for a while and a wheel came off another. But at last they arrived, and there stood the new college building and the President's neat clapboard house waiting nearby, with candles lit in the windows and a meal already cooked by a thoughtful neighbor. Indeed, that neighbor, a Quaker, housed them all that first night.

For the next few days Mary was busy helping Esther settle. It was certainly all a bustle and confusion with professors and students continually appearing to ask questions, and the babies underfoot and everything topsy-turvy. But at last order grew out of chaos; the students and professors retreated to the newly completed Nassau Hall with its chapel, offices, classrooms, and living quarters; one black servant was engaged to cook for Esther and another to help with the children (the redemptioner woman not having come with them); and Mary had her first leisure. In it she wrote to Prue.

Princetown, N.J.
December 2, 1756

Dear Prue,

Well, we are here! And I entertain mixed feelings about being here. Princetown is but a small village. It has only a Quaker Meeting House and a few scattered homes and these are completely surrounded by dense forests in a region as yet but thinly populated. With no navigable water nearby there is no trade, no coming and going of people, ships or cargo and the town exists in a dead calm.

I suppose you are looking for me to come home soon but, Prue, things are just beginning to liven up for me here now. There are landed gentry in the area—the Stocktons who have a fine house called "Morven" and the Leonards who own "Mansgrove"—and these two families often have guests of importance as visitors, Esther tells me. When they do, the Burrs are always invited to meet them and of course they will include me, too. The college boys, though young, are gay company, and one of the professors is not too dreadfully old for me to enjoy. There will be teas and dinner parties and concerts aplenty, Esther says, and she thinks I should stay longer. Besides, she feels she ought not to let me start on the journey home in the face of bad winter weather. Only yesterday she told me to write you this, adding that she did not want to talk of my leaving her until spring.

I have not yet spent any of the money you gave me, except to pay the dressmaker, so you need not fret on that score. I am saving it against the time when I may visit New York again. How I do long to do that! Be sure and let me know if Matt ever gets there as I could then put myself under his protection and the Burrs would not worry. You see, I am really quite set on seeing morc of New York before I return home, so please write me that you do not mind my prolonging my visit.

Your loving sister,
Mary.

Prue received this letter late in January, and she read it and reread it, trying to wrest from it whatever secret thoughts might lie hidden between the lines. Mary sounded more contented than she had in her earlier notes.

Was it because of the young college lads and the not-too-ancient professor? Or was she seeing Nicholas Fanshaw? That hardly seemed possible, Prue thought, if his home were still in Newark, for the distance between there and Princetown was too great and the roads nigh impassable in winter.

For a long while Prue stood at the window in her bedroom staring out in silent thought, seeing, without seeing, the empty white road, the bare brown trees bending in the wind, the bleak cold outline of the snow-covered hills in the distance. And it came to her, with a little jump of her heart, that perhaps Mary might never come home again.

But that was a wild idea which Prue at once dismissed, forcing her mind back to the question that she must now at last answer. Should she write Mary of the stories she had heard about Nicholas Fanshaw? Prue had never been able to confirm or dispel them as rumors, although Abigail Dwight who had moved to North Parish in the fall had written that the same tales were going about in that area, with the added report that Nick spent his money as quickly as he made it by gambling at cockfights and horse races.

Prue sighed to herself. Where there was smoke there was usually fire, she thought, and she fell into deeper and deeper concern.

If only David were here to help her decide what to do! But David and Johnny, who had been home for the harvesting, would not return now until time for spring plowing.

She sighed again and turned the letter in her hand, meaning to read it a third time, when she discovered a postscript had been added on the back of the last page.

Prue! Esther has just received a written invitation from Mrs. William Wilcox expressing the desire to have me—me!—spend a week at the Wilcox mansion in New York over New Year's! The river is now frozen solid so that I can get there easily. And of course the Burrs approve. Oh, Prue! This is what I have been waiting and longing for! *New York.* I shall take all my best clothes, of course, and I shall not come back until I am quite ready. And in case you wonder how I will get there—I will flag the Philadelphia-New York stage wagon here. In Newark I will stay over night with friends of the Burrs who will provide horses and an escort to Communipaw where the river is narrow and I can be sledded across. I shall not attempt to go by sloop, as I came, for there are too many disastrous tales of ships foundering and being lost forever in winter storms. Mr. Burr has made me promise to give up the attempt altogether if there is a thaw and the river ice melts. But never fear! I shall get there! And without drowning, too!

Mary! Mary! Why such great eagerness to reach New York? Not because of the pock-marked young man who will be your host. That I know. Is Nick there?

The more Prue asked herself that question, the surer she became that he was. He had not been in Newark, which accounted for the subdued tone of Mary's early letters. But there she had heard he was in New York. Perhaps he had opened his store there. Oh, if only he had! If only he had settled down at last to a measure of responsibility! One could not run a store in a community and at the same time steal from one's customers and gamble one's profits away. It was a thought to which Prue clung.

Quickly now she planned her letter. She would be careful. She would simply write the local news and gossip and casually include the tale about Nick. But she would ask no questions, add no homily, no word of caution. Just—there it was. After that Mary must use her own judgment. So deciding, she went at once to her task.

Stockbridge
January 28, 1757

Dear Mary,

I was glad to hear from you and learn you are enjoying yourself. I hope your visit to New York will be all you anticipate and I agree with Esther that you must not try to make the journey home until spring.

There is not much news here. Abigail Dwight took her family to the greater safety of North Parish last fall when there was another Indian scare at Fort Massachusetts and I miss her greatly. She wrote me recently of a story she had heard which concerns the pedlar, Nicholas Fanshaw. It seems he is reputed to have stolen some articles from the houses of people with whom he traded. It is said, also, that he is quite a gambler. I do not know if these stories are true or not but I thought you might be interested.

Please extend my greetings to both Esther and Mr. Burr. Pa sends his love. Mark and Faith are both shooting up tall. You will be surprised when you see them again—and this cannot be too soon for me. My prayers and thoughts are with you constantly.

Your devoted sister,
Prue.

Prue sealed and tied the letter and then sat with it in her lap for a long moment as she suddenly realized that she was sending it too late, after all, for Mary would have been to New York and returned to Princetown by now. Yes, she was sending it too late, and her heart grew heavy with worry.

Still—better late than never. And she rose and summoned Zeke and sent him through the wintry cold down to the store where the letter would be picked up the next time the stage wagon came through on its way to Albany.

It was fortunate for Prue's peace of mind that she could not follow the journey her letter made. The missive, passing from person to person on its hazardous trip, slipped once from hands too numb to hold it and fell, unnoticed, to the ground where it was promptly tramped into muddy slush snow by the impatient hooves of the postrider's horse. There it lay until, by chance, a new arrival at the inn discovered it, picked it up and carried it inside. But by then it was mostly pulp, the address completely illegible, so it was tossed into the fire.

Chapter 7

For Mary that first visit to New York was the kind of existence she had vaguely imagined for herself without ever believing it might be hers.

She found herself living in the most sumptuous, most talked-of house in the city, where a double stairway went up from the great front hall, where crystal chandeliers glittered in all the rooms, where her bedchamber seemed a full block long and where every one of the leading families was to be met—the Livingstons, the Kennedys, the Stuyvesants, the De Lanceys, the Beekmans, the Morrises.

Yet she was not dazzled, for it was no more sumptuous than the Stocktons' Princetown home, Morven, or the new house that Judge Leonard had just moved into opposite Nassau Hall. And—to Mary—people were always just people. She was not aware that these she met made up a coterie in the growing metropolis, a veritable "little court" in which the governor ruled as king. When, like a king, he appeared in his magnificent, gleaming coach, drawn by four (sometimes six) horses prancing in elegant, glistening harness, with watchful lackeys sitting aloft in fine, richly colored livery, he was—to Mary—simply one of the sights the city had to offer her.

And the fashionable Promenade, near Trinity Church,

which was the show place for this evolving little court, was another. Here, against a background of stirring band music, paraded British officers in scarlet coats and gold lace, together with the smartly dressed ladies of the town followed humbly by their Negro waiting maids. That she was a part of the show on the arm of her escort, William Wilcox, was only natural. And William, watching her covertly out of small appraising eyes, was pleased at the ease with which she fitted into his picture.

Never would she forget that gay, incredible week as she was whirled from one affair to another. A tea here, a dinner there, a sleigh ride some other place. One time William took her and another couple as far as the Blue Bell Tavern on the Kingsbridge Road nine miles north of the city, where spiced cider and little rum cakes were served in front of a huge, blazing fire before they started on the cold ride back. Another evening a group met at Ranelagh Gardens—("At last!" Mary murmured to William)—where the music and the dinner made a superlative combination. And, fitting climax, on New Year's Eve everyone who was anyone was invited to Archibald Kennedy's palatial home on Broadway for the banquet held in his fifty-foot-long parlor. Such elegant gowns as Mary saw on the women that night! Such striking jewel-colored suits as were on the men! And such a feast of good things as were served to eat! It was all fabulous.

Then, when midnight struck, the New Year was ushered in with a din of firearms outside and a popping of toy guns within. Balloons were tossed into the air and wantonly punctured amid laughter. Ribbons floated down from the chandeliers, and girls and men became entangled in them together. Music broke forth from a band hidden behind a screen, singing started, and everyone went a little wild with champagne and excitement.

But at last this waned and died, and the guests began drifting away. Outdoors a fresh fall of light snow blanketed the city as Mary and William stepped forth into it, and she saw little round cushions of white resting atop the poles holding the candle-lanterns which the law required before every seventh house. They had decided to walk home and, as they moved along, she heard the town crier ringing his bell and calling out the hour.

"Four o'clock and all's well!"

Four o'clock. It was an ungodly time to be abroad, Mary thought. But in no way was New York so strict as New England. Sunday here, for instance, did not commence on Saturday night as it did at home and in the Burr household. Oh, she could live forever in New York and be happy—if she could only find Nick.

"What are you thinking, Mary?"

His interruption of her thoughts filled her with impatience. He was always asking her that. Always trying to poke his way through into her mind. Stifling her feelings, she answered, "I was just thinking how much I love New York."

William, pleased, said he was glad she did. It was on his tongue's tip to say more, but he thought it would be wiser not to speak after such an intoxicating evening. Better wait until the morrow and see if he still felt the same way.

So they came to the Wilcox home and had a few short hours of snatched sleep. Then after a late breakfast Mary put on her red-velvet dress and her matching bonnet with the black feather curling down and her black sealskin coat, and William's father ordered the sleigh and he, with Mrs. Wilcox and Mary and William, all set out to pay calls. For that was the custom. The entire city went calling on neighbors throughout the entire day. It made a merry round. But somewhere along the way the older Wilcoxes were separated from Mary and William.

"It doesn't matter," he said. "Someone else will bring my parents home. And I am glad to be alone with you, Mary," he added, with heavy, measured purpose.

Mary made no answer, for she had not heard. Long before this she had fallen into the habit of paying little attention to William's remarks—most of them were incredibly dull. Now, tucked warmly under a bearskin with the sleigh bells jingling in her ears, she was thinking unhappily of the imminent ending of all this sociability. What was worse—the end of her chance to find Nick. She had known he would not move in the circles in which she was moving; nevertheless she had hoped against hope she might see or hear something of him. Yet never a glimpse had she had. Oh, if only she need not leave tomorrow! If only in some way she might prolong her stay without prolonging her visit! For she did not believe she could endure the close companionship of William Wilcox another day.

"You aren't listening," he reproved her.

She roused herself. "I'm sorry. I was thinking that New York is such a very friendly place. I had no idea it would be like this. Today, for instance. Everywhere we went it seemed like one big family."

He cleared his throat and plunged. "Would you—eh—consider joining the family, Mary? With me?" he asked.

Before she could give a reply, she caught sight of Annetje Wicoff standing by the side of the street in a small fur cape and fur hood. Yes, it was indeed she, staring in surprised recognition of Mary and then frantically waving her tiny muff.

Quickly Mary put out her hand and laid it on William's arm.

"Please! Stop a moment! I see someone I know."

More than a trifle annoyed that his meaningful words had gone unheard, he drew the horses to a standstill. Annetje came running up, her round face scarlet with the cold and wreathed in a pleased smile, and Mary introduced her before the Dutch girl could speak.

Then—"Whatever are you doing here?" Mary asked.

"I come to visit my parents. They live off Bouwerie Lane beyond Mister Stuyvesant's house. Jan not here on account the cows need be milked. You never come back and see me," she finished reproachfully.

"No. I—I couldn't."

"You not found the one you look for?"

"Yes—no—"

Annetje smiled as if she understood. "I like speak with you some time maybe," she said questioningly, and Mary nodded.

"You be here in city long?"

"I leave tomorrow, Annetje."

"Why not come my mother's house? Is plenty room. We go back together then Wednesday week. You help me with baby. Ja?"

"Oh, that would be nice! I—I could send a note to Mrs. Burr by the ferry man—the one who sleds people across the river. He'd pass it along so the stage driver would get it, wouldn't he?"

"Ja." Annetje stepped back and bobbed her head to William. "You will bring her?" she asked.

"If that's what she wants," he agreed coldly.

"She does. Come the first farm beyond Stuyvesant's house. Is good. Ja!"

The horses sprang away as William touched them with his whip. When they were out of earshot, his voice was sharp with anger as he spoke to Mary.

"Who is she?"

"Who is she? Why, she's a Dutch girl I met in Newark."

"You shouldn't bother with her."

"What do you mean?"

"I mean—" impatiently, "—she has no importance. She is nobody. Why do you bother with a nobody?"

"Why, William Wilcox!"

He turned his face toward her, and now she saw it cold and closed-in and small-looking, as well as pale and pock-marked. It was a revelation of a totally new William. Even his voice was different, for it was shaking with suppressed fury over Mary's ignoring of his proposal, which, he now suspected, had been deliberate.

"You surely don't mean to go there tomorrow, do you?"

"I surely do!"

"But I tell you she is nobody!"

"Everybody is somebody." Mary spoke quietly but with an anger equal to his. "And if all the people you know must be well-connected, then you probably shouldn't be entertaining me. I'm a nobody, too."

"You are a friend of the Burrs. And of the Edwardses."

"Oh! So I'm acceptable because of my friends! Well, then, Annetje is a friend of mine!" she retorted.

He did not reply, and she said nothing more. But the question he had asked her before they met the Dutch girl was left unanswered. And the next day it was a Negro servant who drove Mary and her gripsack to Annetje's mother's house in the Dutch hamlet east of Bouwerie Lane. William had left his farewell for her in a note saying he had to absent himself "on important business," and Mrs. Wilcox's farewell to her young guest was markedly cold.

But it did not matter. Mary was glad to be gone, and she settled into the simple country life with a pleasure that surprised herself. What manner of person was she, anyway, that she could so enjoy luxury and the glitter and pomp of society and yet know relief when she left it? It was good to be in a small plain home again. And it was good to talk with Annetje.

"I told Jan about you, Mary," she said, the first time they were alone together.

"You did, Annetje?"

"Ja. And he not like my sending you after Fan Shaw. He say what I did not know the day I see you. He say there are two brothers. One is gone away, and the one I send you after is the no good one. Annetje very, very sorry."

"You couldn't help it if you didn't know."

The Dutch girl nodded.

"Jan told me—and then you did not come back—and Annetje worried." Her blue eyes surveyed Mary anxiously. "Now you say true. He not hurt you—that no good one?"

"No, Annetje, he didn't hurt me."

Annetje sighed with relief. There was a little silence. Then Mary asked a question.

"Does Jan know where's he's gone? The other one? Nick, his name is. Nick."

"Nick. Ja." She shook her head. "Jan only say he gone." She looked at Mary questioningly. "You want Jan and me should watch for him?"

Mary did not hesitate.

"Until I see him, Annetje—until I know certain things—I can't forget him. Yes! Watch for him. And let me know."

* * *

Esther met Mary's break with the Wilcox family with a sharp rebuke. When Mr. Burr went to meet the stage wagon (she said) and Mary was not on it and the driver gave him her note, Aaron was much upset. He had thought—they had both thought—Mary was safe with their friends, but who were these Van Kemps she had visited, anyway? It was not a familiar name.

"The Van Kemps," Mary explained, summoning the polite smile she had promised herself she would employ with Esther in such circumstances, "are the parents of Annetje Wicoff who lives in Newark. I came upon her one day when I was walking, and we've been friends ever since. Really, Esther! I don't know why you're making such a fuss. There was nothing wrong in what I did. My stay at the Wilcoxes had ended, so I went to visit other people I knew—people who are entirely respectable and honest, as Mr. Stuyvesant could tell you, being their neighbors. Besides, we are all brothers in God's eyes, aren't we?" she finished demurely.

This silenced Esther. But the little difference strained the relationship between the two girls. Esther could not help but wonder what Mary might do next, and Mary wondered too, for she found life in Princetown dull after her exciting visit in New York. Perhaps she ought to go home. But she could not bring herself to leave with Nick not yet found. She could not leave, anyway, until spring came and the river thawed so that ships could once more sail up it.

Spring came. And with it a guest arrived to lecture at the college, bringing with him a copy of the latest *Weekly Post Boy*. A newspaper being a luxury and a rarity, mostly to be found in taverns where all might read who stopped, this one in the house was eagerly seized upon. Mr. Burr read it first, then Esther, and finally Mary had her chance.

She perused every word eagerly, but the item that

riveted her attention was one that appeared at the bottom of an inside page.

> Saturday last arrived here two privateers, the brig *Hester,* Captain Bayard, and sloop *Prudence,* Captain Martin, with their prize ship. She is a beautiful ship, almost new, of near two hundred tons, and laden chiefly with cocoa. Though 'twas rumored there was also a vast horde of pieces of eight, these have not been visible.

Matt! Matt had returned from the west and gone back to his waiting ship and his old business—privateering! And now he was in New York! Oh, she must go there again! At once! She had told Prue she would go if Matt came, so Esther could not possibly raise an objection. Now thank fortune for the Van Kemps! She could stay there with them.

But another news item caught her eye as she turned to read once again the notice about Matt.

> Mrs. Steel takes this method to acquaint her friends and customers that the King's Arms tavern opposite Broad Street is now enlarged into a more commodious house where she will have it in her power to accommodate gentlemen, with conveniences requisite as a tavern, but also with genteel apartments which she doubts not will give satisfaction to every one, including ladies, who will be pleased to give her that honor.

Ah! Mary would go there. She would have much more freedom there than at the Van Kemps—and what Esther did not know would not hurt her. After all, in this day and age, women did venture much alone. They traveled alone, went into business alone—Dutch women did, anyway—and lived alone if they had to. Yes, she would stay at Mrs. Steel's. She had enough money.

Thus it was that, shortly afterward, on a day in April

when the world was at its loveliest, Mary set forth once again for the metropolis. There, advised by Mrs. Steel, her landlady, that the Fly Market was a favorite place for the victualing of privateers and that ship's captains were usually to be seen there, she began to haunt it. But to no avail. Matt was not to be found anywhere. She saw a number of fierce-looking, sunbrowned individuals wearing broad red sashes over their left shoulders, fancy jackets, white knickerbockers, heavy gold chains and richly mounted pistols in gaudy belts—privateers, for sure, she told herself—but none of them was Matt. Finally she ventured to address one of them. He was big and burly and wild-looking in the face, but she had seen him lift a child across a mud puddle and throw food to a slinking cat, so she thought he might be safe. Looking up from under her bonnet, she spoke to him in her clear, cool voice.

"I'm searching for a Captain Martin of the sloop *Prudence*. Can you, perchance, tell me his whereabouts?"

"The sloop *Prudence?*" The man lifted a thick, ringed forefinger and pointed seaward. "Thar she goes now, Miss. An' I reckon Cap'n Martin is on the quarterdeck this very minute. Headin' for his new home in Charles-Town, Ca'lina, he is."

"Oh, *no!*"

Mary gazed after the finger. There, already far out on the blue water, were to be seen the full white sails of a sloop. Was it truly Matt's? Had he gone, indeed? Had she missed him? She turned back to the man beside her, her face registering her dismay and disappointment.

"Are—are you sure that's the *Prudence?*"

"I'm mighty sure, Miss."

Slow tears welled up into Mary's eyes. She had so counted on seeing Matt! She had planned to enjoy his companionship here in New York. What places he could —and would—take her to that she had not yet seen! Perhaps even to a play put on by the British officers. She had never seen a play in her life and wanted to discover how wicked it was. And how proud she would be to appear with him on the Promenade and introduce him to some of the people she had met when visiting William Wilcox! She had meant to tell him, also, about Nick and ask him to help her hunt for him. Annetje had thought Mary might even see Nick here in the market, for it was a place to which everyone came some time. But she had not glimpsed him any more than she had Matt. She had consoled herself by thinking that if anybody could find Nick for her, Matt could. But now none of all this was possible. Now the whole point and promise of her stay in the city was gone.

"Too bad, Miss." The stranger rested his thumbs in his belt and surveyed her with curiosity as he spoke. "You'd ought to've gone straight to his ship fust thing. Then likely you'd ha' seed him for sure." He hesitated, but before he could say what he was certain he ought not to say, Mary had turned and was walking away from him.

She walked with blinded eyes, not seeing anything or anybody, though the Market was crowded. It was a voice that brought her out of her brooding dejection. A voice singing behind her, richly, softly, caressingly.

"Rosa, will ye be mine now, mine now, mine now?
Rosa, will ye be mine now? Oh! Rosa, sweet!"

She whirled, unbelieving. But it was Nick! Yes! It was truly Nick this time! Bronzed, blue-eyed and handsome, with his black hair neatly brushed and tied beneath his hat. There he was, without a pack, and looking very affluent in a new blue coat, buff trousers, buckled shoes and a flower-strewn waistcoat, strolling along alone in a gay, nonchalant manner.

"Nick!"

Had she screamed it? Or whispered it? She never knew. Anyway, he turned, his face registering surprise, incredulity, delight, and, for a second, embarrassment. Then he was striding toward her with both of his hands out.

Chapter 8

"So you did not forget me, after all." Mary's voice sang the triumphant words.

"Forget you? Did you think I would?"

"You said you might."

"That was because I thought I ought to. But then—" His blue eyes smiled down, his voice enfolded her. "Then I found I couldn't."

"Why did you think you ought to, Nick? Didn't you know—"

"Didn't I know what?"

They were walking through the crowded Fly Market, oblivious of it, her hand on his arm and his holding it fast there, his feet by instinct leading them towards Maiden's Path, a well-known courting place on the Collect. Only a few couples were there this early in the day, and bushes and trees obscured them.

"Didn't I know what?" Nick repeated, and he brushed off a stump with his hat and handed Mary down to it as if it were a throne and she a queen.

Mary looked up at him, and he saw her eyes brave and bright and tempestuous with her ardor and her new-found incredible happiness.

"That I loved you," she answered softly.

For a moment he said nothing but only continued to

gaze down into her upturned face, his own expressing a myriad of emotions. Pride, surprise, joy, and confusion were all at war there. Then, abruptly, he dropped to one knee and took her hands in both of his.

"Mary! Mary!"

"Nick–" She was suddenly tremulous and uncertain. Was that the most that he could reply? Only her name? She drew her hands away and a pretty dignity fell on her.

"Perhaps I have been too forward," she said. "But I thought you surely knew. You told me you did. That our feelings were just the same. However, yours–yours may have changed by now."

"No." He captured her hands and held them fast. "It's not that."

"Then what is it?"

She leaned towards him, her lips unconsciously parted, her breath, warm and fragrant, fanning his cheek. Quickly he glanced about. But they were as good as alone in this copse, the sound of splashing water and of voices coming but faintly to their ears. There was opportunity for a kiss and he gave it to her, not reckoning on the depth of passion with which she would return it. Slowly, then, and a bit startled–for she had been unresponsive before–he released her. But she would not lift her head from his shoulder. She would not let go his enclosing arms.

"No," she whispered. "Hold me, Nick. Kiss me again! I've waited so long–"

And now she tipped her face to his, her eyes blazing, so that he, too, caught fire and swept her into his embrace with the fierce unrestraint she remembered. When at last he set her free, this time she was pale. But there was no mistaking her happiness when she spoke.

"So long I've waited–not sure–But now! Now I am sure! Oh, Nick! When shall we be married?"

It was hard for him to believe. She had waited for him, she said. Three years she had waited, and now she wanted to marry him. How was he to reply? He sat back on the grass, his hands clasped about his knees, and looked at her for a long moment. Did she not know that he was not the marrying kind? She had wakened to passion. Had she not wakened to wisdom, too?

"How can we be married?" he returned, finally. "We are both exactly as we were last time we met. You a fine lady, me—a pedlar."

"But I thought—" Her glance went over him. "You look so prosperous—and when you weren't to be found in Newark I thought for sure you must have opened your store here."

"Here?" He was delighted that she could think that of him, but he shook his head. "Not yet, though that is my dream. That is what I shall do some day." His voice expanded with confidence as he talked. It was always this way. When he said it, it became nearly true. He went on: "At the moment I've just returned from the southland. Business was excellent down there, so"—he gestured toward his clothes—"that accounts for my elegance. I even have some money left over." And his smile flashed with a childish kind of wonder at himself that this was so.

"Nigel told me you'd gone to make your fortune. And you have!"

"Nigel?" Astonishment swept away the smile, and a look of consternation followed. "Wherever did you meet Nigel?" he demanded. Then her earlier words came back to him. "Oh! You spoke of Newark just now. Have you been there?"

She nodded. "I've been visiting the Burrs. You remember our minister, Dr. Edwards? His daughter is Mrs. Burr.

And it was there while walking one day that I met Nigel. Tell me about him, Nick."

A look of caution came over his face. "How was he when you met him?" he asked guardedly.

"He had been at the tavern."

He struck one closed fist into the other open palm. "I suppose so! Did he behave badly?"

"He did not hurt me," she told him, as she had told Annetje.

He looked relieved. Then he swung about and sat with his back to her so that she could not see his face, but she knew by his voice that it was full of an angry, baffled helplessness.

Nigel was his charge, he told her. On his mother's deathbed when Nigel was born, Nick had promised to watch out for his younger brother. He, himself, at the time, had been not quite ten years old.

"But I couldn't look out for him! I had to scramble for a living for the two of us and leave him with whatever woman would bother with him. What else could I do?"

Mary's hands reached out and touched his curly black hair in light, quick sympathy.

"Nothing," she murmured. "But had you no father?"

"He'd left us months before. Not for him a pregnant woman! All he wanted was the fun of life. He'd left us," he repeated, "without anything. No money. No food. Not even a roof over our heads. A neighbor took us in and did for Ma." A note of pride came into his voice as he finished. "Ma was a lady. Whatever I am that's any good I get from Ma."

Mary's hands continued to move through his hair, their light, scft touch conveying her understanding better than words. Suddenly he caught them and drew them around and held them against his lips for a moment as if he would never let them go. But, just as suddenly, he flung them away and stood up before her, his face clouded with his confused anger, his mingled relief and regret at finding a decent reason for turning away from this girl.

"Nigel's another reason why I can't marry you," he said.

She looked puzzled. "I don't see why."

"Because he's my burden. I can't ask you to help carry it."

"But why should he be a burden? He's—how old, Nick?"

"Not yet seventeen."

"Even so, he's a man." The color flew to her face as she remembered Nigel's saying the same thing to her but with a different intent. "I mean—he's able to take care of himself, isn't he?"

Nick dropped to the ground at Mary's feet and began pulling up blades of grass. His motions were quick and angry as were his words.

"Oh, he takes care of himself! He's sharp—that one. He never lacks for money. But—" He broke off. "I don't understand Nigel," he said. "I don't understand him at all. I never have." He stopped, for he had no way of describing this brother of his. Indeed, no two people could possibly have been more unlike than they were, the one so gay and spendthrift and charming, the other so taciturn, close, and ugly. Yes, ugly. As if he deliberately kept the fires of hate burning within him against the whole hateful world.

Nick went on, "We live together when I'm home, but when I'm away he lives alone. I've tried to get him to come with me on my trips. But he won't. It's then I worry about him. He goes to the tavern too much."

"Perhaps he's lonely," Mary suggested softly. "There he'd likely always find people."

"Lonely? He doesn't like people. It's the cards. He plays to win—and he most always does. It's the drink, too. He likes them both. He likes a brawl, as well, and he's quick with his fists if anyone questions his game." He threw a small stone towards an inquisitive squirrel as he finished. "I never know how I'll find him when I get home. Drunk, dead, or in jail."

"Oh, Nick!"

He looked at her, his dark brows drawn together. "He's born for trouble. That I know, as sure as I know I'm here. And that's why I can't marry you, Mary. I can't drag him into your life." He spoke firmly, his mind made up. In the beginning Mary had knocked him off his balance, but now he knew it would never work. She was not for him.

Mary was silent a long moment.

"Nick," she said at last, quite simply, "if Nigel is your burden, he's my burden, too." He started to remonstrate, but she lifted a small, peremptory hand. "That's the way our life together must be. An equal sharing of everything. Thus we'll double our joys and halve our troubles." Her eyes, lifted to his, were twin stars.

He made a sound, then, like a half groan. For in her quiet persistence he sensed the strength he himself wanted and did not possess. But he said sharply, "You forget! Leaving Nigel out, I'm still only a pedlar. If I give that up, I've no means of livelihood. And if I don't—Do you dream I could ever ask you to rove the countryside with me?"

"You need not ask. I'll just tell you I'm coming. I'd love it. I've always wanted to see the world. And—Oh, Nick! What it would mean to me to see it with you!"

He looked at her, a sense of helplessness spreading slowly over him. For he saw with perfect clarity all that she was—sweet, fearless, strong, and generous. Indeed, more. There was in her, he now knew, a hot and reckless love for him that was dazzling. How could he turn from all this? Shouldn't he, instead, seize what she offered, marry her, and so, perhaps, better himself? He could! He was bound to no other woman. And yet—and yet—to settle down as a farmer in that desolate, cold, northern outpost of Stockbridge—to give up his freedom—

He said, a bit harshly, "You don't know what you are saying!"

"I do! I do! We could get a wagon. Why couldn't we? Show people travel in them. I saw one in Newark. Why couldn't we do the same thing? We could make it like a little house inside and wherever we went we'd have it to live in."

She was pressing him hard, using all her wits and beauty and palpitant, eager warmth. Every moment that he listened further undermined his will, changing his wavering uncertainty into consideration until—suddenly—it was a decision. Yes! He would marry Mary! With her by his side, he would, at last, be able to effect the savings he'd never managed alone, and, in very truth, end up with the store he'd dreamed of all these years. He'd not mind settling into a store. He could stomach a store, but not a farm.

"I could help you," Mary went on, as if she read his mind.

"What would your sister say?" he asked abruptly.

"She would not approve," Mary answered honestly. "But if she knew the peddling was to be for only a short time until we saved enough—or if we did not tell her until we actually saved enough—"

"I'm a bad one at saving, Mary."

"You make it. I'll save it." She waited, watching his face. So much of the persuasion today had been hers, she was thinking. It was a little bit strange, but she did not care. She had resolved long ago he should not escape her again.

"I love you, Nick," she said now softly. "And if you truly love me, the store—Nigel—everything—will work out for us."

He would believe her. Why shouldn't he believe her? And he caught her to him and once again kissed her without restraint. When he let her go, she knew she had her reply, and it left no doubt in her own mind and heart.

"Come!" she said, rising, and holding out her hand. "Today you have money. You told me so. So today we start looking for our wagon!"

* * *

They did not find the wagon. Not that day nor the next nor the next. But they found a wheelwright who said he could make just what Nick had in mind. It would take weeks, he said, and would cost considerable. But he would do it.

"Do it, then!" said Nick grandly.

Never had he been so happy, for he saw his future now both secure and prosperous. With Mary it was bound to be so. Together they would make one more trip to the southland where he was certain he would be able to sell all that he could carry down there, and when they got back, he would at last be in a position to open his store.

"Here in New York?" Mary asked, her eyes shining.

"Here in New York," he promised confidently.

Mary's happiness equaled his. The world, inviting, enticing as it had always been was wide before her, and, exploring it, she would have Nick by her side. When she reached Carolina, she would hunt up Matt, where (the stranger privateer had said) he had chosen to settle in

Charles-Town. Matt must meet Nick. She was sure the two would like each other. Were they not both adventurers and vagabonds? Then, after Matt sanctioned her choice, she would write Prue of her wedding, but until that time she would keep it secret from everyone. Surely there was nothing wrong with this. It was *her* life, wasn't it? And she was not a child.

Nick was a trifle uncertain as to the wisdom of her decision, but he disliked argument and, besides, the easiest way was the best way for him. Prue might raise objections beforehand, he agreed, but after their marriage became an accomplished fact she would surely accept it.

"And so the Burrs mustn't know, either," Mary concluded, growing more and more certain of her course.

She continued to stay at Mrs. Steel's. Nick had had the great good luck to run into a sailor he knew, a Captain, who gave him permission to sleep aboard his ship that was tied up at one of the docks for repairs. It was neither clean nor comfortable, but it cost nothing.

"Think of the money I'm saving, Mary!" he told her jubilantly.

She was as jubilant. They would need that money for the wagon, and Nick, she could already see, was inclined to improvidence. He loved the generous gesture, the lavish life. A bouquet of flowers for her to wear. A fine meal. A trip to the horse races on Long Island and—for fun—a little betting there on either Mr. De Lancey's or Mr. Morris's fine steeds. Once he took her to eat at a place where he introduced her to an Indian dish—suppawn—and where there were oysters of a tremendous size and lobsters over a foot long. Another time at a Dutch place, she tried little oil cakes, puffards, rolliches, and kisky-Thomas nuts.

Yes, he loved the fine life, the rich life. Sometimes

Mary felt that betting might be a serious weakness with him, for if it wasn't a horse race it was a cockfight. He could never get by one. But she would not let this trouble her now. She would just watch sharp and hold him in check so that all his money would not slip through his fingers before ever the wagon was finished. It was not easy, though, for he resented being curbed, and she came to discover he could be ill-tempered as well as gay. Oh! He was not perfect! Not by any means! But then—neither was she. And he could so easily make her forget his imperfections.

So the days went by, falling more or less into a regular pattern. Every morning Nick went from the ship where he bunked to the wheelwright's shop to see the progress that was being made on his wagon and to suggest changes or improvements, for he knew exactly what he wanted and was bound to have it so. Then they would meet for lunch and spend the afternoon together, and though they never went to Ranelagh's or the Promenade or any of the places where Mary might run into the friends she had made through the Wilcoxes, they explored other places that were as interesting. Once Nick's friend, the Captain, escorted the two of them all over his ship. Another time they went across to Brooklyn on the ferry which they summoned by blowing the horn hung from a tree on the shore, and they picnicked in the country there. On still another day they joined an excited crowd, and, like small children, followed the city's two fire engines as they raced along on their solid wooden wheels to a blazing house. Long twilight hours they spent high on the bluff at the Locusts, a favorite haunt of lovers. Oh! New York in the spring with Nick was as near heaven as Mary could get until she was married!

But the wheelwright took longer to do the work than they had anticipated. Meanwhile Mary's own funds were disappearing and she did not like to write and ask Prue for more, since that would lead to questions. It would be better, she decided, if she returned to the Burrs and waited there for Nick. When the wagon was ready he could drive it to Newark and she would meet him at Annetje's. Annetje and Jan, then, could go with her and Nick to the Magistrate's office where they would be married. Or perhaps he would perform the ceremony at Annetje's house. It would seem more like a wedding if it were done in a house. She did not know how she was going to avoid the required publishing of the banns, but perhaps she could meet the legalities some other way. She had heard it was possible by obtaining a governor's license, and she at once thought of Governor Belcher. But no. He knew the Burrs too well, and her own family, too. Her secret would be out at once if she went to him. Here in New York, then, before she left, she must get the special permission. Thank fortune, she was of age and could do this!

It was when she and Nick were on their way to the governor's house that she saw and just barely managed to avoid Mrs. Wilcox. Heavens! If she were stopped and questioned by someone who knew the Burrs—! They, of course, thought her safe at the Van Kemps' all this time. They would not approve of her staying at Mrs. Steel's, nor of her daily meetings with Nick. Best to leave at once before any rumor inadvertently leaked to any busybody here and through him—or her—to the Burrs and to Prudence.

Therefore, in June Mary returned to Princetown.

* * *

She came back to meet, once again, a strongly worded rebuke from Esther. Since Matt had departed before Mary could see him, why had she stayed away so long? It had been weeks! What had she been doing all this time?

"I suppose visiting around with new friends! Mrs. Wilcox saw you once with a strange young man unknown to her. Truly, Mary, you draw men the way flowers draw bees. And your long absence has disturbed me. It does not look seemly for you to be so free. I finally wrote Prue that I was vastly troubled."

"You wrote Prue that?" Mary's eyes held angry sparks.

"Yes. I thought I should."

"It was quite unnecessary!"—stiffly. "Prue knew where I was. I wrote her myself." She paused. "I shall write her again today and tell her I hope your letter did not worry her unduly."

She swept with great dignity up to the privacy of her room, but her dudgeon was reflected in her note.

Dear Prue,

I have just returned from my visit in New York where I had a most enjoyable time although I unfortunately missed meeting Matt. He had just sailed for Charles-Town. Now that I am at the Burrs' again, I find Esther disapproved of my remaining on alone and that she has written you to that effect. For this reason, I feel, dear sister, that it is time I ended my visit here before we have an open quarrel. My independence is so thoroughly frowned upon and resented—as if it would bring disgrace on this house—that I can no longer endure it, for I cannot be any different. I did not think to remain the whole year with Esther, anyway, but the time has flown and when I am biddable I think my company is enjoyed. I do not know at this moment just exactly when I will"—here she hesitated, writing finally—"take my departure, but I will write you as soon as my plans are made.

Your very loving sister, Mary.

* * *

Prudence, reading this, drew a great sigh of relief. Mary was coming home! Soon—soon—she would be here. Then Prue would have the answers to all her questions. Then she would learn why Mary had never once mentioned Nick to her. There could be, she thought, but one reason: her sister had met so many other men who interested her far more that Nick was forgotten by now.

"I've been foolish to worry so," Prue told herself. "I've been very foolish."

Still—it seemed a bit strange that Mary had never once mentioned the rumor Prue had passed on to her about the pedlar. Yes, that was just a bit strange.

* * *

June was hot in Princetown. July was hotter. Young Aaron, always a frail child, fell ill and ran a fever. When he recovered Esther had to worry about her husband, who, despite the enervating climate, maintained a heavy schedule of activity. Wouldn't he, she asked, sensing his weariness, take a short vacation and go up to Stockbridge where it was so much cooler? She herself could not leave the babies in such weather and would not risk taking them, but he could visit her father for her.

Mr. Burr agreed. He would go in August. Did Mary wish to return with him or would she wait with his wife until he came back? If she would wait, he would be glad, for he disliked leaving Esther alone. Mary was thankful he had made the request, for she had heard nothing from Nick since she had left him in New York and she was both puzzled and anxious. The wagon should have been finished long ago and he should have been in Newark before this. What had happened? If anything had, why hadn't he informed her?

"What message would you like me to bear to your sister?" Mr. Burr asked, just before he departed.

"Please explain why I am staying longer—to keep Esther company—and tell her I will write her my plans just as soon as I can," Mary answered.

Is was as much as she could say.

* * *

When the president of the college returned from the Berkshires, he looked ill to both Esther and Mary, but the only complaint he made was, "I am very tired."

Tired—yet he could not rest. A visit to Elizabethtown was the next requirement. There he must procure from the authorities exemption of his students from military service. The summer campaign against the French and Indians had been disastrous. Fort Ticonderoga had fallen and also Fort William Henry. New Jersey had never been more stirred. The whole Hudson Valley seemed in imminent danger of falling into enemy hands. As a result, men everywhere in the state were flocking to enlist, but Mr. Burr did not want to see his new college deserted if he could help it, and since legal exemption was honorable, he must secure it.

Having succeeded in that mission, he paused in Newark on his way home to preach a sermon in his old church, though he was not feeling well enough to make that extra effort. Back, then, to Princetown, and from there to Philadelphia to attend to more college business. It was a great shock to him to learn, when he reached home once again, that his old friend, Governor Jonathan Belcher, had died of a stroke a few days earlier and he—Mr. Burr—had been requested to deliver the funeral sermon. In vain Esther protested against his acceptance of this task, but he was obdurate before his sense of duty.

"I can do it. I must. I will," he told her.

He sat up all that night to write the sermon. The next day, despite a fever, he went to Elizabethtown. There, almost completely exhausted, he barely managed to speak his words. It was not surprising to Esther to have him return and take to his bed a very sick man.

Within twenty-four hours everyone knew it was no ordinary sickness. His fever rose so high that the children were sent out of the house to stay with neighbors. Indoors a deep hush fell. Friends entered softly. Servants whispered. Esther tiptoed in and out of her husband's room, pale, distraught, absorbed.

Mary was appalled at this sudden crisis. Was it her duty to stay? Or was she simply in the way? The children, attended by their nurse, were in good hands up the street. They did not need her. The cook was sufficient, the neighbors more than kind and thoughtful. And only Esther could do the nursing required. What was there for her—Mary—to do? She should never have come back here from New York, she told herself. She should have gone straight to Annetje's. Could she go now? Oh, dear, no! It would look too heartless. Yet how could she stay here any longer with her own feelings torn by secret fears because of Nick's continued silence? Had he, too, caught the war hysteria and joined the militia? She hardly thought so. Besides, he would never do that, without seeing her again first! Oh, what should she do?

It was Esther who answered the question for her. She came to Mary one day, her lovely face ravished with her anxiety, and said, "Mary, I feel sorry to be such a very poor hostess to you through your last weeks here. It must be very dull. But with Mr. Burr so ill I cannot think of anything but him."

"He is all you should think of," Mary answered quickly. "I ought not to be on your mind at all. And if I am, then I am being the worry I don't want to be, and it is time I left." She hesitated. "I meant to go, anyway, Esther, you know, after Mr. Burr returned from Stockbridge. But I won't go if there is anything I can do here to help you."

"There's nothing." The tears filled Esther's eyes. "Nothing at all. The doctor says we must simply wait for the fever to run its course. It may take weeks. And besides its being dull here for you, you may be exposing yourself to danger. I would never forgive myself if you caught the fever, too. I do truly think, my dear, that you should go home."

"You're sure? You're quite sure you feel this way?" And at the other's nod, Mary spoke with a rush of warm impulsiveness. "You've been wonderfully good to me, Esther! How can I thank you for all you've done and for your abounding hospitality? I have loved being here with you, and I'm sorry if I ever distressed you with my headstrong ways."

Esther smiled faintly. "I should have remembered that you have a heritage of good common sense that will always hold you in balance. I fear I spoke hastily and harshly at times. Forgive me. And I must, in turn, thank you for all the help you have been to me."

They kissed, and then Mary said, "I'll go pack now, Esther."

Esther nodded, but she looked uncertainly at Mary. "Are you—Are you going straight home from here? Or will you linger in the city first?"

"I may linger a while," Mary returned. "But you are not to worry. Just remember my heritage of common sense."

Yes, she was thinking. She would linger in New York until she located Nick—if she did not first find him in Newark. She would go to Annetje's first; then, if she must, on to New York. But she had to find him! To fail meant a forlorn return to a dull and lonely existence, probably forever, on the farm.

* * *

Mary found Nick in Newark. Jan went to the two-room cabin where the two brothers lived and brought him back to Annetje's. He came in so radiant, so jubilant, that all Mary's anger, which had been slowly accumulating against him, vanished. But she did manage a mild remonstrance.

"Why didn't you send me word you were here, Nick? I worried."

"My sweet, I just arrived myself last night!"

Mary looked her bewilderment. "You mean it's taken all this time to build the wagon?"

"No. But—" He checked off on his fingers. "Following the wagon I needed the goods to fill it. And following the goods, I needed a horse to pull it. And following the horse and the goods, I needed the money to pay for all that. In fact, I needed the money first. The wagon cost a sight, Mary. I had none left over for anything else."

"Wherever did you get it, then?"

His blue eyes sparkled, his white smile flashed, he snapped his fingers. "I was lucky."

Cockfights? Horse races? But she would not ask. He was here with all that they must have for their venture. That was sufficient for the moment. Nor did he offer to elaborate. Instead, he pulled Mary past the smiling Annetje and the sober-faced Jan out of doors with him. For he had driven over in his wagon and had stopped it a short distance from the house where it was hidden in a clump of trees. It was there that he took her now.

"I can't wait for you to see it," he said, with the glee of a small boy. "You'll be surprised, I know."

And surprised she was, as he handed her up the little steps at the rear into the hooded vehicle that was to be her home in the future.

What a marvel of contrivance it had turned out to be! Far more comfortable and better outfitted than she had dreamed, with bunk beds along each side and two lockers with drawers at the foot of each bunk, with a narrow chest running nearly the full way down the middle, and, forward of this, behind the driver's seat, a kind of bureau for her that had a chair fast to the floor before it. Everything was fast. Nick's twin-rifle gun slung in straps to the ridgepole, his musket easy to reach in a stand by the whip socket, the iron fork, spoon, and skillet handy for a quick meal, the tin plates tucked away together, the hanging cups and saltbox, the brass lamp screwed tight above her bureau—These were all fixed so that nothing would bang or fall down or break, no matter how rough the road. And all the woodwork was painted spang-up new in a soft, green color!

"For you," Nick told her joyously. "I'd never have bothered with paint just for myself."

Oh, she was proud to bursting over it all! Moreover, the bunks had feather beds and good blankets on them, and there was even a strip of carpeting on the floor by hers. Little murmurs of appreciation and praise kept coming from her as he continued to point out this and that comfort and convenience, but when he opened the drawers and showed her the neatness with which he had stowed away his wares, she was speechless. No woman could have done better.

What had he? Why, everything a body could wish for.

Papers of brass pins, fine linen thread, button cards, garters, Bristol needles in beeswax, colored ribbons, red Carlisle stockings, glass beads, small knives, combs, cheap jewelry, whangs, handkerchiefs, tracts, Bibles and catechisms. These were the little things. In another locker that had been divided into compartments there were bottles of peppermint essence, of bergamot, of wintergreen extract and bitters. Hair oil was here, too, and Seneca Snake Root and opodeldoc. Not to mention red cedar, wormwood, cloves, aniseed, and rhubarb. One locker, besides her bureau, had been left for her clothes, another for his. There also was an assortment of domestic necessities—cutlery, a tin box of tea, a box of sugar, a box of nails, twine, scissors—each thing fitting precisely into its allotted space.

"Nick! It's wondrous!" she said, at last. "I never dreamed it would be like this!"

He pointed, then, to the canvas roof hung with more articles than she could take in at a glance: nested Indian baskets of birch and ash, brush splints, beaver hats, strands for caning chairs—everything of little weight. In a small cart that was to be trundled along behind were heavier goods such as iron pots and pans, axes, firearms, boots and shoes, wooden bowls, trenchers and cups, to say nothing of their own provisions and tools—all packed away tight under a stout canvas top.

"You've thought of everything," Mary marveled.

"I've tried to." His eyes were dancing with his triumph. Oh, it was a good beginning, all right! he was thinking. And then he leaned down and pulled open deep drawers that ran the whole length of the narrow chest in the center of the wagon.

"Here's the best," he said. "I saved it to show you last."

She gasped. For there before her eyes lay heaps of shawls of finest cashmere and the loveliest colors imaginable. Bolts of cloth were here, also, sheerest paduasoy of Italian weave, English lawns, Scotch tweeds, silks from China and Japan. And laces from everywhere.

She looked up at him, awed. "You must surely have been *most* lucky to be able to buy all this, Nick."

He closed the drawers as he answered carelessly, "Oh, this isn't paid for. A merchant let me take it on trust. When I get back I pay him for whatever I've sold. What I don't sell I can return to him."

Mary said slowly, "I never heard of an arrangement like that. Is—is it—reputable?"

"Why, of course!" He pinched her cheek. "When you've been in trade as long as I have, you'll learn things like that."

"But—but suppose something happens to it? Suppose it gets rained on—or ruined one way or another? Or suppose someone gets into our wagon some time and steals it?"

He shrugged. "We won't suppose anything so terrible." He frowned down at her suddenly. "What are you trying to do? Spoil everything?"

"No. No! Of course not!"—quickly. "I was just—" She put her hand out in apology. "I'm sorry, Nick. You know what you're doing, I'm sure. It's just—well—I was worried. I'm—I'm ignorant, I suppose." She paused, as she saw his face light before her apology, and went on with all her usual, eager warmth. "I do truly think it's a wondrous wagon, Nick! And I know, when you sell all this—we'll have our fortunes made."

"That's what I intend." He drew her to her feet and there in the closed-in privacy of their wagon, his face came close to hers till all she could see was the hot gleaming blue of his eyes, and all she could feel was his near warmness smelling of soap and pomade, and all she could hear was the beat of his heart and the soft urgency of his whisper.

"Now! Let's hurry up and get us married!"

And beneath his kisses, her world fell away again, rocking off into darkness so that she was only able to nod her acquiescence.

PART TWO

❦

August 1757–January 1758

Chapter 9

NEVER WOULD MARY FORGET her wedding day at Annetje's. Nick was in such a hurry. He was in such a hurry he would not even let Jan go for his brother, Nigel.

"No!" he said, frowningly. "I've had my fill of Nigel. Let be! He knows I'm to marry. I told him. Did it matter to him? Not an owl's hoot. Off he went to the tavern just the same. You found him there, Jan, when you went to ask him my whereabouts. Well, I'll not have him disgracing me at my wedding."

Mary felt that was wrong. Nick's only brother—indeed, his only relative—not to be present? She had thought about Nigel a good deal since Nick had told her about him, and the more she thought the less she remembered him as he had appeared to her and the more he reminded her of the way Matt used to be. Always unhappy. Always seeming to hate everyone. And why? Because Pa hadn't been willing for him to do what he wanted with his life. Perhaps Nigel had a dream, too, and no way of realizing it. She had said this once to Nick when they were in New York, and he had told her Nigel's dream was just to make money.

"But what for? What does he want with it when he gets it?"

Nick had shrugged. He thought all Nigel wanted was

just to have it. Certainly he held onto it tight enough!

"But hasn't he ever said—"

"The only thing he ever said that I can remember is that he didn't intend to live in a pigpen all his life. He calls the cabin a pigpen! Well, whose fault is it that it is? He's the one stays home. He's the one should clean it up. But if the roof leaks he just moves out from under the drip. I tell him he's living where he belongs."

"Perhaps," Mary had ventured slowly, "if he felt someone cared about him—what he is and what he becomes—some woman, I mean—"

Nick had laughed. "Lord! Who would? He'll have no friends!"

Mary had gone on as if she had not heard. "He's never had a mother, you know. Matt had Prue. Prue always loved Matt no matter what he did. Even when he ran away and never wrote for years, she kept on loving him. It seems as if he must have known. What else brought him back?"

Nick asked curiously, "What are you driving at, Mary?"

"I was just thinking—if I could make Nigel feel I really wanted to be his older sister—" She stopped, wondering if this would ever be possible. "What I mean is, I just don't believe he is all bad the way you make him out to be. No one is, Nick."

Very earnest she looked as she said this, very sweet, too, with her big brown eyes soft and her scarlet mouth in a pleading half smile. Nick called her a lovely angel and kissed her, and there the matter was dropped. But today—the day of their wedding—she ventured to argue again.

"I don't believe Nigel will disgrace us, Nick. Not really."

Nick flew into one of his quick tempers and turned on her rudely.

"I tell you—No! I'll not have him here! That settles it!"

Mary subsided. Nick shouldn't speak to her that way, she thought. Certainly not today of all days. But she said nothing more. So Jan, his thin, dark face sharp with disapproval of all this unseemly haste, went out to bring a minister or a magistrate or a justice of the peace to perform the ceremony, while Annetje bustled about laying the best cloth on the table and getting out the best plates and cups.

" 'Tis a good thing I bake yesterday," she said. "Now we have pork cakes. You never eat pork cakes? I cook chopped pieces with spices, almonds, currants, and raisins and then flavor all with brandy. Is good! Ja! We have pork cakes for this wedding, anyway. But I wish you stay, so after we can have a shivaree. It's fun!" And her round, rosy face took on a knowing, mischievous look. "It's not Dutch custom. Is New England. You not like?"

Mary shook her head. "No, thank you, Annetje. How could we stay here, anyway? You haven't room."

"Oh, Jan and Annetje could sleep in the barn one night."

But Mary shook her head again.

Accordingly no shivaree was planned. Indeed, for a short while when the puffy, important, fussy little justice of the peace came back with Jan, Mary feared they might not even have a wedding. For he looked at the permission she handed him that had been signed by the governor, and said, "But this is the New York governor. You must, therefore, be married in New York."

"He never told us!" Mary answered. "And how can we get one signed by a New Jersey governor now? Governor Belcher died a few days ago and no one has been appointed in his place yet."

That was true. The justice pulled his lip and admitted

that it was true. And of course previously the New York governor had presided over New Jersey's affairs, so perhaps now, too, until a new man arrived—

"If you don't marry us, we'll live in sin," Nick put in at this moment and winked gaily down into Mary's shocked face. "We'll live in sin and everywhere we go I'll say the justice of the peace in Newark drove us to it."

"Come! Come! Young man!"—testily. "We have troubles enough here with runaway marriages without you adding to them. Are you of age, Miss Martin?"

Nick's humor vanished before the reproof. "She's of age! And so am I. I am also sick and tired of all this palaver. Will you or won't you marry us? Though you don't deserve it, I am contemplating double the usual fee."

Mary smiled faintly at the alacrity with which the justice drew his Bible from his pocket then. Yes, Nick was in a hurry, all right. Why! He hardly wanted to wait to eat Annetje's delicious pork cakes and drink Jan's beer before he was for starting.

"I aim to get to Trenton before dark," he said impatiently.

But they did not get to Trenton before dark because, a mile or so before they came to it, Nick drove his wagon off the road into a cleared space in the woods, and, with tenderness and passion and hunger, took Mary into his arms.

* * *

Oh, the glory and the beauty and the joy of those first few weeks of married life! Nick made a wonderful lover, knowing, gay, imperious, tender, irresistible. Nothing was strange and nothing was terrifying in the sweet intimacy of his embrace. Nothing was discouraging, either, not rain or heat or blowing dust, before his buoyant nature. The crowded wagon, the sketchy meals, the lack of privacy and proper bathing facilities—all these were minor hardships to be turned into laughing matters. For was she not seeing the world as she had always wanted to see it? And was not her guide and companion the handsomest man to be found anywhere? The most devoted? The most attractive in every way? If only Prue could glimpse her now and see how happy she was! Well, the first time they stopped anywhere long enough, Mary would write her. So, in an aura of delight and excitement, she went through the days.

And how she loved to hide within the wagon and listen to Nick making a sale! (He had asked her to stay inside, because, he said, she distracted him.) Not a customer ever escaped him. All bought something, however small and trivial. For he combined a quick wit, a sweet cajolery, an ardent interest in his prospective buyers with a charming or droll enthusiasm for his own wares. Thus the toilsome journey down over the dull flatlands of South Jersey was made interesting.

But, oh! It was scorching weather in which to travel, and there came a day when the shimmering heat waves rising from the ground made Mary feel dizzy so that she crawled back from the front seat, past her bureau, till she could stretch out with closed eyes on her bunk bed.

It would have been better, she thought, as she lay there, if they had waited till later in the season before setting forth. October would have been a good time. In August and all through September the land still burned, the foliage drooped, and not even the nights brought respite. What had been their hurry, anyway? Still—the memory of his impatience brought her a flooding sense of warm, rich happiness and pride. It was wonderful that he loved her so he couldn't wait for her even a moment longer than necessary. It was truly wonderful. But if only the wagon wouldn't jounce so!

* * *

Nick, driving, was completely unmindful of any discomfort, for he had things on his mind. They had come a long way from Trenton by now, he told himself with satisfaction. Now they were down in The Pines, that vast, irregular tract of land crossed, long before this, by surveyors and dotted over with lumber mills. It was a lonely area, wild and still heavily timbered. Wolves roved here at night and sometimes their howls came disconcertingly close to the wagon, making Nelly, the mare, tremble and whinny, and plunge against her rope, so that Nick would have to climb down, gun in hand, and quiet her.

But it was a good land for the traveler for it abounded with food. There were deer aplenty, more squirrels than you could count, to say nothing of wild turkeys, partridge and other fowl. Nick had no fear of traversing The Pines. The Indians in this vicinity were friendly when you met them, and Tom Bell and other highwaymen were not likely to appear around here.

So, whistling, he drove the endless miles cheerfully, sometimes stopping at a lumber camp to pick up a few fat pine knots that were always handy in the dark, sometimes gathering some laurel butts or "niggerheads," as they were called, that he would later whittle into tobacco pipes. He was clever with his hands, was Nick. And he had told Mary that when they came to the Eastern Shore of Maryland, they would stop for a few days and then he would have time to make things. He would make a spinning wheel out of persimmon wood, he said. And the short gum pieces he had picked up as discards could be turned into good wagon hubs and mauls. They would live like royalty on the Eastern Shore when they reached it, he promised her, for down there you could have any kind of fish out of the water you wanted. You had your choice of oysters and clams and turtles and terrapin, and he didn't know what all else. With, of course, quail and duck and every kind of meat that stalked the forests.

The further south he went the higher rose his spirits. He did not seem to mind the heat as Mary did. He did not mind but one thing, and that was a nagging memory of Nigel.

He would go over and over his last day with his brother, telling himself that he couldn't have done anything different, that it was Nigel's fault things had turned out as they had. And, in truth, it was! If he had not been so stingy when he hadn't needed to be—if Nick hadn't spent his last cent to outfit his wagon—if the man in Newark selling him all his hardware hadn't expected Nick to stop and pay for it before he left town—

Well, that's the way it had been. And he supposed he should have known, knowing Nigel. But he had believed that when he drove up in his fine wagon before their cabin, Nigel would be proud that his brother was getting nearer to the fortune he'd always said he'd make. For Nigel could see for himself it was on its way, it was no longer empty talk.

He'd seen, all right! He'd come out at Nick's happy shout to stare in astounded unbelief at the sight before him. He'd inspected every bit of the wagon and he'd gone over Nelly's mouth and feet to find some way Nick had been stuck. But he'd found none. Then he'd said, in his mean, suspicious way, "How're you going to pay for all this?"

"It's paid for," Nick had replied quickly, jubilantly. He did not tell of his "arrangement" about the cashmere shawls and bolts of goods in the center chest. Why should he? There'd been no papers signed. The whole thing had been merely a matter under discussion when a diversion in the form of a fire next door to the New York shopkeeper had made that little man forget the uncertainties of a future deal with Nick before the greater uncertainty and peril of the present moment. In the excitement, Nick, seeing his opportunity, had helped move all the goods to a safer place, and by the time the fire was out the contents of the shop were both inside and outside, with the shelves in such disorder and confusion it was no wonder the poor shopkeeper did not know Nick had taken what he wanted and stowed it away safely under his canvas top. "I'll be back tomorrow to finish our talk!" he had called out, waving aside thanks.

Only, of course, he hadn't gone back. He told himself that the man had been on the verge of letting him take the stuff, anyway, so why bother? Instead, he had left the city and traveled all night, paying a fat sum to be ferried in a hurry across to New Jersey on a scow. All the next day he had traveled, uncertain that the shopkeeper had even discovered what had been done as yet but taking no chances. Then he had hidden for a day to rest Nelly and had finally reached Newark with only his hardware left to buy.

They knew him in Newark. There he was liked and trusted. For Nick had shrewdly been careful about his reputation at home, knowing he would always have to return there. So when he had said to Josiah Dibble, with whom he had often traded, that he would settle the next day for his hardware, Josiah, impressed by his new status with a horse and wagon, had believed him. Nick had meant to borrow the money from Nigel. He knew Nigel had money. Nigel always had it, for he was unusually skillful at cards. And Nick had been sure his brother, too, would be sufficiently impressed, as Mr. Dibble had been, to lend him some.

But what had happened? Nigel had refused point-blank to lend him a farthing. Nick hadn't asked at first. At first he'd just talked easily and confidently of his future.

"It's not far away now—my store," he had said. "One more trip to the southland and I'll be able to set it up. I'm trying to make up my mind whether it'll be in Newark or New York. Newark, I think. Mary likes Newark. Mary's the girl I'm going to marry. She's waiting for me now. She's the one who's prodded me into all this. She believes in me, you see, and when a woman believes in a man he can do anything. I wish you could find a woman like my Mary, Nigel."

Nigel's lip curled. He said, "Who is she?"—not really caring to know, only thinking she must be a rare one to have snared Nick so fast and so tight.

"Her name is Mary Martin. I met her in my travels to Stockbridge years ago. Never could forget her. Nor she me. Then she came to Newark to visit—What's the matter?"

Mary Martin, Nigel was thinking. The initials on the sweet-smelling handkerchief he had plucked from the bodice of that girl hunting for Nick had been M.M. He had kept it. He didn't know why, unless its fragrance and its fragility had made him think more than ever of that other world he meant some day to enter when he could leave this pigpen. She belonged to it. The handkerchief told him so. Perhaps if he kept it, he might meet her again and somehow— His vague thought always ended here, except that, following it, he was glad he had only frightened her that day and had not really hurt her.

He said carefully, "Did she say she'd been this way looking for you?"

"Yes. And met you." Nick's glance narrowed. "She wants to see you again."

"She does!"

Nothing could have told Nick more clearly than his brother's startled surprise that Nigel had given Mary no reason for ever wanting to see him again. Reaching out, he caught the boy's shoulder and held it hard.

"What did you do to her?"

"Nothing."

"You did!"

"I tell you I didn't. I tried for a kiss but she wouldn't have it, so I let her go. Ask her!" he finished boldly, with a sudden, swift insight into the kind of woman Mary must be. Certainly she would never have said a word of their meeting that might trouble Nick, whom she loved. He repeated, "Ask her."

"I did."

"Well?"—with a sharp, upward glance.

Nick relaxed his hold. "She said the same thing, that you did her no harm."

"I told you!" And, after a moment, "She's—different from the others you've known."

"Yes. She's different."

"What does she want to see me again for?"

"You remind her of a brother of hers. An older brother that gave the family a lot of worry and heartache. But he turned out all right. She thinks you can, too."

Nick could not guess the feeling that had come over Nigel at those words. It was not gratitude. It certainly was not humility. It was not even surprise. It was more a hard, grim pleasure that his own secret belief in himself, alternately wavering between confidence and unsureness, had been supported. And by what a person! The heights to which he saw himself rise in that brief moment were dizzying. He would show her, he resolved. He would show her how right she was.

It was then that Nick put forth his request for a loan. He hardly expected immediate compliance, but he was not at all prepared for the anger with which Nigel refused him. Nick (Nigel had thought), who would have been happy to be a pedlar all his life, was being given a chance to rise into a new world of prosperity. Nick, unstable and weak, had secured this chance by winning for a bride a lady who would help make his rise possible. Nick, deceitful braggart with only a glib tongue and good looks in his favor, was the one of the two to have this luck, when it was he, Nigel, who had the ambition to better himself, who could hold onto his money to fulfill that ambition, and who asked no help of anybody. Where was the justice?

So Nigel blazed forth his refusal, and Nick blazed back. But it did no good. Next Nick tried coaxing, then shaming his brother. To no avail. At last he gave up.

That is, he pretended to give up. But when Nigel went off to the tavern down the road as usual, Nick instigated a hunt for the place where Nigel hid his winnings. Did he bury them outside? Nick thought not. There were no trees on the place, and Nigel would have been too easily spotted at his digging. The cabin, then. In his mattress? Beneath a loose board? Behind a chimney brick?

He found it, finally, in an old sock wrapped about with a dirty cloth and stuffed into a crack above Nigel's cot to keep the wind out. An obvious place, and clever of him to be so obvious. Here it was under his eye all the time. Here, by a glance, he could tell if it had been touched. What had made Nick pull it forth when it had been there like that for weeks and months, he didn't know.

Anyway, he had found it—and just in time. For almost at that moment Jan appeared, sent on from the tavern by Nigel, to tell him Mary was at their house. In all haste Nick climbed into his wagon with Nigel's sock safely stowed away, and, with Jan beside him, drove off. Thinking that Nigel, at any moment, might return to the cabin, discover his loss, and set out in pursuit, Nick had hastened the wedding and his departure with Mary. There had not, of course, been time to pay Mr. Josiah Dibble.

But he could explain that when he went back—if he ever did go back. Right now it seemed to him that it might be smarter to stay in the south and open his store down there. New Bern was a nice little town. Yes, New Bern might be just the place.

He stopped his whistling to call out to Mary. "Come on back up here with me, honey! I'm lonesome!"

He was not unfeeling, Mary told herself. It was just that he didn't know what it was like to mind the heat. Anyway, she loved him, and she would have tried to please him no matter what. So she crawled out from her bunk bed and made her dizzy way to the front seat.

"Feeling better?" he asked cheerfully.

She nodded. At least she could pretend she was, she told herself, as she gave him a small, wan smile.

Chapter 10

PRESENTLY THEY CAME to the Delaware River. They crossed at Cooper's Ferry and then followed along the water's edge till they reached New Castle, and, at last, the Eastern Shore of Maryland. How far away now Martin Manor and the hills of Stockbridge seemed! To her own surprise—for she had never thought she would miss them—a wave of nostalgia swept Mary at this realization. But soon she would be stopping for that week's rest Nick had promised and when she did she would surely write Prue. The very act of writing would, in a way, bring home nearer.

Not that she wanted to return. Oh, no! Not yet. The world was just beginning to open before her, for one thing. Besides, Nick had already sold a great deal of his merchandise and had taken in a considerable sum, and Mary's confidence in their future was mounting. Indeed, she had even begun to think they might not have enough goods to last them till they reached the wealthy southland. But Nick told her not to worry. He would manage.

She did not worry, either. Not in that way. But she did wish he had taken her suggestion and returned the beaver hat and the wooden bowl to the woman who had bought them at the Ferry. Nick had gathered them up by mistake with the other stuff that remained unsold and had put them back into his wagon. Then, just as the scow pushed off, the woman had come running to the river's edge demanding her goods. At first Nick had not understood, but Mary had, and had told Nick he could still throw them ashore. However, by the time he had climbed up into the wagon and found them, the distance between ferry and shore had widened too much and he could only stand shouting at the woman that he was sorry but she would get them when he returned.

"You could give them to the ferry master," Mary had suggested, at which Nick had scowled and said in a low voice, "I don't trust him. He'd keep them himself and then where would I be? No. The woman will have to wait until we come back this way."

"But, Nick, do you really think—"

"Leave be!"—sharply.

It was not the first time he had spoken to her like that, and Mary was angered. After all, she had only been trying to help him. And she still thought the ferry master could have been trusted. It was with this small shadow of a disagreement lying between them that they set forth along the Eastern Shore—that wild and lonely land with houses and towns spaced at great distances and rivers and forests separating these so that the going was slow and more than ever tiresome. Fortunately Nick's annoyance at her vanished almost as quickly as he had given it expression, and their way in time came to be livened by his singing. He loved to sing and he had a good voice and a fund of songs. Some of these were charming and some were ribald and shocked Mary. But her shock was amusing to him and she decided she had better get used to his songs as she was having to get used to his quick bursts of temper and his impatience with her for her "squeamishness"—as he called it.

For this had not lessened but had increased as they journeyed, and he, always healthy himself, found illness in others an irritant. It was, however, nothing she could control. It was the pitiless sun and the heat and the jouncing and bouncing causing it, she was sure. She tried her best to continue to hide how she felt, but there came a morning when the sight of the uncooked slab of bacon, slippery and slimy in her hand, nauseated her beyond the possibility of concealment. Retching and gasping, she leaned against a loblolly pine while Nick stared at her in a curious, waiting silence. Finally she lifted her shamed, streaming face.

"I'm s-sorry—"

"Better go lie down," he told her briefly, and he cooked his own breakfast. All that day while Mary lay miserably under the hot canvas on her bunk bed, able only to swallow and keep down nothing but tea, he gave her no attention. Indeed, he hardly spoke to her but held himself in a silence until that night after supper (and he cooked that himself, too) when he said they would head for Oxford where they would rest for a time and where she might be able to see a doctor. His tone held a note that might have been anxiety. She took it for that, anyway, and so found consolation for what had seemed to be an earlier indifference. But she felt too miserable to do more than murmur that she would be thankful to stop.

* * *

My, but it was good to be in civilization again, Mary thought. It made her feel better just to gaze out at the busy docks where a number of sails were outlined against the blue sky and where a multitude of all kinds of folk swarmed in a beehive of activity. Sailor men were there, bare-chested, long-haired, dirty and hearty, strolling by to search out diverse entertainment. Black slaves were there, glistening in their sweat as they unloaded boxes and barrels from the cavernous holds of the ships. Captains were there, swaggering and arrogant. And wealthy plantation owners, elegantly clad, were stepping down from their elegant carriages. Ladies, too, beautifully gowned, sparkling and confident with the knowledge of their allure and well-being, lent richness and color to the scene.

Mary's eyes held a luster for the first time in weeks as she gazed through the open flap of their wagon which Nick had brought to a standstill in a grove of tall holly trees close to the teeming wharves. He had left her now to go to inquire about a doctor, and she was alone. It was a joy to have the wagon quiet beneath her at last, but it was a still greater joy to be so close to people again.

People! Barefooted, woolly-pated urchins darting about the stacks of lumber, the piles of skins, the bags of wheat, and heaps of tobacco that lay ready for shipment on the docks. A line of newly arrived Africans, their chains clanking as they walked, making their way to the auctioneer's platform. A group of girls, pretty as flowers, laughing and chatting with British officers in their scarlet and gold. The Governor of Virginia and his lady just coming down the gangplank, preceded and followed by attendants. The factor, chief of the warehouse of Foster, Cunliffe and Company—a name that appeared on all the boxes and barrels—was surrounded by sharp-faced agents come to buy what he had to sell.

Mary gazed, entranced, until a high shout came to her ears.

"Doc! Hey, Doc!"

Quickly she turned her head. There, coming through the trees, was a rotund little man riding barefoot on a barebacked mule, a small kit held balanced carefully on the mule's neck. His broad-brimmed straw hat was pushed far back on his forehead; his gray jacket was wrinkled and soaked with his perspiration. At the shout he stopped his mule and waited for a small girl with flying yellow locks who came panting up to him.

"Please, Doc! Pa says can you come right away? It's a boy and Pa says—"

Mary heard the doctor's chuckle. "If it's a boy and he's here, what's your Pa want me for?"

"Well, Ma's bleedin' somethin' turrible an' he says—"

The doctor was already turning his mule. "Where do you live?"

"Oh, Doctor!" It was Mary speaking from her wagon and at her hesitant voice he looked around and found her above him peering through the canvas flap. "I'm—I'm not really sick bad but—but if you could come see me after you see the little girl's mother—"

He nodded. "I'll be back."

All afternoon Mary waited for his return. And all afternoon she waited for Nick, too. Where was he? What was he doing? She heard the passing men speak of horse races and her heart grew heavy within her. But surely he wouldn't—not when he'd gone off for a doctor for her—not leave her here alone—

The sun was low in the sky before the barefoot, rotund little man on the mule returned. By now the docks were nearly empty and quiet brooded over the waterfront. Mary lighted the brass lamp above the bureau and in its faint fitful light faced the doctor and told him how she had been feeling.

"I suppose it's just the heat," she finished. "I'm not used to it. I've always lived in the mountains. But whatever it is, I would like to be able to eat a little something and keep it down for a change." And she cast him a small, pleading smile.

"Hhrmph," said the doctor, squinting his eyes up and patting his medicine kit. "Well, there's nothin' here but a jar o' calomel, a lancet, an' a syringe with a nozzle like a twelve-foot shotgun. Don't see as any o' them'll help you. Tell me—" And he began to ask her questions that puzzled her and made her blush in the semidarkness. But she was relieved at the words he gave her in reply.

"Nothin' to worry about—your nausea. Plenty o' women have it right after they're married. Fact is, it 'most always comes. But it goes, too. Likely the heat an' the jouncin' you speak of made it worse—yes. Still, I'll warrant it'll be gone in another few weeks. Jes' take it easy as you kin an' tell your husban'—Where is he, by the way?"

"I—I—don't know." She could not bring herself to say what she feared.

"Hhrmph. Well, tell him t' stay home an' take care of you from now on. You look a mite peaked." He reached out a pudgy hand and patted her briefly on the shoulder. "Don't let nothin' upset you. You're goneter be all right. You livin' here in Oxford?" he finished.

"Only for a week. Then we'll move on to the southland."

"Hhrmph. Jes' as well to move on. Oxford's been a thrivin' city an' still 'pears to be. But decay's settin' in. Yep! Place is runnin' downhill. French an' Indian war's a-doin' it. Our tobaccy's dark Orinoco stuff. England won't buy it. Never has. An' the French have jes' one buyer in London, 'count o' the war, and that man's smart enough to play off one importer ag'inst another till he gits all he wants at his price." He scratched his head thoughtfully. "Yep. An' I sh'd know. Hear it enough everywhere I go." He scratched again. " 'Sides, Baltimore's kind of rivalin' us as a seaport, now. But mos' folks ain't aware yet. They don't know. Another two-three years an' this place'll be deader'n a doornail. You mark me." He stood up and looked sharply around. "Nice little wagon, this. Wouldn't mind havin' one like it myself. Mule's ornery now an' then. Like a lot of folks." He chuckled. "Well, I'll be goin'. Reckon your husban' 'll be back soon. Gittin' dark."

She nodded. "What do I owe you, Doctor?"

"Pshaw! What'd I do f'r you? Nothin'. Well–gimme some o' those brass pins there for my wife if you want."

Now she was alone once more. She drew the flap tight across the opening so that no curious person could peer in, then lay down in her bunk bed. She was not afraid. There was the sound of music coming to her from off one of the streets–a fiddle it was–and the stamp of feet and voices and laughter. No, she was not afraid at all. But she was worried.

She must have fallen asleep, for she was wakened by a slight sound as of someone reaching in through the door flap. She had left the lamp burning, and in its light she saw that the fumbling hands were Nick's. She was about to speak when she heard him whisper to someone behind him. "Wait out there. My wife's asleep."

She pretended she was. She did not need eyes to know what he was doing. The squeak of the long drawer as he pulled it out from the center chest told her too well. The rattle of money in the tin box they kept there–yes. He was after their savings. She could hear them being poured out into the waiting hands of the man outside.

When the stranger had gone and Nick had fastened the door flap again and turned to pull off his shoes and shirt, he saw Mary's eyes wide open and fixed on him.

"You lost at the races," she said.

He nodded slowly. Now he had to lay low and chew pokeroot. But the remorse and humility that filled him did not make that difficult. Christopher! How bad he felt! Yet angered, too, that he must apologize for what he had done. Coming to her, he dropped on his knees and buried his head against her shoulder.

"I know what you're thinking," he said, his voice low and penitent. "And I'm thinking the same. I could—I could kill myself. That's a fact. I don't know how—I mean, I never had such bad luck as I had today." He paused, waiting for a word from her, but none came. He lifted his head. "I won at first, you know!"—eagerly. "If I'd only stopped then! But—I thought—I mean! It was for both of us—" His voice changed before her continued silence, grew husky and uncertain. "I hate myself, Mary. You can't hate me any more than I hate myself. But if you'll give me a chance, I'll make it up. I swear I will! And I swear, too, that never again—" His arms tightened about her. He nuzzled his face in her neck like a little boy and whispered, "Mary? Say you forgive me! I don't deserve it, I know. I don't deserve anything. I'm not near good enough for you. It—it scares me sometimes to think how I'm not. But—this time—say you forgive me."

There was a long silence. Then—slowly—her hand lifted and her fingers began to move lightly through his hair.

"Oh, but Nick!" she murmured brokenly. "I don't see how you *could.*"

"I know. It just comes over me. It's powerful and I can't seem to—but it won't happen again. I vow it won't."

What more was there to say? Their savings were gone. Every cent. But there was still the future. He was good at selling. And he had promised to behave.

"Mary."

"Yes?"

"I want you to know I didn't forget about the doctor. I asked. They said he's riding circuit and is expected here any—"

"He's already been here."

He jerked upright and stared at her. "You mean—*here?*"

"Yes."

She could feel a tenseness come into him as he voiced his next question. "What did he say?"

"He said just what I've been saying. It's the heat and the bouncing and jouncing. He said it would pass."

She heard him draw a long breath as if he were relieved. Why had she ever thought he was indifferent? He asked, "Is that all he said?"

"Yes. Except—he said for you to stay home and take care of me."

"I will. I will!"

* * *

On, then, to Cambridge with its church surrounded by a low wall of bricks in the very center of the city. Then to Salisbury where the vivid green tuckahoe grew in solid masses high above the water line along the shore. And still further down to the little town of Princess Anne. Here they paused again in their journey.

It was here that Mary at last wrote to Prue, but it was a short note, saying only that she—Mary—was well, that she was on her way to Matt's, that she sent her love and would write more later. She did not mention her marriage and because of that she did not, after all, mail the letter. When her confidence in Nick had fully returned, she thought, when she was happy again, as she had been in the beginning, then she would add that news and send the letter.

The trouble was that the doctor had been wrong about her squeamishness. It did not disappear as he had promised. Nick had tried to coax her appetite by careful cooking, in the gentle art of which he possessed considerable prowess. There had been a day in their travels when he promised her "marsh rabbit" which, he said, had a "flesh as succulent as terrapin and tender as wild duck." He went hunting for it first and would not let her see it when he brought it in. The next day he was as busy as could be preparing it, soaking it in salt water, parboiling it, changing the water, and cutting it up. When this was done, he added onion, red pepper and salt, also a piece of fat back. Then, after it was cooked tender enough to suit him, he made a delicate gravy and served it with honest pride. To her own surprise, Mary ate some and enjoyed it. Not until then did he let her know that what she had eaten was muskrat. At the word Mary promptly vomited.

"Now that's silly," he exclaimed, in angry disgust.

"I know it is. I'm sorry."

"If a thing isn't named to suit you, you throw it up!" He stopped short and gave her a quick, sharp look. "I thought that doctor told you you'd not be sick any more? That 'twasn't nothing ailed you but heat and jouncing?"

"He did."

Nick was silent, his face a thundercloud. "Looks like he was wrong," he said at last, curtly.

And ever since then he somehow made her feel that she was more a burden to him than a pleasure. She could not say how he conveyed this idea. Perhaps by singing less, perhaps by not listening to what she said and then failing to answer when she asked a question. Or perhaps only because he was cross whenever she wasn't feeling well.

Anyway, they came to Princess Anne and paused, for this was a pleasant town and there was money in it. The people were "quality," Nick said, and the houses—great, white, "five-part" mansions, with handsome cornices, heavy paneled doors bearing enormous brass locks—looked prosperous. Nick got into some of them with his wares, but Mary was content to lie on her bunk bed and look out through the open flaps at the huge sycamore trees that formed a lofty green vault above the street. Lying so, she would listen idly to an old song that was wafted to her almost daily from somewhere down by the water.

"Juba do an' Juba don't.
Juba will an' Juba won't.
Juba up an' Juba down.
Juba all aroun' de town.

"Sif' de meal an' gimme de husk,
Bake de cake an' gimme de crus',
Fry de pork an' gimme de skin,
Ax me when I'se comin' agin."

It was a haunting song with a melody that somehow combined a sad resignation with cheerfulness, and it brought tears to her eyes as she lay there. Why, she did not know. Was it because she, like the singers, longed for a full measure of riches and must content herself with less? With acceptance rather than the earlier ecstasy of fulfillment? With faint foreboding rather than full confidence? She could not say.

Nick sold four of his twelve cashmere shawls here. They brought a good price and he was pleased, but one of them nearly got him into trouble.

He had just hitched up Nelly and was packing up

preparatory to leaving the place after the sale of the last one when an irate little old lady with pale blue eyes and white wispy hair marched up his steps and poked her head unceremoniously in through the door flap.

"You! Pedlar!" she said in a commanding tone that held both scorn for the likes of him and a righteous, fearless anger. "You took back my shawl aftah sellin' it to me. I don't know how you did it, but you did. An' now I've come to get it and I'll thank you to hand it over to me without a fuss."

"Why, ma'am!" Nick turned toward her in shocked surprise and with his politest manner, while Mary viewed the scene as if she were an outsider. "How can you say a thing like that to me!"

"I can because it's the truth. And I'll have no words about it. You sold me that shawl, and I paid you for it. Then I was called out of the room for a minute and when I got back you was packing up your bundle and my shawl was gone. I never noticed it till I went over the heap of stuff I bought and found it missing." The pale eyes flashed, the wispy hair quivered. "Now give it me! And quick about it!"

Nick bowed low to her and said pleasantly, "Come in, ma'am, won't you, please? Now, then. Here's the bundle I brought back just as I fetched it. I only just this minute laid it here, and I haven't opened it yet. Would you like to open it for me? If your shawl's inside, I'll apologize on bended knee for my mistake." He gave her his most engaging smile and concluded, "I've been called a heap of things, ma'am, in my time, from snake to mule and worse inbetween I'd not like to repeat. But—" Here his voice grew grave and reproachful with an injured dignity. "—I've never been called a cheat before, ma'am, and I'm frank to tell you I don't relish it."

The little old lady merely sniffed as she jerked open the bundle Nick had indicated. In angry haste she went through its contents, but the shawl was not to be found. Mystified, but not yet defeated, she cast a sharp look about the wagon.

"It must be somewheres else in here, then."

Nick waved his hand with an elegant air of nonchalance. "You're welcome to search anywhere you like, ma'am. Indeed, I'll help you." He pulled open drawer after drawer for her, finally coming to the long drawer in the center chest. "Here are the shawls I haven't sold yet. I have eight left. But none of these—see!—not one has the rose center that yours had." He shook his head and laid the shawls back with care. "I'm sorry, ma'am, for your loss, but I wonder—"

"You wonder what? Speak out!"

"I wonder if you questioned your own servants before you came here to accuse me?"

"I'd trust my house servants with my life!"

"With your life—ah, yes. But a black woman can't wear a life the way she can wear a gay, colorful cashmere shawl." Nick's blue eyes were sparkling and the notion came faintly to Mary, watching him, that he was thoroughly enjoying himself. "Didn't I hear you ask your Chloe to carry an armful of things upstairs for you?"

"You did." The old lady looked at him, a little less certain of herself now. "Well! I'll say this to you, young man! If you're right, I'll come back here and apologize to *you* on bended knee. But if you're wrong, I'll come back with the sheriff." She turned toward the door flap and saw Mary for the first time.

"Who are you, if I may ask?" she inquired.

"I'm Mrs. Fanshaw," Mary told her quietly.

"His wife?"

Mary nodded, her dark eyes grave and unhappy with the concern this incident stirred in her. The little old lady looked for a long moment into them and into Mary's pale, heart-shaped face, worn to a delicate thinness by her illness. When she spoke again her voice was gentle, though her words were caustic.

"Too bad," she said, and went out.

"Blast her impudence!" Nick exploded, when she was gone from earshot. "That's a fine thing for her to say! What did she mean by it?"

"Oh, I don't know, Nick!" Mary answered wearily. "Nothing much, I guess. Anyway, don't get excited about it."

"I'm not excited! I'm not one bit excited! But I know one thing! I'll not stay in this danged town another minute! All I've had is snoots and insults ever since I've been here. We're off—*now.*" And he climbed over into the front seat and picked up the reins. "You can straighten out and pack back there while I'm driving."

"But—Nick! Suppose she doesn't find the shawl on Chloe?"

He whirled about and at the blaze in his blue eyes she shrank away.

"Is that my fault?" he demanded. "Whose side are you on, anyway? Hers? Or mine?"

"Why—yours, Nick, of course."

"Of course!" he mimicked. "Sometimes it's hard to be sure." Then he swung about again and shook the reins on Nelly's back. "Get on!"

What had he meant, Mary wondered? Hadn't she always been on his side? Or was he thinking back to the time at the ferry when she had wanted him to leave the beaver hat and the wooden bowl with the ferry master?

She did not know, and she could not guess. She knew only one thing.

Nick was not the same, gay, lovable, charming man she had married—or was it she who had changed? It was hard to tell.

Chapter 11

POCOMOKE, where the cypress trees lined the river on both sides, their tops overhung with dripping gray moss, their gnarled knees twisted grotesquely together above the deep dark waters. A sinister-looking place, this Pocomoke. Mary was glad when they pushed on to Accomac, and still gladder when they left that earliest English settlement and drove along the strip of Virginia to its point from where they could get a sailing vessel across to the mainland again. Perhaps it would be cooler on the water, she told herself. Perhaps on the water she would feel better.

But the sloop that carried them from Cape Charles to Cape Henry had to cross a choppy sea, and her misery increased fourfold. To add to her misfortune, she slipped on the deck and fell and broke a bone in her wrist which could not be properly cared for until they came ashore two days later. Even then no doctor was to be found before they reached Norfolk, and by that time the bone had begun to knit of itself, leaving a horrid little lump where no lump should be.

It was in Norfolk that she finally mailed her letter to Prue without additions or changes. And it was in Norfolk that she had her first glimpse of herself in a long mirror since leaving Newark. (How she had missed a mirror!

But even a small one was hard to come by.) For a reason not clearly thought out she no longer stayed inside the wagon when Nick was selling his wares, and if he was invited into a house she went with him. It was in the front hall of one of these Norfolk homes that—with a shock of surprise—she saw herself. What a sight she was! No wonder Nick had changed toward her. Frowsy hair, wrinkled gown, and eyes staring dully out of a white, drawn face which she hardly recognized as her own. Why! She was an old woman already! A veritable hag! Oh, she must get busy and pretty herself at once, though how she would manage, with her wrist still wrapped up and hurting, she didn't know.

But she tried. She tried the harder as Nick met with greater and greater success in this thriving little city. For success restored him to her as he had been and—at last—she felt happiness returning like a slow, warm tide.

"I told you!" he would say gleefully, pouring the day's earnings into her lap and bringing his sparkling face close to hers. "I told you I'd make up for what I lost!"

Yes, he had more than made up for that unfortunate day in Oxford. The tin box was half full again, the heavy coins making a pleasant sound in her ears. In addition, Mary was finally feeling better. If (she thought) she had only waited till now to send her letter to Prue, she would have been able to tell her of her marriage. Well, she would simply have to write again.

But the days slipped by and she did not seem to find the time. There were the marketing and the cooking and the wagon to clean and her own clothes to care for, and her hair, that she had so long neglected, to wash and brush. There were visits to make, too, for Mary had a way of establishing friendships, and homes were opened to her, sometimes out of curiosity about her, sometimes out of a pity she did not suspect, but most often out of an interest in and liking for her own bright, sweet charm. Nick was glad of this. The more friends she had, the more quickly suspicion of him fell away and the more easily he sold his wares.

He got out the rest of the cashmere shawls in Norfolk one day and in so doing discovered among them the one with the rose center that he had sold to the little old lady in Princess Anne. In a pleased surprise he held it up for Mary to see.

"Now wherever in the world did that come from?" he exclaimed.

Mary shook her head, her wonder equaling his. She had not been able to find it in all of her cleanings. Yet here it was, neatly folded like the others and lying with them as if it had always been there.

"We'll have to send it back," she said, trying to think through this puzzle.

"Send it back? How?"

"I don't know. But we must."

"I don't even remember that old woman's name," Nick said carelessly. And he stepped lightly down from the wagon, the cashmere shawls over his arm. This time Mary did not follow. She was tired and wanted a nap. She wanted to think about this mystifying shawl business, too, but before she could come to any conclusion on that, her eyes closed and she fell asleep. Nick, returning, woke her to hear his news. He had sold three shawls, he told her jubilantly.

"Oh, good!"

"Yes, it is good." He laughed and came to her and sat down on her bunk bed, his arms framing her body, his glowing, confident face close. This was her Nick. With him in this mood, other memories fell away and she smiled in happy response up at him.

"When I've sold two more shawls, we'll move along south again—" He broke off. "Why? What's the matter?"

Mary answered slowly and with a little wistfulness in her voice. "Oh, Nick! Must we go on? I've been thinking that—Well, why couldn't we stay here? Settle down, I mean, and you open your store here. Why shouldn't we? I'm so afraid I'll be sick again if we start traveling! And this is a nice place. We've made friends—"

His quick frown interrupted her. "You'll have to let me run my own affairs," he said shortly, and rose from beside her.

The scarlet sprang to Mary's cheeks at this unexpected rebuff. He was always so touchy on that point! She could never say a thing. Although she was angered she answered quietly enough, "But your affairs are mine, too, now, Nick, I must remind you. Our affairs are joined."

He looked down at her for a moment. "Joined?" he repeated impatiently. "Well! It seems to me you're doing your best to pull them apart."

"Whatever do you mean?"

"I mean—stop criticizing. Stop finding fault. Let me manage things the way I always have. That's what I mean!" And he flung out.

It was the next day that he told her they were leaving. "I've sold my other two shawls," he announced, "so we'll get going at once."

This time Mary said nothing, and he went out to harness Nelly. She could hear him whistling out there to himself. Presently he called to her.

"By the way, I had some news today. Your friend, Mr. Burr, died."

Mary's shocked face appeared in the door flap.

"Mr. Burr? Esther's husband? Oh, Nick! How did you learn this dreadful thing?"

"Some traveler brought the word. 'Tis said Princetown's to have Mrs. Burr's father, Mr. Jonathan Edwards, for the new president."

Mary hardly heard. She was trying to realize Mr. Burr's death. To be sure, he had been a seriously sick man when she left. But she had never thought he might really die. Why, he was still young. And now Esther was left alone with those two babies. Grief for her friend and contrition that she, Mary, had not remained to help her through such a tragic time overwhelmed her. She sank down on the bunk bed and became lost in her thoughts and was not aware of the approach of someone to their wagon until she heard an angry voice outside.

"Well! Mr. Fanshaw! I reckon I'll take a look inside here, anyway!"

Unceremoniously a man's head appeared at the door flap. When he saw her there, his tone changed slightly.

"I ask yo' pardon, Missus. But my wife jest bought a cashmere shawl from yo' husband along with a lot of other stuff and when he left she couldn't find hide nor hair of it. I figgered it had got back in here some way."

Mary looked at him like one stunned. Oh, no! she thought. Oh, *no!*

"Come in," she said, after a moment. "Come in and look around. I'm sure Mr. Fanshaw wants you to."

"Yes! Tell him to look around all he wants!" Nick called from outside.

She remained on her bunk bed, her eyes downcast, trying not to think, trying not to believe what she could not, after all, help but believe. Only—where did he hide it? A low, respectful voice broke into her thoughts.

"Mind if I look under yo' mattress, ma'am?"

She rose and sat down on Nick's bunk which had already been examined along with every other nook and cranny in the wagon. The place was a mess! Her heart swelled with resentment at the indignity and shame she was being made to suffer, and the fingers of one hand rolled around and around the little lump on her other wrist. Outside she could hear Nick humming as he backed Nelly into the shafts. *How can he?* she thought.

"Beats me," the man said, at last. "But 'taint here."

She looked up, her dark eyes wide. "No."

"You don't know nothin' about it? No, you don't, I kin see that."

"I only wish I did"—very low.

"Well—"

He went out. She heard Nick say cheerfully, "Any luck?"

The man swore softly. Nick called after him, "I not only have to sell goods to the women, but I have to keep track of what they do with 'em after! It's too much. Tell your wife to ask that little black slave girl of hers if she knows anything about it."

He came up the steps of the wagon, whistling again. At sight of the upheaval within his whistling stopped.

"Why! I'd ought to call that fella back and skin him alive!"

Mary said, "Where is it, Nick?"

"Where is what?"

"The shawl you sold—and stole back."

His hand shot out swiftly and struck her a stinging blow on the cheek. There was lightning in his blue eyes and thunder in his low, furious voice.

"How dare you say a thing like that to me!"

"Because it's true."

He looked at her standing there with her cheek reddening from his blow. Then he swung about. But as he climbed past her into the driver's seat, she saw a corner of the cashmere shawl which he had wound tightly about his own body, hanging down beneath his coat. Yes, there it was. She stared blankly in a sick, horrified revulsion at Nick's back. Then she made her way across the lurching wagon and dropped onto her own bunk bed. As she buried her head in the pillow, she broke into tempestuous, silent weeping.

She was weeping for Mr. Burr's death and for Esther's bereavement; for the illness she herself had suffered and the disfiguring lump on her wrist; for the hot, flat land that lay behind her and the unknown land that lay ahead; for the hills of home that were so terribly far away, and the dignity and love and beauty that lived in Martin Manor; for the letter she could now never write to Prue telling of her wedded happiness; for the blow Nick had struck; for his anger and his trickery and his deceit. But most of all she was weeping for the loss of her love for him.

For it was gone. Bit by bit it had trickled away, till now there was nothing of it left. Nothing at all. And what she could do living with Nick without love she did not know.

So she wept.

Chapter 12

THIS WAS ANOTHER Nick with whom Mary set out along the Dismal Swamp road toward North Carolina. A Nick no longer gay, no longer a whistling, singing charmer. How could she have guessed there were two men living in the likeness of one? For this Nick was not only thoughtless and weak and given to moods of reckless gambling. This Nick was a thief.

The word scorched through her, drying her tears at last so that she was able to sit up and think what she would do next. She did not know. Only one thing was certain. She would never weep again over anything that Nick might do. Whatever came, she would find a hardness and a strength with which to meet it.

She climbed out presently and sat beside him on the high front seat, not because she particularly wanted to, but because it was too hot to remain inside. In silence they rode, and through the silence. It was a terrible thing in the Dismal Swamp—that silence! It pressed about her like something evil. It held eyes behind all the thick, close trees. It held smothered sounds. It lived in the black swamp water on both sides of the narrow trail. It lived in the dank dripping bushes. It lived in the tall treetops. It swooped on silent wings and slithered into dark pools, leaving only a faint stir of air or widening rings of water in its wake. It was something both alive and dead, and it contained a sinister, eerie threat. At last her fear of it grew greater than her heart sickness, and she began to talk to Nick simply to break it.

She did not speak of the shawl. She knew about the shawl and would never mention it again. She spoke, instead, of the country through which they were traveling, asking countless questions, partly to inform herself, partly to keep her courage up.

Was that the Roanoke they had crossed a way back? What were the trees that grew here with roots like knobby knees sticking up out of the water? The black snakes that hung down over their path—were they poisonous? How far was it, anyway, through the wilderness? Did Indians live hidden in its depths? If so, did Nick have his gun loaded and ready to shoot in case one appeared? And was he certain they would come to a tavern before night fell?

"Hold your tongue!" he shouted at her suddenly, worn past forbearance by his own corroding shame and fear and growing uncertainty about their future together. For Mary knew him now. Never again could he deceive her with any words. And, knowing him, what would she do? Hold her knowledge like a whip over him? He could never stand that! Nor could he crawl in penitence forever. He should not have married her. He'd known it all along. He was what he was, and he could not be different. But he was married—and now what? It was a puzzle he could not solve and which drove him in its torturing doubt beyond all self-control.

At his rebuke Mary straightened as though a ramrod had been thrust behind her back, closed her mouth tight, and, with her dark eyes fixed on the wet straining flanks of Nelly, sat without speaking again for the rest of the day.

When, at dusk, they reached a tavern in a small clearing, she said only, "There is not room for us both in the wagon tonight," and waited in a proud, unbending silence.

He stared blankly for a moment and then, without a word, went in and secured a room for her upstairs.

What a place that tavern was! When Mary first stepped inside she could hardly get her breath for the foulness of the air, so filled was it with tobacco smoke and the fumes of corn liquor, ale, and beer. It was dirty, too, the floor covered with the mud of men's boots, spittle, hens' droppings, spilled food and drink. This was seeing the world, she thought, a trifle wryly, and picked her way with care past sprawled figures and leering faces to the steep wooden steps that led to the tiny loft bedroom.

Safe there, she called for hot water, and, when it was brought, she bolted the door and washed her whole body, as if she would wash away the stain of all contact with Nick. Then she dressed herself again, for a moment wondering why her dresses all felt tight these days when she had eaten so little for so long. But the thought passed, and she gingerly lay down on the narrow, hard, lumpy bed. She did not want food. The thought of eating in this place sickened her. She wanted only rest and quiet in which to think.

As yet she had no plan for the future beyond getting through the swamp. But even had she tried to see past that point, it would have been impossible because of the rousting and quarreling and dicing and card playing and cockfighting that went on the whole night through below. Once clumsy footsteps softly made their way to her bolted door, and a hand tried it, but she held silence and presently the footsteps clumped down again. Had it been Nick? But this night, anyway, she would have to herself.

Finally she fell into a troubled sleep, only to waken

in the dawn at some disturbance outside. Rising, she went to the window, and saw, to her shocked horror, that it was Nick getting ready to drive off. Yes, there he was in his high seat gathering up the reins with never a glance toward her window.

"Nick!"

The scream tore from her throat and, turning, she snatched at the bolt on her door and rushed down the stairs. Through the Great Room she flew, past fallen benches and snoring, slobbering clouts, with the innkeeper, startled awake also and still wearing his slatternly apron, running close at her heels.

As she reached the wagon, Mary paused only long enough to flash a look of dark furious scorn up at Nick before she climbed inside.

"The innkeeper wants his pay for my room," she said then coldly.

"He's had his pay," Nick answered. "He owes *me* money now." And he climbed down and went after the innkeeper who had suddenly gone back inside. For a few moments there was the sound of a hot argument, but presently Nick reappeared, climbed to the driver's seat once more, gathered up the reins, and, with dogs yapping in a frenzy at Nelly's heels, they started on their way.

Mary lay on her bunk bed without speaking, her mind in a turmoil. What had happened? Could Nick possibly have drunk so much last night that this morning he had forgotten he had a wife? Or was it because she had not unbarred her door to him that he had felt justified in shaking her off? But to leave her in such a foul place! Without funds! And at the mercy of whatever brute might choose to molest her! It was incredible.

Nick's voice interrupted her.

"I thought you hated me when you wouldn't let me

in last night. And I couldn't blame you. I—" Suddenly he pulled Nelly to a halt and turned and let her see his face. Never had she thought it could hold such self-abasement, such contrition, such despair—and humble worship, too. "Oh, Mary! Mary! This time I can't even ask your forgiveness," he said. And there was a world of sadness in his tone, for the future that had once been so bright and promising now was arid as ashes. And his fault. All his fault.

In spite of herself, a stab of pity went through her. She said, in soft weariness, "Never mind, Nick."

"But I do mind. Why do I break your heart? And mine. And mine!" He made a sound like a groan.

"Never mind," she repeated.

He shook his head. "It's spoiled. I've spoiled it." And there was an unexpected dignity in his admission. "But leastways know this. I was planning to leave you only because I love you. No other reason. I gave money to the innkeeper for you, and I made arrangements with a man there to drive you back to Norfolk. I could do no more. Nor could I do less." He stopped. He had turned from her now and was staring straight ahead of him as he talked. "I really do love you, Mary. You are the one right thing that has ever come into my life, but you are better off without me." He stopped again, his face working with his emotion as he waited for her reply. But he waited without hope. For it was as he had always known in his heart it would be. He could not live up to her. She was too far above him. No, he could not reach up to her—indeed, he did not altogether want to—and yet he did not want to drag her down, either. This, anyway, out of yesterday's turmoil and trouble, he had finally resolved he would never do.

Mary was gazing at him, only half believing his words.

Yet why should she not? He had not once tricked her. He had only tricked others.

"I'm sorry," he finished. "I thought it was the best way but—well—I'm sorry."

"I'm glad you're sorry," she said, at last in a tired, gentle voice.

He flapped the reins on Nelly's back, and the wagon moved on. There was nothing more for either of them to say.

* * *

No need to give the details of their dreary crossing of North Carolina's seemingly endless stretches of arid land broken by occasional stands of tall pitch pines, rickety Negro cabins spawning naked babies, grunting pigs and scrawny chickens and wizened cows running wild along the sandy track. But one thing came clear to Mary as they crawled along.

Pity was not love. Nor was it trust. And come what may she would not, without either, spend the rest of her life with Nicholas Fanshaw. Plainly now she saw him, a man in whose blood ran a wild fever. It was a fever that consumed him, when it was on him, lifting him out of all common sense and to all manner of risks. She could remember as if it were yesterday the sparkle of excitement that had burned in his blue eyes when he had confounded the little old lady in Princess Anne. Nor did Mary think that, had his trickery been found out there and he had been jailed by the Sheriff, the punishment would have cured him. The threat of being caught in some deceit was only a whip to this lust of his, for to him life was but a game to be played for fun and to be won by hook or crook.

Well, Mary could not live that way. As soon as they reached a sizable town she would tell him so and seek conveyance north again. Home! She would go home gladly—her thoughts broke off there. What, she asked herself, had become of all her eager zest for life? Her restless curiosity and desire for adventure? It was gone, like her love for Nick. Now there was nothing. She was empty—and cold.

She went back to her planning.

She would go home. By ship this time, for never would she repeat such a journey overland. She would ask Nick for the necessary money on the promise that when she reached Martin Manor she would return it to him. Surely he would give it to her, for hadn't he, at the inn, without any request from her, been ready to let her depart? Had even made arrangements so that she might? Yes, she would leave him and take her chance on God's punishment for breaking her marriage vows. Prue had risked His anger once by not going to church for a while because of Johnny and had come safely through. She would do the same.

When they reached New Bern she would speak to him. New Bern was on the Neuse River which ran into Pamlico Sound. Surely there would be a gathering of ships there, and it would be easy to find one heading north. She was thankful her squeamishness had finally left her. It would make the sail back to New York much pleasanter.

As to Nick's feelings—she knew that he loved her in his way, but he did not love her as David loved Prue, nor as Mr. Burr had loved Esther. There was nothing protective or giving in his love. That was the difference. It was selfish. It asked for too much, and she no longer had anything to give.

So determined, she arrived with Nick in New Bern. But there she came to a wholly unexpected realization when one of the ladies of the town made a casual reference to her "condition."

"Condition?" Mary asked.

"Oh, you can't fool me," the woman answered, smiling. "I've had four myself."

"But, of course! She's right!" Mary thought suddenly. The nausea—the tight-fitting clothes—the doctor's words at Oxford: "Plenty of women have it after they're married" —how could she have failed to know before? Merciful heaven, she was going to have a baby! Nick's baby!

And for the sake of Nick's baby it was more than ever necessary that she leave Nick. Now more than ever she must make haste to return to Stockbridge. She would most certainly not risk bearing her child at the side of a ditch or in some foul tavern along the way. But what would Nick say? Uncertain, she did not reveal her discovery at first. Later that same day, however, on waking from a nap, she saw Nick standing by the center chest, an odd look on his face, and then the news burst from her.

He said nothing for a moment, only looked at her strangely.

"Are you sure?" he asked finally.

"Yes."

He said slowly, "I've been thinking so for some time, though how we'll manage with a baby—" He broke off. "Better see a doctor, Mary. I hear there's one lives in this town."

He went out. For a while she remained on her bed. You couldn't tell, she thought, from the way he spoke and acted, whether he was pleased or not. But she thought not. Presently she rose and went to the long center chest to get some money from the tin box that held their earnings so that she could pay the doctor.

The box was there, but it was empty. The drawer was empty, too. She stared blankly down at it for a moment, and then she slowly closed it and opened the other long drawers.

They were all empty.

What had become of the bolts of Scotch tweeds and English lawn and Italian paduasoy? Indeed! What had become of the last four cashmere shawls? Stolen? But they had never both left the wagon at the same time. Lost in betting at a cockfight, then? Ah, that was it! Back there at the tavern in the Dismal Swamp Nick must have lost everything. Or had he left these things as part of the "provisions" he had made for her journey back north without him? She did not know, and she could not guess.

She rose from her knees before the chest in the grip of a familiar emotion—pity mingled with anger—and went to another drawer where Nick kept the small items he had for sale. These, at least, were here. Remembering the doctor at Oxford, she selected some brass pins, a few ribbons, and a bottle of opodeldoc and dropped them into the deep pocket of her dress. Then she stepped out into the late sunlight of the day.

In many places she had been she would not dare venture forth alone, but New Bern had impressed her pleasantly upon their arrival earlier. It was an old town, settled by the Swiss and Germans and having along its shaded streets many fine mansions, large and square and painted white, with widows' walks atop the roofs. There were small cottages here, too, with a long sloping slant from the ridgepole to the ground in the rear. And everywhere you looked you saw little square window glasses and fanlights above the front doors—a sight happily familiar.

Nick had said there was a doctor in town. Well, she would find him. She would ask the first person she met to direct her to him.

She moved quickly along the street to the corner where there was a tavern. Here the excited voices and cheers of men caught her attention, and she turned her head. In the dusty yard at the rear a cockfight was in progress, and there she saw Nick, kneeling in the dirt, his handsome face bright with a tense hopefulness. A wave of sick fury swept through her at the sight.

Yes, there he was, betting again. Trying, no doubt, to win back the fortune he had lost in the swamp. Trying to retrieve his bad luck so that he might return to her in triumph and say, "See! Now the baby will be taken care of." Or so that he might return in shame to murmur—"It was for you. For you and the baby. I won in the beginning! I ought to have stopped there, but—Well, I'm sorry."

Oh, Nick! Nick! Being sorry isn't enough. And what are you using for money to bet with if ours is all gone? Or did you fill your pockets just now when I was asleep? A belated memory of his odd look came to her—the look she had seen when she first wakened—and it told her this guess was right.

With her lips set firmly she hurried past, averting her gaze from the sight of him, thinking suddenly that if her child turned out to be a boy-child and were like Nick—

Oh, she would never let him be like Nick! Once she got safely away she would never see Nick again. She would bring up her baby at Martin Manor under the good influence of Pa and Prue and David. So surrounded, it could not help but take on worthy qualities.

So busy was she with these thoughts she did not see a tall man coming toward her until he was almost upon her. Then, as he courteously stepped off the narrow walk to let her pass, she stopped.

"Oh! Excuse me," she said.

Warm gray eyes set in a lean and somber face looked down into hers with surprise as he waited for her to continue.

"Could—could you direct me to a doctor, please?"

"I might, lassie."

"Thank you. Where does he live, then?"

He had seen, from the proud tilt of her head to the tips of her buckled shoes, that she was an uncommon girl. Her dress was modish, though tight-fitting, her kerchief clean, her bright brown hair a pretty confusion of brushed, gleaming curls. But her lovely face, shaped like a heart and coming down to a point at her chin, was too white, her eyes too big in it and holding now a look of uncertainty and fear. She was, moreover, a stranger in town, as her question revealed. A young, bonny stranger, unattended, seeking a doctor. His glance swept her again, and when he spoke concern sounded in his voice, for he was one to pat the stray dog, to pick up a homeless kitten, to drop a coin into a withered old palm. Moreover, he was nearly twice her age. Why! She could be his daughter—almost. At least if he were married, she could.

"Lassie, be ye in trouble?"

For a moment she did not comprehend. Then, as the implication of his question became clear to her, she drew herself up, and the color flared into her cheeks.

"No! And never mind your impudence!" She swept away, her head high.

His voice followed with its right Scottish burr: "Turn the corner to y'r right. 'Tis th' wee white house." Then, interested, and having nothing else to do, he turned and slowly followed her.

She did not see him when she came out a while later,

for dusk had fallen and he stood in deep shadow. Nor did she hear his following footsteps as, once again, her thoughts absorbed her. The doctor had told her he believed she must be four or five months pregnant. Well, now, to inform Nick of the certainty.

Making her way back past the tavern to the small grove of trees where their wagon was, she could not find it. Startled, she peered through the gathering gloom. Then she darted about among the trees, looking everywhere. But truly there was no wagon to be found.

Had she mistook the grove? Had she, at the tavern, made the wrong turn? Hastily she retraced her steps. No. There was only one lane ending in trees. The other led to the village.

A bolt of fear went through her like an electric shock. Then, in a rising panic, she rushed to the tavern door and pounded on it before she flung it wide and stood on the threshold in the half light from within.

"I—I'm looking for my husband," she said to the innkeeper who was alone in the Great Room mopping up the long table before the fireplace. "He's a tall man with black, curly hair. He was here at the cockfight this afternoon. Do—do you know which way he went from here?"

The innkeeper, squint-eyed, with a greedy look on his heavy jowled face, came close to her.

"Lady," he said, his glance holding a bright watchfulness, "Lady, he lit out o' here. He lost all he put up an' he lit out."

He waited, his tongue moving over his loose-hung mouth, his eyes speculative, cautious—and hopeful.

Mary looked at him a little wildly for a second, then, through stiff, whitening lips, she said, "Did—did he leave any money—any note—or anything—with you for me?"

The squint eyes glittered, but the answer came readily enough. "No, ma'am. Not a thing. He jest lit out."

She nodded and turned away. Outside she stood in a stunned uncertainty in the darkness, trying to believe what had happened to her. Nick was gone. He had driven off and left her alone in a strange place without a cent, knowing she was with child. Once before he had tried to do this—(he had known about the baby, then, too, she thought now, even if she hadn't)—and now he had gotten away. But that other time he had provided for her, planned for her safe return home. This time he hadn't. Or had he? And was the innkeeper lying to her? Or was it Nick who had lied to her before? She would doubtless never know. Slowly, as if in a horrid dream, she moved along the street.

The ringing of a church bell in the early evening stillness gave her her first direction. In a church it would be quiet, and she could think. In a church there was safety, too, and a measure of protection. She made her way towards the peaceful sound, entered into the dim stillness, and dropped to her knees in the last pew which she found empty.

How long she stayed there she did not know, but gradually her thoughts cleared.

She should have known this might happen. Right from the beginning there had been warnings of Nick's undependability—if she had cared to note them, but she hadn't. —"Not for him a pregnant woman! All he wanted was the fun in life"—Even Nick's words about his father had not stirred a tremor of alarm in her.

Not a pregnant woman for Nick, either, it seemed. All he too wanted was the fun in life. The easy way that led nowhere. The ready money, no matter how it was got.

With the new strength that had come to her, Mary thought, "Well, all right! That part of my life is over and done with. Nick has gone because he didn't care any more. Perhaps he never did. Well, all right. Now what?"

Chapter 13

SHE COULD GO to the doctor and ask his help. But he had been a harsh and crabbed old soul, taking with poor grace her offer of pins and ribbons in payment. Now, recalling the lean sharpness of his seamed countenance, she knew she could not throw herself on his mercy. She doubted he had any.

The minister? Would the minister lend her money for her passage home? If she had her marriage paper he might. But that was gone with the wagon. And she had no wedding ring—it was one of the things Nick had always been going to buy for her and never had—so the minister might not believe her without her marriage paper or a wedding ring. He might only tell her what an awful end awaited her for her sin and do nothing but pray for her soul. Anyway, it was likely he had no spare coin. What minister ever had?

The thing to do, perhaps, was to make her way to the river road and along it to the sound. Once there, a ship's captain might take pity on her. If she used Matt's name—Yes, that was what she would do. That was the way she would get herself home.

Then a new thought came. Could she go home now? Home was the place she had wearied of and left so happily. Moreover, she had never written back of her marriage.

Might not Prue and Pa question the truth of that if she told them of it so late? Might not they, too, doubt she had a marriage paper since she could produce none? Oh, they would take her in, all right, even without it. Mary could not imagine Prue's great warm heart refusing her love and protection. And though Pa might look at her with his black eyes filled with a sharp and bitter disappointment, he, too, would make her welcome.

But did she want it that way? Did she want to return to Stockbridge—to Martin Manor—contrite and humble and—yes—shamed? She would be a woman without a husband and with a child about to be born. The whole town would talk. She was married—but she had married secretly. Why? Perhaps she hadn't really been married, after all. What had she to prove it? Oh, the tongues that would clack! And the guesses that would be made! So it had been when Matt had run off. The scandal had provided conversation for weeks and months, hurting both Pa and Prue deeply. Did she want to hurt them that way again, even though there would not be a grain of truth in all that might be said?

Yet if she did not go home, what would she do? How could she take care of herself and her unborn child? She did not know! It all made her head spin.

She was roused from her thoughts by the final singing, and, pulling herself to her feet, she slipped from the church ahead of everyone and out into the night. Once again soft footsteps followed her, and once again she failed to notice them. This time her distraction led her to the edge of town, to the river's bank where she sank down, undecided what course to follow and feeling more and more desperate in her indecision.

Staring at the black water whose tiny waves were tipped with moonlight, it occurred to her that there lay one answer. She might wade out into the stream and lie down. It would be quite simple. But she did not want to die! All she wanted was to begin again. To write a fresh page on the book of her life. There must be some way to manage this.

A cold wind began blowing off the water, and she shivered a little. Further down where the river widened into the bay she could see the white sides of ships at anchor. There was one in particular, hung from bow to stern with lanthorn lights as if some revelry were taking place on board. The ship's captain, maybe, was giving a party to friends from the shore. She could hear faint music now, and she thought how happy and untroubled those people were, while she, alone and friendless, had no place to lay her head this night.

The sound of carriage wheels came to her from the road that ran along the water's edge, and she rose to her feet, thinking whoever it was might give her a lift if she dared ask for it. The conveyance was coming from town on its way, most likely, to the gaiety aboard the ship. Presently it hove in view, a great white coach drawn by four beautiful black horses, a Negro groom in elegant livery atop the high platform in back, two postilions galloping alongside and two outriders bringing up the rear. In the pale moonshine Mary could see silver buttons all atwinkle on the groom's jacket. In the swaying lanthorn's light she could glimpse within the coach the green velvet of upholstery, the glitter of gold lace beneath the cuff of a man's dark coat, the white, laughing face of a woman with a cascade of dark curls falling over snowy shoulders only half hidden beneath her scarlet cloak. And then the coach jolted into a deep hole and came to a stop, and a man's head, his black hair smoothly clubbed, was thrust through the open window, and a man's commanding voice shouted, "Avast there! Have a care!"

"Matt!" Mary screamed and flung herself forward.

But her frenzied cry was lost before the confusion of sound that followed—the galloping of hooves as the outriders closed in, the deep excited words of men all talking at once, the squeak of wheels and creaking of leather harness and groan of coach as the horses heaved to pull it from the hole. Besides, a hand had closed over her mouth and a strong arm about her had drawn her back and away.

Frantically she fought and bit and scratched, but to no avail. The arm was iron and would not let her go until the coach was gone. Even then the man spoke before he released her.

"Have no fear o' me, lassie. I would help you, not do you harm."

It was the Scotsman who had directed her to the doctor's office, speaking with his odd, rich burr.

"I've been following you. You denied you were in trouble, but you are. And deep. Your man has deserted you, and you don't know what to do or where to go. Well, I'll tell you, do you come with me to a place where we can talk."

"I wouldn't need you to tell me if you had only let me alone! That was—"

He broke in. "First, permit me to introduce myself. My name is Alexander MacDonald, First Mate o' the sloop *Prudence.*"

"The *Prudence!* Why, that's where I want to go! Oh, take me to him! Take me to Matt, please!"

"I will. Or I'll bring him to you. You have my promise. But first a bit of food and a bit of talk, for there be things you must make clear to me as well as things I must make clear to you."

There was no help for it. So she went with him back to an inn—not the inn where the cockfight had taken place, but another—where they had a table before an enormous fireplace.

Never would she forget that inn! The great fire was presided over by a muttering Negro woman who looked like some kind of a witch stirring an evil brew. Around her were pots on spiders, pots on hooks, a rack of iron spoons, ladles and other implements. Over the fire two spits were turning that were driven by springs and weights, one holding a ham, the other a sizable turkey, while in nearby cauldrons stews bubbled and potatoes boiled and clams steamed, the whole filling the air with a wonderful mouth-watering odor. There was a candle on their table, and in its flickering light the dark wood walls glowed warmly and Alexander MacDonald's face, clear to her now, showed itself somehow both gentle and stern as he leaned toward her.

"And now tell me, child," he said, after plates of food and coffee had been brought them. "What precisely are you to Matt?"

"Why! He's my brother!"

"Your brother! Oons! And I thought—" He stopped. "Your brother's known many a woman," he said. "You'll forgive me."

She smiled wanly. You could reach a point, she discovered, where shame could no longer shame you. Anyway, she could not blame him for his thinking, the way she had traipsed the streets by herself. He went on, then, slowly, puzzling out loud what to do.

"You cannot go to your brother in your present fix. And here's the reason. He's on his way to winning the hand of a very lovely lady, one of the fairest in Charles-Town. And one of the proudest. Myrtle's visiting now in Edenton, not far from here, and the party aboard Matt's ship is in her honor. You understand 'tis no fitting moment for you to burst upon him with your difficulties. 'Tis not the captain can help you this time. 'Tis only Alec himself. Aye. Alec must do it. You trust me, child?"

She nodded. She remembered about Alec. Matt had told of him and of their friendship the last time he had come home almost four years ago.

"You must stay here the night, then. 'Tis a respectable place, and you'll be safe. Tomorrow I'll bring your brother to you." His gray eyes smiled with sudden warmth into hers. "We must find a way to give you good care till the wee bairn is safe in the world. And I'm thinkin' I know the way."

Tears, then, welled up in her for the first time, and she had a hard time to whisper the words she must say.

"I've been so headstrong and foolish, Alec!"

"Aye. But we're all that, some time or other. We scourge it from our natures with whip lashings o' grief and regret, and then we're made sensible. Providence be thankit!"

"Prue—my sister—never was so foolish."

"You cannot be sure. She might have been, in another way."

"Oh, no! Not Prue! I wish I were like her." She looked at him, unconsciously beseeching. "You must think poorly of me," she finished, very low. "A girl who will run off secretly with a pedlar and who is deserted by him surely holds a despicable place in a man's mind."

There was a strange fateful instant of silence, though why it was fateful she had no idea. Then he said gently, in a voice that seemed to send a singing vibration deep into her proud, bruised spirit, "Far from it, lass. Pity I feel. And tenderness. And grave concern. But not scorn. And now tell me: has this Nick broke your heart?"

"No!"

"You dinna love him any more?"

"I never did love him, Alec. Never at all. I thought it was love for a while. But it wasn't." She lifted her candid brown eyes to his. "I used him," she said. "I used him to escape from a house of sickness and to avoid going home, which was my only other choice. That's the whole of it, I see now. So I suppose I deserved what I got."

"You're honest, Mary."

It was amazing how much better she felt in his presence. The feeling of having disgraced herself was still on her, heavy and dark, and all the worry for the future, but none of it was any longer a burden she was unable to bear, for Alec was sharing it with her.

"What's your plan for me?" she asked him. "For Matt to take me on his ship?"

"No. He cannot do that. There's no woman aboard. And he's not one to thole a kittle cargo."

"What does that mean?"

"It means he cannot abide a difficult cargo. And a woman aboard is always difficult."

"But—he could leave me somewhere, couldn't he? On some island—"

Alec shook his head. " 'Tis a daft notion. There's nowhere safe for you. I'd never be certain—Matt would never be certain—" He broke off. "Leave be with your thinking! Trust me."

"I'm sorry"—contritely.

Matt came the next day, a new Matt such as she had never seen before, all his burly weight trimmed down, his beard gone, his face clean-shaven, his manner polished and sure. He was dressed in a striking blue uniform with gold buttons and buff breeches that gave an elegant appearance to his big frame. Had it not been for his voice and his eyes she would not have known him either last night or now. But now she saw that in his black glance there glimmered still the old bright impatience.

He bent it on her as she stood before him waiting his judgment on her, and in it she saw a deep anxiety for her, mingled with harassment. For this untoward happening might well founder the ship of love he was so delicately maneuvering into port. A runaway sister who had married beneath her and been left stranded, as Mary had been, would be looked at askance by the aristocratic Averys. Yet her expression now, both proud and humble, penitent and defiant, told him silently that she had chosen her path, as he had chosen his, out of the necessity of her nature, and she would take the consequences of it and pay the price. The courage he read there that underlay her silent pleading for tolerance and help gentled him. After all, it must not be easy to be a woman and walk the same tracks like a blind mule in a treadmill year after year till you grew too old to do aught but sit in a rocking chair. Mary had always been too high-spirited for that.

He put a heavy hand on her shoulder and said, "Mary, Mary, you are like me, 'tis plain as a pikestaff. And where we get this wild streak and itching foot, I know not. But I'm fair cured. I hope you are."

She nodded. "I am, I think." She hesitated. "You'll help me?"

"Yes!" Alec spoke now. "You've clabbered his noddle, 'tis true, but he'll help you, all right."

"I don't want to go home." Mary spoke quickly—and a little wildly in her fear that he might make her go home. "Not yet! Not till I can go with my head up. It isn't fair," she went on, seeing Matt's frown, for he had thought to ship her quickly off to Prue without Myrtle's ever knowing about her. "It isn't fair at all. I—I don't deserve anything so easy. Oh, don't you see what I mean? I'm not —I'm not good enough to go home yet. I won't tote my troubles to Prue's door! She's carried more than her share already. I'll carry my own! When I've proved I can, then I'll go. Not before, Matt."

She stopped, breathless, not seeing the admiring light in Alec's eyes as she finished. All she saw was Matt's discomfiture. But before he could find voice, Alec spoke.

"I've a plan. Now hark to it, the two of you."

He had a relative, a cousin, he said, named Jeanie MacDonald. Her home was in Cross Creek, not too far away. If Matt approved—and made a generous enough offer—Alec thought Jean would let Mary stay with her and her husband until after the baby came. By that time Matt would have returned from his cruise, could pick her up and take her and her child to his new home in Charles-Town.

"You'll be there in time for his wedding," Alec concluded. "And all that need be said then is your husband was not able to be with you."

Mary listened in a curious state of mind, feeling helpless and unsure. Her defiance oozed away entirely now that she had voiced it. She was able only to lean like a willow on their decision for her. Indeed, what choice had she since she had refused so firmly to let Matt send her home?

So it was settled, and that afternoon Matt and Alec accompanied her to Cross Creek to the neat little house on Green Street where Jean MacDonald lived. Jean, tall, with glittering glasses above a grim mouth, heard Alec's introduction and Matt's request, with her arms folded forbiddingly across her meager chest. But there must be a heart there, Mary told herself, otherwise Alec would not have suggested her. And Mary was right, for, without apparently paying any attention to Matt's suggestion as to finances, she gave him a curt nod.

"She can stay. I'll nurse her myself. Life takes queer twists," she added, as if to exonerate herself for befriending a girl who, for all the men's talk, might be unmarried.

Matt turned to Mary, relief in his face and in his voice that the present, at least, was taken care of—and far enough from Charles-Town so that no rumor would reach Myrtle's family. As to her going there for the wedding with her child, as Alec had suggested—well, he'd see about that when the time came.

"Good-by, then, Mary," he said.

Mary looked up at him. "Matt, I—I have no clothes other than these on me. I'll need things—"

"Blow me down! Of course you'll need things." He stood there, stripping money from his wallet as if it was leaves from a tree, and filled her hands. She wanted to thank him and could not. She also wanted to thank Alec, whose eyes had hardly left her face through all the talking, and Jean MacDonald, and her great silent man of a husband who had nodded acquiescence to Jean's decision when he had joined them in the little parlor. But no words came, and presently Alec and Matt were both gone, and she was alone in the bedroom to which Jean led her.

She sat quietly in the rocking chair in the small, cheerful room, neat as wax, that was to be hers for the next four or five months. She was thinking that if ever she had learned that a single act can never be a solitary thing just affecting her own life, she had learned it now. When she had gone off with Nick she had been so sure she had the right, for it was only herself doing it. Now she knew that whatever action she took was like dropping a stone into water from which ripple out ever-widening circles. These had reached to touch three people already. No, four, since Jean's husband could not be forgotten. And the shore was still distant!

PART THREE

❦

January 1758–April 1759

Chapter 14

IT WAS JANUARY when Matt and Alec left Mary at Jean MacDonald's house, and it was March when her baby was born prematurely. The birthing was not easy, and Mary's memories of it were always hazy. She never knew what went wrong, but her little girl lived for only a few moments and (Jean told her later) it was a wonder she, herself, lived at all. When at last she was able to crawl out into the sunshine again she felt utterly beaten. She had not strength enough left in her to grieve over her loss.

Jean worried about her because of her failure to regain her health and insisted that she go out every pleasant day to lie in the fresh air. Mary did as Jean bade her, but the hours she spent in her chair were filled with a nothingness. Staring with lackluster eyes, she tried to plan her future only to turn from the effort in weak helplessness. Future. What future had she? Life, which only a year ago had beckoned her alluringly along an unknown road that held a promise of delightful surprises around every curve and beyond every mountain, now stretched out a flat and empty desert over which she must toil to the end of her days. That was her future.

For, as Jean had pointed out, Mary was still married in the eyes of the Lord and the Church, and until she was free there would be nothing but the desert.

"I'm caught in a web of my own spinning," she thought to herself, and wondered whatever Matt would say to her when he came back for her. He would not want her as an invalid in his house and at his wedding, she was sure. His kindness and generosity had already exceeded what she might have expected from this swashbuckling, vital, impatient brother of hers. But an invalid called for special attention. An invalid could throw a wet blanket over such a festivity as a wedding. And an invalid called forth questions—the last thing Matt desired. His own adventuresome past had been one of high excitement and derring-do, with a fortune made out of it. By contrast, Mary's experience was drab and shabby, even somewhat shameful. He did not want it known any more than he wanted his own affair with the Indian girl known. No, unless Mary could make him proud of her, could add honor and joy to his wedding, he would not care to have her there.

Yet how could she go home? How could she face that long journey alone in her present weakness? Or the curiosity and pity and scorn that would be meted out to her when her story became known there? The idea was now more repugnant to her than ever.

These were the thoughts that possessed her all the time and that were going through her head on the warm April afternoon when Jean and her husband left her alone in her chair on the lawn. She was lying with her eyes closed when she heard the gate latch click and, looking up, she saw Nigel Fanshaw coming toward her. For a moment she could not believe her eyes. But, though somewhat better dressed and walking with a steady purposefulness rather than at the shambling gait that had been his earlier, it was the same rangy figure and black tousled head, so like Nick's, that she remembered. The face, set in sullenness, was, at first glance, the same, too.

In that instant, life seemed to stop within her. Then it poured through her veins in such a torrent that she could scarcely speak his name for the smother of emotion in her. How had he discovered her whereabouts? And why had he come? Had he, perchance, news of Nick?

He walked directly toward her, his head thrust a little forward between his shoulders, his dark glance opaque so that she could not guess the answers to her unspoken questions. His face, she now observed, had matured since she had last seen him and had taken on a resoluteness that, with his smoldering look, gave it an appearance of strength. He looked to be a full-grown man, she thought, whose way in life was determined and already embarked upon.

"I've found you," he said, and there was a note of triumph in his voice for his success.

"Yes. How–however did you do it?"

" 'Twas fair easy to trace a pedlar's wagon. Especially when the pedlar left behind a string of folks angered by his cheating of them." At her instinctive gesture of pleading protest, he stared, then he said incredulously, "Surely you know by this time what Nick's like!"

"I know"–very low.

The dark eyes narrowed on her quickly. "Kind of makes you shamed? Kind of makes you think you'd ought to pay back something to the ones he's cheated?"

"Yes, of course, Nigel. It troubles me. It's always troubled me. But how can I? Those people are way north, and I'm here."

"Not all of them are north."

"What do you mean?" She looked at him uncertainly, aware now that he was driving toward something, that he had a purpose and that it might not be a good purpose, but that he had, too, a will which would let nothing stop him from achieving it.

"I'm here," he said. "I'm one of the ones Nick cheated. Belike the very first, before you and he went off."

And he told her his story, his gaze never leaving her face as he talked, clearly seeing her recoil and her deepening humiliation. For she had to believe him. It explained too clearly Nick's unwillingness to let Nigel come to his wedding. Oh! She could die of shame, hearing that story! And yet there was pity in her heart, too. For Nick, with a brother so selfish and unfeeling, as well as for Nigel who had been so wronged. She felt, too, a proper anger against the two of them for involving her in ways of thinking and acting so alien to her.

"How much was it Nick took?" she asked, at last.

He named a sum. Startled, she shook her head. "I haven't that much, Nigel. If I had, I'd give it to you."

He took her answer quietly, turning it over in his mind as if to examine its truth and determine his next move. Then he nodded.

"How did you track me here?" she asked.

"Nigh every one at New Bern saw you with two men at the inn, one in the uniform of a ship's master, the other speaking like a Scotsman. It was the Scot asked the shortest way to Cross Creek here. When I learned that, I followed. You've been sick," he finished, changing the subject.

"Yes."

"You lost your baby."

"Yes." (He'd found out everything, she told herself, in a dull wonder.)

"Do you know at all where Nick's gone?"

"No. Further south. That's all."

"I'll find him." He looked at her questioningly. "When I do, should I bring him back to you?"

"Oh, no, Nigel! *No!* My life with Nick has *ended!* It's over. It's finished. I never want to see him again."

She felt herself trembling and near to tears and wished he would go away and leave her. Why didn't he? She could be of no help to him.

He broke into her thoughts.

"You were too good for him, and he had to let you go. But if you belonged to me, I'd never let you go."

There was an odd ring in his voice, a challenge in his lightning glance that startled Mary.

"I'd make myself as good as you," he went on. And then he drew from his pocket a sheer white handkerchief, clean and neatly folded, that he held out towards her in his outstretched palm so that she could clearly see the initials on it—M.M. "It's yours."

She nodded, her breath coming faster as she remembered how he had snatched it from her bodice that day long ago. She was alone again now as she had been then, and no doubt he knew it. Was he telling her that he was the stronger of the two of them and could do as he liked with her if he chose?

But he was putting it back into his pocket and saying unexpectedly, "I'm sure sorry for the fright I gave you that time. I didn't rightly know—till I'd takened this—that you were different from the other women that chased Nick. I kept it," he went on, "because it's the first thing I ever had from your kind of world." He stopped, and his coal black eyes took on a bright, determined gleam as he continued. "It's the kind of world I mean to live in some day myself—same as you do. It's the world I'll get my start in as soon as ever I have back what Nick took from me. How soon will that be?" he finished.

"How soon?" she repeated, not understanding. "Why, as soon as you find Nick, I suppose."

"Bah! Nick won't have it. You know that! He won't have tuppence. It's you who'll have to give it to me. You said yourself just now you thought you'd ought to." His voice changed, softened. "I know Nick's used you bad, too. But—" He hesitated, then finished angrily. *"Some* way there'd ought to be fair dealings!"

She was silent, her mind turning every which way in the tangle in which she found herself. Indignation, commiseration, a sense of justice and a natural fear—these all made up the tangle. Both times she had seen him, Nigel had stirred up a tumult in her, she thought, but in the same breath she told herself how it had been she who had said he needed only an interested woman, someone like an older sister, to make something of himself. Now, as if he knew that, he was asking her to be one to him and so help him.

"All I want is what is due me," he finished.

"I've told you I didn't have that much."

"Your brother has."

She shook her head. "I can't ask Matt for anything more. You don't understand how much he's already done for me. I'll give you what I have now but—really—I can't ask him for more."

Nigel never moved. He simply stood with his dark eyes holding hers.

"Listen!" he said. "I found out a lot back there in New Bern. I found out for certain that your brother's rich. He's got ships. He's bought himself a big house in Charles-Town. And he wants to marry a hoity-toity Southern lady. Well, she wouldn't be pleased to learn he had a brother-in-law fit only for the whipping post and the jail." He stopped, and Mary looked at him, her heart thudding sickly. "You ask him," Nigel ended. "I'll wait around till you do."

He went away, then, walking with that new purposefulness, and she knew he would wait as he said. Oh! What a sorry state of affairs she had contrived, not only for herself but for Matt, too! If he should be angered and defy Nigel—what then? Nigel had told her plainly enough. He would go to Charles-Town and spread word about Mary's husband, Matt's brother-in-law. If Matt yielded—dear sakes alive, what would that let him in for? Because if Nigel dared demand money now, wouldn't he do it again? How could they—she and Matt—know when he would feel fully repaid? When would his threats end? In her sick and nervous condition she could see Nigel's shadow hovering over them forever.

* * *

If Mary had not been such a low-spirited wraith of herself, so full of self-condemnation and despair and fear, it is possible that Matt might have blasted Nigel right out of the town in one of his terrifying bursts of wrath when he came back to Cross Creek late in May. But the white, frail, frightened look of her alarmed him and he could not add to her torment by any threats against Nigel.

"Nick's and my affairs are still joined," Mary told him in anxious weariness. "I can't deny that. And I know he'll not pay Nigel even though Nigel finds him." She lifted her glance to Matt's huge figure which seemed to fill entirely her little square bedroom. "This may sound queer to you, Matt, but I feel responsible for Nigel's getting the start in life he wants. It's as I told you: I bear Nick's guilt with him. I can't help it. Besides—" She hesitated, then went on. "Besides, there's no one else in the world to care if Nigel succeeds or not. And—and someone ought to care about everyone. I mean everyone ought to have an anchor they can hold to."

Matt's black eyes, that could be cold and hard as ice, warmed as he looked down on her. "Now you sound like Prue," he told her. "All right. I'll pay this sum. But it'll be the end, and he'll know it."

Mary nodded in relief and he went away. However, he took with him a rising anger against Nigel's presence here, his knowledge of Matt's affairs and his demands which could not be refused. He found Nigel with no trouble, paid Nick's debt, secured the lad's signature to a statement that it was paid in full, and then ordered him to leave him and Mary alone in the future. He spoke with such a force and fury that it would have frightened any one else, but not Nigel. He listened, his dark opaque eyes never wavering from Matt's black flashing ones. Yet he did not shrink. Nor did he answer back. It was the damndest thing, Matt told himself, as he strode away. It was as if Nigel had been memorizing the pattern of his—Matt's—words and behavior for future reference.

When he returned to the little house on Green Street, Jean called him into her sitting room where Alec waited.

"Sit you down," she ordered, her glasses glittering upon him. "And you, too, Alec, for you're not leavin' yet. The two of you must understand what lies ahead of you. Your sister," she went on, addressing Matt, "does nothing but weep. And 'tis more than the rascal, Nigel, troublin' her. She's had full time to think, and all her thoughts have taken her nowhere. She's at a blind alley, and 'tis a dangerous spot for her to be. Tragedy behind her and nothing before." She shook her head. "What she needs, if she's to pull out o' this slough o' despair, is diversion. A sea trip would pick her up something wonderful with all its strange sights. Also, the width o' the waters below and the heavens above might give her a new view on the smallness o' herself and her affairs. So 'tis my advice to you, Cap'n Martin, to take her aboard your ship for the one more cruise Alec says you're taking afore your wedding."

Advice? It was a command, and Matt, accustomed to giving commands himself, recognized it as such. He had thought to be married after the cruise he had just finished, but Myrtle's mother had put him off, saying she could not be ready, and he had decided on another voyage to the Caribbean in the interim. But—a woman aboard his ship? He did not like it. While he hesitated, Alec spoke.

"You do not want the lass here with you longer, Jean?"

"No."

"And she is not fit to travel north alone?"

"No, she is not."

"Then—"

Matt made a fierce gesture of protesting resignation. How like Alec to spell out for him the only possible course he could take!

"Do you pack her gear, Jean MacDonald, and we'll be on our way," he said.

There was no help for it. But perhaps good would come of it some way, he told himself.

Chapter 15

NEVER IN ALL HER LIFE would Mary forget that cruise on Matt's ship. She was so weak that Alec had to carry her aboard, but from the moment she saw the white spreading sails fill and felt the surge of the sea beneath her, she began to mend. It might have been the bracing air or it might have been the feeling that she had truly left her unhappy past behind her on the shore and was about to commence a new life, that worked the cure. Or it might have been Matt's words to her and the challenge that lay in them, or all of these together—plus something more she had not anticipated or dreamed of.

Matt had given her his own cabin, a generosity that touched her deeply, for it was a sumptuous place with every possible comfort: fine silken Oriental rugs, carved teakwood furniture, linen sheets sweet with cleanliness, and silver service on the trays that bore her meals. Oh! Matt could be hard, and he had been errant, but—as Prue always said—there was goodness in him, too, and Mary discovered it anew on that trip.

He came to her the second day as she lay in the bunk he had yielded to her, and sat down beside her to take her thin hand in his.

"Do you know why you're here, Mary?" he asked, his black eyes piercing hers. "Let me tell you, then. You're here for just one reason. To get well so you can represent my family at my wedding when we return."

Mary gave a little gasp. "You really want me to? Oh, Matt!"

"I really do want you to." He paused, a frown on his face. He felt positive it was doubts about him and his background which had made Mrs. Avery postpone Myrtle's marriage to him. Despite his prepossessing and overwhelming personality, despite the glamor cast over his life at sea and the attractiveness of the financial success he had won from it, there remained this uncertainty in her mind. Was the newcomer wellborn? What of his family? For she, herself, was a "true Charlestonian," descended from a family that had settled there in the time of the Lords Proprietors, and inclined to regard all later comers as less than her equal. Mr. Avery, it must be said, was less hesitant. He was living under heavy financial pressure with a large mortgage on his property now due, which Matt stood ready to pay off. No scruples about "sacrificing his daughter," as his wife put it, hid his desire to avail himself of the relief offered by his prospective son-in-law. Myrtle, blowing first hot and then cold, drove Matt wild. For too long, to one of his impatience and ardor, this had been the situation. But if Mary could appear—the Mary he remembered from a few years ago, who had been all sparkle and grace and charming eagerness, and who bore in her looks and manner the marks of breeding Mrs. Avery wanted to see—then surely that woman's doubts would be laid at rest.

He repeated, "I do most certainly want you to. I want to show you off, Mary. I want to let Myrtle's folks know what a fine family I come from. So get well and do me proud."

Mary looked at him, thinking how much she owed this

brother of hers and how much she wanted to repay him. If she could do as he asked—If she could be present not as a sorrowful ghost but as the fine lady he wanted her to be—it seemed a great deal for her to do, however, and so she said slowly, after a moment, "Prue's the one, Matt. Prue could shine for you better than I ever could. You ought to ask Prue."

"I did ask her some time ago. She can't come. She's with child."

"She is! How wonderful! How is she feeling? When is the baby coming?"

"I don't know that. She said she was fine. I wrote her about the baby three months ago and got an answer just before we left."

Mary's voice took on an anxious note.

"Matt, when you wrote her, what did you tell her about me?"

His black eyes met hers steadily. "Not a word, Mary. How could I know what you'd want said? You'll write her yourself when you're ready."

Mary fell back against the pillows in relief. Matt's understanding and kindness were beyond belief. And he needed her. If Prue could not help him, she—Mary—must.

"Matt," she said, lifting her eyes to his, "I'll get well. I promise! And if I'm not certain I can do you proud, I'll—I'll jump into the sea!"

He smiled. "You'll do me proud, all right," he said confidently. Then he rose. "What's past is past," he went on, looking down at her. "I had to learn that the hard way myself. What's past is past. For you and for me—both. No use to hold onto it."

He was telling her that as he had put Marie out of his life, so she must put Nick out of hers. She did not remind him that she was married to Nick as he had not been married to Marie and that it made a difference. But she would remember that later. Right now she would forget it—because he had asked her to.

She nodded silently.

* * *

The weeks slipped by. And the islands slipped by. The anchor would drop, and Mary, on Alec's arm and a little stronger each time, would go ashore to explore. This was seeing the world as she had dreamed of seeing it, in a luxury and in a safety such as she had never known with Nick—but, better than that, in a slow-growing return to health and happiness.

All thanks to Alec for this last—Alec, to whose watchful care Matt had entrusted her. Alec, forever by her side, shielding her from too much sun or too much wind, encouraging her to a little greater endeavor each day, leading her gently but firmly out of apathy to interest, out of languor to laughter, out of uncertainty to confidence. Dear Alec! If he could be on her desert the rest of her life she would not mind its aridity at all.

The islands rose before Mary's eyes, sometimes in a cluster of high peaks topped by sparkling white chapels, sometimes appearing only as dark, crumbling shapes half hidden by a sunlit haze, sometimes as a sharp green point of land covered with feathery palms and reaching out into a blue sea, sometimes as a chaos of soft verdant hills enclosing a turquoise harbor, and sometimes—though rarely—as broad flat stretches of fields, cane-covered and golden. But always they were different, yet always alike in their heat, their somnolence, their strangeness. And from each Mary usually brought back some one vivid memory.

Martinique, with its yellow houses topped by scarlet roofs, its royal palms and tall, proud, handsome, queenly women, its sudden-falling dusk cut by thousands of fireflies, its soft-voiced children—"I askin' you fo' one franc, baas!"

It was there while she and Alec were drinking a mixture of rum and lime with syrup and water at a small table set out of doors that Mary came to understand how loyal, how devoted Alec was to Matt. She had known it, of course, from the very first moment down by the river in New Bern, for he had made it clear then when he would not allow her to interfere with Matt's party aboard ship. But now his continued kindness to her brought it home more sharply every day. He wanted her to get well so that no shadow would be cast by her on Matt's impending marriage. There was no other reason—or was there? She felt impelled to find out.

"You love my brother very much, don't you?" she said to him that day, and she put down her glass to peer into his face that was shadowy now in the dusk.

"Matt is an interesting man to me," Alec replied, after a moment. "Summat like the son I've never had."

"Why! He's only a few years younger than you! You're nowhere near old enough to be his father!"

He turned his head sharply toward her. "You don't think so?"

"Of course not! You—you just want him to be happy, isn't that it?"

"I doubt he knows how to be happy, lassie," he replied, going sober suddenly. "Matt cares too much about Matt," he continued. "But if this Myrtle he's to wed—if she can but play the right tune on the strings o' his heart —Matt could be a great leader of men." His tone grew graver. "There's trouble brewin' in this world, lass. There's rumbles of war in the air, and our country will have need of a man like your brother. I would not choose

Myrtle for Matt myself, but since he has chosen her—well—what he'll make of himself is in her hands. And I'm for giving her every bit of help that's possible."

His slow, thoughtful words, his undercurrent of anxiety, but most of all his great respect and affection for her brother touched Mary deeply so that she put aside her own inexplicable feeling of disappointment before his reply and laid her hand on his.

"I, too, want to give him all the help possible. And—and thanks to you, Alec, I begin to believe I can."

He turned her hand so that he could clasp it warmly. For a moment they sat thus in silence, while to her ears came the sound of softly splashing water from a fountain, and through the darkness winked the thousands of little fireflies, and from a window above drifted down the gentle twang of a guitar as a man's voice rose in a melodic love song. For some reason unknown to her she felt the threat of a rising tide of tears.

"But I couldn't—without you," she heard herself saying in a low voice that trembled.

His hand gripped hers suddenly and then as suddenly let it go. He stood up.

"No weeping now, Mary," he said brusquely. "I'll have no weeping. Come! 'Tis time we went to the ship."

The tears stayed in an aching lump in her throat as she rose and followed him. But why should she want to shed tears at all?

* * *

Guadeloupe—lofty, rugged, and volcanic, with the scarlet-splashed Mount Soufrière rising to blue-green heights, with the town's roughly cobbled streets divided by a central gutter down which water flowed incessantly, with its women placidly smoking clay pipes in the shade, and its girls, heads bound in bright turbans, long pendants swinging from their ears, tossing their colorful flowing skirts with an inviting abandon.

"The market place here is quite a sight," Alec told her. "We'll go there first."

So to the market place they went. There Mary saw mangoes and breadfruit piled in neat pyramids, fish laid out in straight military rows, and bananas carefully tied in bunches of three.

There was a festive atmosphere about the place that day and a turbulent excitement, for it was Mardi Gras time and the three-day revel would begin that night. Already some boys had donned their grotesque masks and costumes and were prancing about the square disguised as clowns, monkeys, donkeys, bulls, or women. The air was filled with laughter and shrill cries as girls tried to guess identities and boys ducked and ran or teasingly clung to their false faces and hopped about in circles defying recognition.

That night Alec took her to a dance palace to witness the *Bal Lou Lou.* It was an experience Mary was never to forget. Starting mildly and with a certain amount of decorum in a dimly lit room, it soon worked itself up into a frenzied orgy as the music grew wilder and the dark-skinned natives, abandoning themselves to the pulsating rhythms and the incessant hypnotic drumbeats, literally got drunk on sound. She pressed closer and closer to Alec, her fascinated gaze riveted on the figures before her as they gyrated and jumped and twitched. Their eyes were half closed and their faces contorted, while animal sounds, shrill maniacal yells and deep groans, broke through the twanging of guitar, the clash and clang of cymbals and pans, the relentless drumbeats. Suddenly the African weirdness, the smells, the harsh sounds, the flickering lights, all became more than she could bear, and she lifted a white face to Alec.

"Take me away," she whispered.

Quickly he rose and, half carrying her, led her down the stairs to the street. But here, too, in the uncertain flaring of torches, was more madness, more leaping creatures in disguise, more snatching hands and stamping feet and shrieks and screams and yells.

Mary murmured, "I think—I'm going—to faint—"

When she recovered consciousness she was lying in a shaft of pale light on the floor of a chapel far from the din, and Alec was laying a cool wet handkerchief on her forehead. Slowly she opened her eyes. There was stillness about her and the fragrance of hibiscus and the soothing sound of falling water beyond the open doorway. Through this she could see the dark shape of a mountain above which a white moon sailed in majestic serenity.

"I—behaved badly. I'm sorry."

"*You* are sorry!" Alec's voice was savage with contrition. " 'Tis I! I blame myself. I should have known you weren't up to a thing like that. Not yet. I was a fool. Will you ever forgive me, dolt that I am?"

He bent over her, his warm hands holding hers close. His face, clear to her as if it were daylight, held the blaze of a deep, tender, loving concern. She gazed up into it, thinking only how wonderful it was to have him caring for her, and then she happily closed her eyes once more.

"Dear Alec—" she began.

But before she could tell him that there was nothing to forgive, that he had been all kindness and consideration, she felt his breath warm on her cheek and then his kiss. It was gentle and sweet and light—like a blessing. For it fell on her forehead and not on her lips.

* * *

They stopped at Monserrat, where Mary ate "mountain chicken" for the first time, to learn that mountain chickens were only plump and tender bullfrogs; at St. Lucia, where she ventured to taste the delicate flying fish. She saw the black cone shape of Saba, which had no harbor and past which they sailed without seeing the Dutch town that nestled in the top of the cone well hidden from the world; Nevis, whose single mountain peak was lost in the clouds above it; Antiqua, where the fine white sand was like velvet to the touch. So many islands there were that Mary's mind became confused. Which was the one where the streets were all steps leading up or leading down? Which was the one where the strike of the poisonous *fer-de-lance* was so dreaded? Which was the one near the Pitons, those two small pyramids upthrust from the sea, where eight echoes could be heard when a man halloed as he passed them?

"I have a hodgepodge of memories to take back with me," she said to Alec one day. "A lovely hodgepodge!"

Memories of color: of an old gray cathedral perched above a foaming brown river; of ebony-skinned gendarmes in gleaming white; of barefoot girls of bronze; of green palmettos wind-driven against a black sky. Memories of sound: of soft slurring voices; of gay accordions; of chiming church bells and of drums: and memories of smells: flower smells, delicate and pervasive; the pungent smell of bananas and mangoes and breadfruit and spices; smells of rum and burnt sugar and coffee.

Yes, she had a hodgepodge of memories—and a hodgepodge of feelings, too. For what was this that had sprung up without words in her heart for Alec? Was it love? How dared she love while she was still married to Nick? Oh! She did not know! She could not say! But whatever it was, it brought happiness back to her face. A subdued happiness, perhaps, lacking the brightness of her unknowing youth, but a soft and glowing happiness that bloomed despite her conscience, that became her well, and that she had learned could be found in thought of others even though she still knew the bleakness of a private uncertainty and fear.

The bleakness was not quite so bleak as it had been because she had discovered that, whatever her own feeling for Alec, he loved her. Despite that chaste kiss on her forehead, he had once, before that, given himself away. She had seen it in his eyes when she had told him he was not so old as to look on Matt as his son. "You don't think so?" he had exclaimed, and the look that had briefly lighted his countenance told her later, as she thought about it, that it had held more than vanity. It—and his voice—had held the leap of a personal and pulsating hope. Yet in the next instant, as if he recognized how useless—indeed, how wrong—was that hope, it had died away and the muscles of his face had stiffened it to a rigid and impassive control.

But Mary had seen, and, incredible and impossible as the truth appeared to be, it brought her the first faint stirrings and gropings of that new subdued happiness. It was like a pallid but warm finger of sunlight reaching through the cold grayness of her days. Alec loved her! Errant and selfish as she had been, and weak and thoughtless in all respects, Alec had yet found something about her that touched his heart. What could it be? She longed to have him tell her. But while Nick was her husband she knew—after that restrained moment in the moonlit chapel—he would never speak.

Still she could hug her knowledge to herself, feeling the cold despair that had held her in its grip thaw slowly before the flickering flame of this new and sweet devotion.

She could watch with furtive eagerness for other inadvertent revelations of his feelings, and she could think how things might be if she were free. She could—if she did not let herself think of Alec and *his* future. For what right had she to tie him to her even by thought?

* * *

At last in November they came back to Charles-Town with its white mansions and brick mansions and tinted stucco homes of strawberry and salmon-pink and lavender; with its amusing chimney pots and hipped roofs and flaring eaves; with its balconies and gates and doorways of exquisite ironwork—and its bloom of flowers everywhere.

"It is a foreign-looking city," was Mary's first thought, as she saw it, sun-drenched and dreaming there by the harbor shores. It was a city that combined everything she had ever seen—the English traditional with the French ornate and added to these unexpected touches of West Indian. It was an opulent, leisurely, fragrant, exotic city—and she loved it at once.

She turned to Matt in whose black eyes an anxious watchfulness of her had long ago changed to relieved approval and confidence.

"I'm not afraid any more, Matt," she said to him softly. "I'll do you proud here, I'm sure!"

Chapter 16

MATT'S TALL, narrow house on the East Battery was open and ready for him when they landed. It was one of those built endwise to the street, only one room deep, with wide piazzas on every floor facing the west and overlooking the gardens. As Matt strode in through the white front door, his house slaves, dressed in pale blue livery, were drawn up in line awaiting his arrival and orders. In the dining room his mahogany gleamed, his silver shone, a great crystal chandelier glittered. In the library, where shelves of leather-bound books rose from floor to ceiling against one end, the wood paneling had been rubbed to a warm and satiny glow. And scattered everywhere were the rugs and other priceless treasures he had gathered from all over the world.

Matt strolled through his establishment with a nonchalant air that did not wholly conceal his pride. And then there appeared in the doorway a slender, gray-haired woman with a voice like silver bells and a smile of such warmth and radiance that Mary was captivated at once.

"Welcome home, Captain Martin! I hope you are finding everything as you wanted to find it? I have done my best—"

"A most wonderful best." Matt, who could put on the

proper air when necessary, bent low over the lady's hand, and then, straightening, led her to Mary.

"My sister, Mrs. Pinckney, who has come all the way from the north to be present at my wedding. Mary, Mrs. Pinckney is my neighbor, who, out of pity for my male helplessness, has readied my house for me."

"Ah, Miss Martin! How very nice that you can be here. I know a little about your family. Your brother has often spoken of you all. I hope you left everyone well at home?"

Thus, easily, without effort and without falsehood, Mary's past was buried. And just as easily was she drawn at once into the gracious and boundless hospitality of the southern city that so happily mingled formality with informality, elegance with ease.

It was Mrs. Pinckney, guiding and guarding her with the utmost tact and unfailing vigilance, who enabled Mary to enter without difficulty into the social life of Charles-Town. Of course she was confronted at once by the need for a whole new wardrobe ("because I went with Matt at a moment's notice"), and Mrs. Pinckney's dressmaker performed wonders in short order. As a result, not for a moment did Mary's appearance give her or Matt any uneasiness. She simply blossomed in beauty and exquisite taste. Mary had thought it might be Myrtle who would thus take her in charge, but after their first meeting Mary realized that Myrtle would never look out for anyone but herself. She smiled sweetly, kissed Mary effusively, uttered little cries of delight over her unexpected presence—and promptly flitted away on affairs of her own. It was Mrs. Pinckney, not Myrtle, who introduced her wherever they went, or who saw to it that she was properly shepherded and presented at gatherings where the older woman was not to be present.

For Mary this new life was unlike anything she had ever

known. Even during that week in New York long ago she had not been treated to such a steady whirl of gaiety as she was here. Here everyone felt it necessary to give a party for the bride-to-be and each party was a little larger, a little more lavish than the one before. It was considered nothing to entertain thirty or forty guests for luncheon, Mary discovered. And a weekend house party at one of the great plantations beyond the city easily included a hundred people. There, amid wealth and beauty unparaleled in Mary's experience, boating, riding, feasting and dancing were the order of the day. It was fabulous.

All this was made possible, of course, because of the great number of slaves employed. On Matt's household staff there were fifteen to keep the place functioning. At first Mary had been dismayed before the thought that it was she who must direct them all, but—once more—Mrs. Pinckney came to her rescue, explaining the duties assigned to each. As a matter of fact, they had been so well trained by Mrs. Pinckney before Matt's arrival that there was little actual direction needed.

"You are so good to me," Mary said to the older woman one day. "Why do you bother?"

"Perhaps because once I was a stranger here myself," Mrs. Pinckney answered. "And I know what it means to be offered a little help." And at Mary's eager show of interest she related her story.

Mrs. Pinckney at the age of sixteen had come here with her invalid mother and a host of younger brothers and sisters. Her father, who had expected to remain with them, had been recalled to Antigua by the British government, and it was young Eliza who had to run his three plantations here. This she did most successfully, and, in addition, taught her younger brothers and sisters their lessons. As if that were not enough, she managed to keep up with the latest reading matter, followed scientific discoveries and, herself, introduced indigo as a crop into South Carolina from the plants sent her by her father.

"And then you married Mr. Charles Pinckney, the Chief Justice here."

Mrs. Pinckney nodded. "I was eighteen. He was a widower twice my age. Many people thought it was dreadful for me to marry a man so much older, but my years with him contained nothing but perfect happiness." She paused a moment, her face soft with her memories. "He died two years ago," she went on in her sweet voice. "And now I have plantations to manage again and two sons to educate—Charles and Thomas. You will meet them when they come home from England." She smiled. "It is because I am alone so much that I have become a busybody in my neighbor's affairs. I am grateful for Matt's tolerance."

"*You* are grateful!" Mary exclaimed. "He is the one. And I, too." And her face was suffused with the warmth of affection she had come to feel for this new friend. But it was Mrs. Pinckney's words about her marriage that stayed with Mary the longest. "He was twice my age . . . but my years with him contained nothing but perfect happiness."

* * *

The days sped by. Names that had been only names at first took on personalities as Mary encountered them again and again. The Moultries, the Rhetts, the Middletons, the Draytons, all became individuals with definite characteristics. Christopher Gadsden, lean and long and tough, was (Mary learned) a man to be reckoned with—a firebrand who was already talking in terms of American independence from England. John Rutledge, calm, quiet, inclined to portliness, was Matt's lawyer. And Tom Izard, whose sister was later to marry the Governor of Carolina, was an attractive young blade with a most flattering manner, who moved lightly and easily from one love affair to another.

There were other attractive young men, too, and Mary met them all. But, charming as they were (as, indeed, Nick had been charming), none of them evoked in Mary any emotional response. Perhaps it was the need to be guarded in their presence, lest, by chance, she let slip something that would arouse too much curiosity about her past. Or perhaps it was a natural and inevitable defense against the kind of charm that had once lured her to disaster. Whatever it was, she found herself turning more and more toward Alec for companionship, preferring his escort to that of anyone else and resting securely in his knowledge of her which was so complete it necessitated no watchfulness on her part.

Again she asked herself if this slow, steady surge of a deep contentment in his presence could be love. Was love no more than a sense of well-being? Where was the ecstasy she had felt with Nick? Or had she been too hurt ever to know that again? Perhaps, if Alec would speak, would voice his feeling for her, if she could feel his touch upon her, ecstasy might spring alive. But not once since his eyes and his voice had betrayed him at Martinique had he let his emotion escape him. So careful was he that there were times when she questioned her memory of that moment, uncertain whether she had dreamed up what she thought she had caught then.

When such doubts came, she grew restive and unhappy and tried to stir Alec to some fresh show of his feeling for her. She would be first demure, then provocative, altogether so tantalizing him that abruptly one day he reprimanded her.

"What are you trying to do, Mary?"

The blunt question, coldly, even sternly put, shocked her into stillness. What had she, indeed, been trying to do? How explain the vague need within her? The desire to come to a final answer that would settle all her disturbing uncertainties? The hunger for the hurting punishment of his arms? No, she could not explain to that severe face. She shrank back, her own gone white.

"You like to play with fire," he went on, not accusingly but with a judicial remoteness that was somehow the more alarming because of its impersonality.

"I–I–" she began, and, shamed and frightened, fell silent.

"In the eyes of the Lord and the church you are a married woman still," he went on. "Never forget that again." He paused a moment, to add harshly, "I don't. And I will not."

Her eyes swam with sudden tears. She knew he was right, that by her teasing she had been trying to provoke Alec into declaring a guilty love which would make him miserable for the rest of his days. For he was too honest, too upright to render his love a furtive thing. She loved him honest and upright–and yet, if he loved her, she wanted to have the comfort of knowing it. Better not to see him, not to be tempted day in and day out into tempting him.

"I think we had better not see each other for a while, Alec," she said soberly.

"As you say," he answered.

But it was Alec she unhesitatingly called upon in her sudden need a few weeks later.

By this time it had been decided that Mary was to be

the Maid of Honor to follow the procession of Myrtle's six bridesmaids. Her gown, peach-bloom in color, already hung beneath a sheet against the wardrobe door. Her matching slippers, wrapped in tissue, stood on a shelf inside. Her mitts, her silk stockings, her lace handkerchief and her airy gauze stole of pale rose and gold, were ready and waiting.

Mary, herself, was ready and waiting, too. Only one thing remained to be done first. She must—at long last—write to Prue.

She was seated at the open French window in her bedroom in Matt's house as she told herself this. From here she could step out onto a balcony overlooking the lush gardens and, by turning her head, see across the high brick wall edging the property to the crowded harbor and the tangle of white-sailed ships that were anchored there. Here, too, she could catch what cooling vagrant breezes might come wafting off the water. But she had no thought now of gardens or white sails or cooling breezes. She was thinking only of the letter she must write.

It would be difficult if not impossible to do. So much had transpired since she had left Esther Burr's house in Princetown almost two years ago. The one note she had sent back from Virginia upon landing in Norfolk had not told anything at all. After that, things had happened so fast and, for the most part, so disastrously, that silence had seemed best until the black interval had passed.

Now, however, it had passed, and Prue and Pa had a right to know about her, and if they did not want her ever to show her face again at Martin Manor they could say so. It was only fair to end their worry over her, for worry they had and would, beyond a doubt, continue to worry until they had certain news of her. She remembered well how Prue had worried over Matt for six long years.

She rose and moved to the table where her escritoire lay. She must tell Prue about Myrtle, too, she was thinking. And about Mr. and Mrs. Avery, who, after their first sharp sizing up, had accepted Mary without reservations. But just as she stretched out her hand to pick up her writing desk, there came a knock at the door.

It was Belladonna, the young upstairs girl who stutteringly told Mary that Amos had sent her up to say a young man below was asking to see Cap'n Martin's sister.

"Didn't he give his name?"

"No'm. Dass why Amos stay down dere wiv'm till you comes."

Mary turned toward the door. What young man would be calling on her in the morning? Mr. Izard? Mr. Laurens? But neither would refuse to give his name when asked. Disturbed, thinking inevitably of Nick, and wishing Matt were here and not on some one of his ships in the harbor, she went slowly down the stairs.

Nigel rose to greet her in the long drawing room. A new Nigel, handsomely turned out in buff trousers and brown broadcloth coat and buckled shoes, his hair neatly tied back, his face lifted by the beginnings of success from sullenness to alertness. Such prosperity as he evidenced did away with her first ready suspicion that he was here to demand more money. And as if he guessed her thought, he said at once in a kind of stiff and injured dignity, "I want naught for myself."

This was a relief, but before speaking Mary turned to the grizzled Amos who was hovering in the doorway.

"It's all right, Amos," she said quietly.

The old servant disappeared, and Mary turned back to Nigel.

"Why do you come, then?"

"To tell you I've found Nick."

Her hand flew to her throat. "Oh! Where?"

"Not far from here. I've been away, or I'd have found him sooner," he added.

Mary, her face gone white, sank down on a chair. Nigel here in Matt's house—and Nick not far away—saints alive! What complications might there not be for the wedding!

"How—how did you find him?" she finally managed to ask.

He shrugged. "A pedlar with a wagon is rare in these parts. Most come afoot."

"Tell me," she said, through stiff lips. "Did he send you? How is he? What does he want?"

"He's sick," Nigel hesitated a moment. "In fact, he's mighty sick." He did not pause for Mary's low exclamation but went on. "He's in his wagon. And 'twas he sent me here for you."

"What is wrong with him? Has he seen a doctor?"

"He's got a fever that keeps him so weak he can't move. And he didn't want to get a doctor till I'd talked with you," Nigel answered. "In his condition he might babble your whole story, and it would be all over town in no time. Your high and mighty brother wouldn't care for that, would he?"

What shall I do? Mary asked herself. What shall I do?

Nigel continued, his dark eyes fixed on her: "I know you said you never wanted to see him again. Only he keeps asking for you. Asking me to find you for him. He's sure you're here. I can't guess how he knows. Anyway, he does."

"We were heading for here," Mary murmured. "He knew Matt was here."

Nigel nodded.

Mary's hand fell from her throat to her lap in a helpless way. She did not know—she did not know. Slowly she asked, "Where is Nick's wagon? How far from here, Nigel?"

"Few miles outside the city." He paused, and she sensed he had more to tell her. Presently it came. "There's naught left in it now. The wagon's stripped. He's sold about everything, even his horse. He hasn't so much as a ha'penny. Or a crust of bread. Leastways he hadn't till I brought him some."

Shocked, Mary said, half to herself, half to him, "I can't bear it. Whatever happened? I can't bear it."

"I don't know what happened. I found him sick—too sick to do much talking. I've been with him a week now, taking care of him."

She looked at him as if she were seeing him for the first time. "You—that was good of you, Nigel. It was more than—than anyone could expect."

He nodded. "I never thought to do aught for him. That's the truth. I figured all along to get my revenge on him. But—" He stopped. What he meant was that he'd had his revenge seeing Nick so defeated while he himself was already well started up the ladder he meant to climb. Only this wouldn't sound right to Mary, for she was soft, and he wanted most desperately to make a good impression on her. So he said, instead, "But, after all, he's my brother. All I've got." And his black opaque gaze met hers so that she could not be sure if this was truly a new, kinder Nigel or not.

"Will you come along?" he finished. "I walked. But I'd be pleased to get a rig for you."

Dear God of heaven! What was she to do? To ignore Nigel's request would be inhuman, if Nick were as ill as he said. Yet to go with him would be unwise, at the very least. Should she call on her good friend, Mrs. Pinckney? But Matt wanted no one in town to know of her marriage, and if he, himself, learned of Nigel's presence in his house he would perhaps throw him out forcibly and refuse to let Mary go near Nick. No, she could not ask Mrs. Pinckney to accompany her. She remained silent and uncertain and torn two ways by her conflicting loyalties.

Then she thought of Alec. Of course! *Alec!*

"You tell me the way to go," she said, at last, "and I'll follow you with a friend."

Anger blazed in his face. "You don't trust me!"

"It isn't that"—quickly. "It's just that I prefer to have my brother's assistant accompany me. Then—then you won't have to bring me back again, for you know how wroth Matt would be if he were to discover you here. Besides, Mr. MacDonald is an experienced and level-headed man whose judgment I respect in case—in case some action must be taken."

Nigel accepted this, albeit unwillingly; he explained the way she should go and departed. Immediately Mary called Amos to send him for Alec who, she knew, could be found at the office down by the Battery.

"But give him my message privately," she added. For a moment she hesitated. How much was this ancient servitor to be trusted? Mrs. Pinckney had said, "He is well-trained and wise. If you ever have any question about anything, trust Amos." Mary went on. "Later, after Captain Martin is married, I will tell him of this call this morning. But until then it would only upset him and no one, excepting Mr. MacDonald, is to know. It will just make trouble. You understand?"

"Yes'm, Miz Martin."

"You must make Belladonna understand, too."

"Yes'm, Miz Martin."

It seemed hours before Alec came, but at last he appeared. His lean face turned grave but compassionate when she explained to him. Matt's face under the same circumstances never would have taken on such tenderness, for Matt had scant use for weaklings, and Matt's own future was more important to him than anyone else's past.

Mary sighed in relief when she heard Alec say, "You did right to call me."

He summoned his own horse and carriage, dismissed his man, and, himself, took the reins with Mary beside him. Together they drove out of the city, past the church of St. Michael, across an open space, finally turning up King Street to the town gate and the sandy waste beyond that was used for drilling troops. Past this they went, and along the rutted road toward the grove of trees Nigel had described. On the way, overtaking him, they picked him up to ride with them.

It was a strange ride. They spoke little. Once Alec turned to Mary, saying that if anyone should spot them and later question her, she was to say that Alec had been on an errand for Matt, going to look over a stand of pines for the building of a new ship; that she had accompanied him for the airing and the stranger with them had been conducting them to the right place.

Mary nodded. How careful Alec was! She never worried when he was beside her. But even he could not help her if, as Nigel had said, Nick were desperately ill and in want. Alec could not, that is, change her duty to her husband which would plainly be to stay by him and succor him. Yet how could she simply disappear just before Matt's marriage? Or where in town could she take Nick without having the whole story come out? No light came through the dark tangle of her thoughts as they rode, and, presently, she saw the outline of the familiar wagon in the trees before them.

It looked forlorn and lonely standing there. And

deserted–without the horse, Nelly. Shabby, too, with its paint worn and peeling and streaks of dirt all down its sides. Yet she should not have been surprised at its condition, for it was over a year since she had seen it. But even as she thought that, she knew that more than time and weather had taken its toll. The wagon looked unloved and neglected. It had become an indifferent shelter where before it had been a home.

The horse's feet made no sound on the thick pine needles and no one spoke as Alec drew rein. So it was in silence that Mary stepped to the ground, and then, with her heart pounding heavily within her, mounted the little steps to the place that had once been the center of her happiness.

Chapter 17

FOR A MOMENT, as she pushed back the canvas flap and looked inside, she was aghast. Despite the dimness, the change was shocking to her eyes, and she was thankful Nigel had warned her. What she saw was a wagon bare of everything save Nick's gun and a few clothes humped carelessly on the center locker. Even Mary's feather bed had been sold, as well as the rag rug that had lain beneath it.

A board squeaked under her foot, and from Nick's bunk came his weak voice. "Nigel? Is it you?"

"It's Mary, Nick."

"Mary—!" The gladness in that escaped breath caught at Mary's heart. She went forward quickly and, dropping on her knees, took the groping hand that reached for her, feeling it strange to her touch in its hot, thin frailty. Behind her Alec entered with Nigel, and they two sat silently on the hard boards of Mary's bunk. But Nick never noticed them.

"You came!"

"Of course I came. Just as soon as I knew—" Mary stopped, too filled with the anguish of her pity. For Nigel had been right. Nick was seriously ill, indeed. He lay before her, wasted to skin and bones, a shocking sight in comparison to her memory of him. Gone was all the sparkle and charm. Gone the bright, resilient spirit, the temper, the bravado, the impatience. Nick was but the empty shell of himself but, perhaps, truer to the best in him than he had ever been before.

"I had to see you," he whispered. "Nigel thought you wouldn't come, but I–"

"You knew I would. I'm glad you knew that, Nick. I'm glad you sent for me."

His blue eyes, a faded blue, heavy-lidded with fatigue and fever, sought her face. "Mary–"

"Yes, Nick?"

He could scarcely push the words out, he felt so far away, but he made the effort. "Did the innkeeper there at New Bern–give you what I left?"

Mary's hands tightened on his and her heart jumped with an unexpected joy. So he had–! Oh, shame on her for thinking so hardly of him!

"Yes," she told him unhesitatingly.

His eyelids dropped. "I gave it him before the cock-fight, just in case. I never meant to take it all that day, but you woke up and I hadn't time to put any back." He paused to gain strength to say the rest. "So I gave it him. I thought–with that–you'd be all right. Better than with me. You'd make friends. You always did, Mary. You'd get to Matt's. But I was worried. I wasn't sure about that innkeeper."

"He was all right, Nick."

"Good. There wasn't anyone else. And I wanted to take care–I really always wanted to take care–" He sighed. "I just didn't have–any luck."

"Never mind all that now, Nick."

He moved his head on the pillow. Then he spoke again. "The baby–"

"The baby died, Nick."

Slowly his eyes opened wide. "I came here to see you and the baby. I knew you'd get to Matt's. I thought I'd open my store—here. That's why I sold everything. It wasn't the Sheriff got it, though—but never mind that. I sold it so's I'd have money—for the store."

Oh, Nick! Nick! Mary thought. Dreaming—hoping—deceiving himself still! She lifted his head and turned his pillow and wiped his wet forehead with her handkerchief. "Don't try to talk any more, Nick. Just rest. We'll talk later."

He smiled. "Mary—my sweet—" he murmured. "Remember that song?"

"I'll never forget it."

A silence fell. Nick's breathing grew quieter and presently he slept. Mary looked around at Alec and whispered, "We must get a doctor for him." And Alec nodded and signaled her to come outside with him where they could talk.

Nigel followed them out and stood silently listening to their words and watching Mary.

"We must get a doctor," she repeated, through pale lips. "We must get him to a decent place, too, where he can be in a bed and have proper nursing." And then a realization of her dilemma swept over her, and she looked up at Alec in piteous appeal. "But I have to think of Matt, too, don't I! Oh, Alec, whatever shall I do?"

"We'll get a doctor first. Mayhap he'll say Nick is too ill to be moved. That would be my guess, anyway. To jounce and bounce him for miles over the rough ground might be disastrous." He paused. "I'll drive back to town now and get a doctor myself." He paused again. "I'll tell him Nick is a friend of mine. Nigel, too," he added, with a glance at the other. "I'll tell him you and I were waylaid by Nigel while we were driving, and Nigel, who had been hunting for me, gave me my first news of Nick's sickness, and because you were with me and the matter was urgent I had to bring you along." He paused a third time. "I'll ask the doctor to keep Nick's presence here a confidence as—as he is in trouble with the authorities and is now too ill to be pestered by them." He stopped. "I think that takes care of everything," he ended.

"Everything but one thing." It was Nigel speaking, and he stepped forward now, his black eyes bright on Alec's face. "Who's to pay for the doctor?"

"Have no fear," Alec told him coldly. "I'll take care of that, too."

Nigel replied in anger, "No! You will not! Do you get him here and I'll pay for his services!"

Alec's eyebrows lifted but he only nodded. "As you wish." He turned and strode quickly to his horse and wagon. "I'll be back as soon as I can get here," he said, over his shoulder. "Or—" he added, "—will you go with me now, Mary, and let me leave you at home first?"

"No." Mary shook her head. "No, Alec. I must stay. I want to stay. I want to hear what the doctor has to say."

Left alone, Nigel turned to her. "We may as well sit down out here, Mary."

"See if Nick is still sleeping first."

He tiptoed quietly up the steps of the wagon to peer in and came back with the report that Nick's eyes remained closed.

"Sleep is what he needs. We'll not disturb him talking here, and I've a mort of things to tell you," he said.

She became aware of him now, as, up to this moment, she had not been. She became aware of him as a man, personable and full-grown, with a man's ambition and a man's strength and a man's determination. And there was, too, more of Nick in him than she would ever have suspected, as, with all of his brother's remembered grace, he swept smooth a place on the pine needles under a tree and handed her down to it. *The way Nick did at the Collect the first time I found him,* Mary thought to herself in surprise.

"Thank you, Nigel."

He settled himself beside here, facing her, and his black eyes met hers with an unflinching boldness that was oddly disturbing.

"Could be you're wondering how I come to be so prosperous," he said.

She nodded.

"I told you I'd been away."

She nodded again.

" 'Twasn't my idea—at first. My idea was to track Nick down. But instead, after Matt gave me the money that was due me, I shipped aboard a vessel that was heading for Charles-Town. I thought I'd look the place over, for I was sure Matt would bring you here finally. I thought—" he went on coolly, "—that I might like it as a place to live in myself."

"Really, Nigel? But—but what did you think you would do here?"

His glinting glance held hers. "I thought, in time, I might do what I found all the leading citizens here doing," he answered. "I might own a plantation."

Mary was speechless. It sounded impossible. Yet was it? Why was it?

He continued, "That was what I thought. But I soon found out I'd need more money than I had for a venture like that. I'm lucky at cards—only that wasn't going to be quick enough." He leaned toward her. "Did you know, Mary, that piracy is still a prosperous trade?"

"You—turned pirate?"

There was no need to be shocked. Matt had been a pirate once. She waited for Nigel's reply, seeing for the first time a long red scar down one side of his neck.

He nodded, his fingers following her eyes and touching the scar. "Yes. I turned pirate. I joined a crew that volunteered for a voyage. There's a plenty of men picked up in Charles-Town for just that. And there's a plenty of pirates' nests along the Carolina coast." He paused. "Well, I joined, for I'd heard tell that each man would get a thousand pounds as his share for one trip." His glance narrowed. " 'Twas true, too. But it's a dangerous life, and I'll have no more of it." And he touched the scar again.

There he sat, cool and untroubled by what he had been, as Matt had once been cool and untroubled, and richer by a thousand pounds than when she had last seen him. He had known smoke and shell-fire, death and destruction, blood and thunder, had robbed and plundered and killed. And by his face she knew that other plans—bigger plans—were seething in his head and, however nebulous now, they were plans that would certainly some day materialize. A little shivering thrill of admiration stirred in her for his force and courage and resoluteness, and she reached out a hand and touched his arm briefly.

"I'm—proud of you, Nigel," she said. "I do not wholly approve of you—of piracy, I mean—still, I cannot blame you for choosing that way for a while. What I'm proud of is your strength and your daring. I—I believe you will succeed in anything you undertake."

"You can count on it." He looked at her with an expression she could not quite fathom. "But whatever I do I want to be near you," he added. "And so I want to know now if you are planning to stay on here after your brother's marriage."

Before she could reply Nick's voice came to her ears, calling her name.

"I'm here, Nick! I'm coming!" she answered.

And she rose and went quickly into the wagon to sit beside him until the doctor came.

He arrived on his own horse, with Alec leading the way in his carriage. He was a tall spare man with sharp eyes and a cold, forbidding manner and plainly not pleased to have such a patient. It was lung fever, in an advanced stage, he told Mary and Alec after he had examined Nick and they had all gone outside again.

"Will he recover?" Mary whispered.

The doctor shrugged. "I am not the Lord to answer a question like that." He glanced back at the wagon. "This is not the best place to assure recovery, but I understand there are—eh—reasons why he would rather not be taken into town."

"You know how ruthless authorities can be, doctor, when laws have been broken," Alec said. "For friendship's sake, I beg of you, if it is not a—a life or death matter, to permit him to remain here."

The doctor shrugged again as he nodded. "It might not be wise to move him, anyway." He turned to Mary. "To answer your question about recovery, that will depend on the care he receives: the food, the nursing. Who will do that?"

"I will, sir." Nigel stepped forward promptly, a suitable expression of concern on his face. "I will see that my brother has the best that can be provided. And I will stay with him and nurse him myself."

He stood in an attentive silence as the doctor issued his orders. There must be food, good food, hot food, nourishing and well-cooked. There must be medicines and tonics administered regularly. There must be no exertion, no worry of any kind, no excitement. Nick must never be allowed to get chilled.

"I'll come see the patient again tomorrow—if I can," said the doctor. "Or the next day. Whenever it's possible," he concluded, a trifle impatiently. And he swung his long, lean figure up onto his horse and rode away.

Mary said, "I'll come tomorrow, too, Nigel. I'll come every day. I'll bring clean blankets—and sheets—whatever he needs. You will fetch me, Alec?"

"If you wish it."

"I do! I do!" Compassion and an overwhelming sense of guilt filled Mary's voice, and now for the first time since she had arrived tears crowded up. Alec laid a hand on her arm.

"You are unnerved. I think we'd best be going. There's no more you can do today. I'll bring the medicines and tonics," he finished. "I'll come back again today, since Nigel ought not to leave Nick alone and he must have what the doctor ordered. But you have done all you should do now."

Mary nodded. "I'll say good-by to Nick."

She went into the wagon and bent over the figure on the bunk bed. "I must go, Nick. But I'll be back tomorrow. Don't worry. You're going to get well. We're all going to take care of you."

He looked at her, and it seemed to her that already his eyes looked less faded and bluer. "You're good, Mary. Can it be you still care—a little?"

"Of course I care."

"And you will come back to me? To live with me?"

For answer she leaned over and kissed his forehead. "We'll talk about that and everything else when you are stronger. Content yourself now that—that I hold you dear in my heart and—and would do whatever is best."

Outside once more she said, her voice breaking, "Thank you for coming for me, Nigel."

"I suspicioned you'd be glad."

"Yes. I was. I—I am. It was kind of you to help him after—after what he did to you."

Nigel made no answer. He had not been kind just because of Nick, as she thought. He had been kind because it had given him a legitimate reason for seeing her again, for showing himself to her in his improved state, for letting her know he was on his way to her world—and to her. Why not? He was a better man already than Nick had ever been, and if Nick should die—the thought that followed, which had zigzagged now and then through his mind, suddenly took root, bringing a blaze to his eyes that Alec saw but Mary did not.

"Come!" the older man said firmly. And he led Mary to his carriage.

On the way home she told him what Nigel had told her of his recent past and of his plans. Talking of Nigel this way steadied her and put off for a while the necessity of facing the dark and difficult questions that must some time be met and answered.

"When he—Nigel—came back to Charles-Town after his first voyage," she said, "he started hunting for Nick again. Oh! I'm so glad he found him, Alec! Suppose he hadn't! Suppose Nick had been left alone there—to die—without help—or my ever knowing—" She shook her head. "I'm glad. Truly I am! And yet—yet I'm frightened, too, Alec. I'm frightened because of Matt and—and all the future."

Alec reached out, and she felt his warm, dry palm on her shaking hand.

"Yes. 'Tis frightening. But the future must wait. It's the present we must think on now. We must be careful

—most careful—that no hint of Nick's presence reaches Matt's ears."

"I know. Yet I must go to Nick, Alec! You—you understand that, don't you?"

"I understand, lass. And we'll manage. Never fear."

His deep gentle voice, his reassuring calm, his immense and endless kindness and care of her made her drop her head suddenly against his shoulder, all her defenses swept away.

"What would I ever do without you?" she whispered. "I should be helpless!" Then she was silent as a blessed certainty shot like a bright rocket through her tormented thoughts. "I can't live without you, Alec. Oh! I know I shouldn't say this! But it's true. I need you. I—I *want* you. I always have. And I guess I always will." She lifted her face then, and he, looking down, saw it white with misery and at the same time glorified by the light of her newly discovered love.

"This is a thing we must not speak of, Mary," he answered, ever so gently. "But 'tis a thought I shall carry most joyfully in my heart forever."

Chapter 18

LATER MARY WAS TO WONDER how she ever lived through the next few weeks. The burden of the necessary secrecy weighed on her heavily. Not to let Matt know! For Matt would never hesitate to send Nick flying from this neighborhood. Even Nigel—now—would not be able to stop Matt, Mary felt sure. For her brother could be ruthless when he felt the need to be, and he would somehow find a way to banish Nigel from the scene, too. She did not know how he could do this, but the knowledge that he would—that he would stop at nothing to insure his marriage—filled her with a cold terror, which, added to the thought that the wreckage of his life would be all her fault, nearly drove her crazy. No, Matt must not find out.

Nor must anyone else guess or even suspect that anything was amiss since, once suspicion was aroused and gossip started, discovery would surely be made. Somehow she must go through her days as if she were lighthearted, happy and gay. She must attend all the functions that were being given in honor of the bride-to-be and she must never be distrait, never by a look reveal that she was not enjoying herself, that anxiety filled her and warring emotions were pulling her apart.

Warring emotions—yes. For how could she wish Nick to die? Yet how could she wish him to live now that the deep, sweet glory of her love for Alec and his for her was known to her? Little had been said, it was true. Indeed, Alec had never mentioned the word love to her, so upright and honorable was he. Yet she was certain. And if Nick lived, how could she bring herself to be his wife again with thoughts of Alec filling her mind and the image of Alec filling her heart? All the hours held a black anguish for her as she asked herself these unanswerable questions.

"I am dancing on dead feet," she would think, as she pirouetted and curtsied in the intricate movements of the lancers. "I am not alive. I hear my voice as if it were someone else's. My laughter, too, sounds strange to my ears. I am simply numb with fear and pity, and an awful sense of wickedness haunts me all the time because I have the wrong desires in my heart. Dear God above! When will this end? And how?"

* * *

For the most part Mary made her visits to Nick at night. Alec, her acknowledged escort long before this for all occasions, would start toward Matt's house as a party ended, and then, when opportunity presented itself, he would circle back through the town to its outskirts and so to the stand of pines where Nick lay in his wagon. Occasionally Mary would be able to go to him in the morning while all the other young girls still slept after the festivities of the evening before.

"I'm not sleeping much, anyway," she would say to Alec. "I might just as well get up and go with you. It is better for Nick, too, not to have his nights broken."

And always in Alec's carriage would be whatever Nick needed—fresh towels and sheets and clothing, daintily prepared foods to tempt his appetite, something to read during those brief periods when he felt like reading.

"You never forget anything," Mary said once. "Oh, Alec! You're dear and wonderful and—I'm fair bowed over with my—my feeling for you!" And she lifted brown eyes so blazing with love through her tears that these were quenched.

But Alec only said gently, "Hush, lass. Not now. Let us not speak words now that we may later regret."

Inevitably notice was taken of her long drives with Matt's right-hand man, but the only interpretation put on them was a romantic one.

"You could do better, Mary," Myrtle would say critically. "He's almost forty."

And Mrs. Pinckney would murmur, "You couldn't do better, dear child. He's a rare fine man."

And to neither of them could Mary cry out the reply she was thinking: "I can do neither better nor worse, for I'm married to Nick!"

Yet for all her own dark turmoil, she never failed to be beautifully tender with Nick when she was with him. To him she gave all of her sweetness and all of her courage, as if, by these gifts, she would atone for being able to give no more.

"Let us not even try to plan for the future yet, Nick," she said to him in the very beginning. "Let us just take a day at a time. That way we won't build up any worries about how we'll manage. Let's—let's live for the moment, Nick!"

And since that had always been his habit, anyway, Nick found it agreeable. Mary's presence by his side, her lovely face near for his eyes to rest on, her smile warming him, and her low, kind voice speaking words of comfort and reassurance—these were enough.

And these, together with the good food and the medicines and the ministrations, wrought an improvement that seemed little short of miraculous to them. Nick gained in weight and strength. Presently he was sitting up in bed for short stretches, and not long after that he was asking if he might not go down out of the wagon and lie under the trees in the shade.

"Wait until the weather is more settled," the doctor told him. "You've all summer in which to lie under those trees."

All summer! Mary heard the words and panic filled her. For she could not stay here all summer. After Matt was married she would have no rightful place in his home. She had planned to return alone to Stockbridge. But now —with Nick?

There was only one answer. She must take Nick away. She—and Nigel—must somehow get him aboard one of Matt's ships sailing to Boston. From there she would manage to reach Stockbridge. Alec would help her with their passage. But oh! What a heartbreak to ask the man she loved to help her go out of his life forever!

"There's naught else to be done," Alec agreed soberly, when she told him of her plan. "Home to the hills is where you surely must take Nick. And Prue will welcome you."

"I've never even written her of my marriage, Alec."

"You will. You'll have time after the wedding."

After the wedding. Everything dated after the wedding. If she could but reach that day safely for Matt's sake! But how was she to live beyond it—without Alec?

* * *

Came the morning when Mary, hearing Nick singing as she and Alec approached, felt the time had come to tell him of her plan to take him home with her. But first she would insure Nigel's help, for she would hesitate to embark on such a voyage with a sick man without his assistance.

"Do you go in and sit with Nick a while, please, Alec," she said. "I want to have a talk with Nigel for a moment." And she beckoned him to her as he stood on the steps of the wagon awaiting them.

He leaped to the ground and strode quickly forward, his face alight. Alec nodded to him and sprang down to go to Nick as Nigel, reaching up his arms, easily lifted Mary from the carriage."

"You're strong," she said.

"You're a feather," he returned. "A lovely little feather."

She was pleased that he and she had become such good friends, and, laying her hand on his arm, she said, "I am going to need your strength, Nigel. I'm going to ask you to lend it to me." And she told him of her purpose. "Will that upset your own schemes for the future, to take time to go north with us?" she ended, and her face lifted to his in an anxious waiting.

For a moment he made no answer as the thought that had zigzagged like a comet through his mind returned. It had returned often in the days that had passed as he had watched Mary, finding her in her solicitous and unselfish care of Nick increasingly desirable. With Mary as his wife, what could he not do? he had asked himself. Certainly all that Nick had dreamed of doing—and more. Far more! Yet if he were really to take his brother's place, whatever was he doing helping Nick to get well?

Now he said slowly, "I have no schemes—except to remain close to you."

Mary said thoughtfully, "You are wonderfully changed, Nigel, do you know it? You are good. And kind. I always knew—" She stopped.

"You always knew what?"

"I always knew you only needed someone to—to care about you," she told him softly.

His black eyes burned upon her. "And you do?"

"Of course. A great deal." She smiled. "Then I will count on you to accompany us. Thank you so much."

"Tell me!" And his voice was as harsh as his words were abrupt. "Have you love in your heart for Nick again? Or is it only pity?"

She shook her head while her eyes filled with tears. "You must not ask me that question, Nigel," she rebuked him gently.

But she had given him his answer—the one he wanted to hear, anyway.

She went past him and mounted the little steps of the wagon to join Alec who was there with Nick. Left alone, Nigel stood in thought, his dark brows furrowed.

So! Mary no longer loved her husband, but she would live with him just the same. She would take him back to her own home there in Stockbridge where, whether he ever lifted a finger again to work or not, he would dwell in security and comfort. It was more than his rascally brother deserved! And (again he asked himself) why was he, Nigel, such a fool as to promise to help Nick to have all this, when he wanted Mary himself?

* * *

Three nights later—and two nights before Matt's wedding—Mary and Alec reached the wagon to find Nigel sitting outside in the darkness waiting for them.

"I thought you'd never get here," he said.

Mary, hearing the tenseness in his tone, asked at once, "What's the matter?"

He stood up without answering. It was a bleak night

with a drizzle of rain in the air and a wind keening out of the east. The storm had blown up late the day before, and all the bridal party was praying for it to pass before the wedding. Because of the storm Mary and Alec had not driven out the previous night.

"What's the matter?" Mary repeated, as she and Alec hastened to Nigel's side.

"Nick's taken a sudden turn for the worse," he told them, without preamble. "He—he's a whole lot worse."

Mary put out a hand and caught his arm. "Nigel! He can't—! Why! He was so well! The doctor said he could make the trip—Nigel! What happened?"

He told her, his voice shaking a little—and low, so that Nick would not hear.

Yesterday had dawned hot. Maybe they remembered? It had been hot and sultry with a blazing sun, and Nick, feeling so much better, had grown impatient of his bed and the stuffy wagon, and had declared that, doctor or no doctor, he was going to get up and go outside under the trees. Nigel had tried to stop him, but Nick had been determined and in the end Nigel had compromised.

He had told Nick that as soon as he himself got back from town with medicines and food, he would help his brother out of doors. And now he put his hand over Mary's that was still clutching his arm.

"But he wouldn't wait. While I was gone he must have half dressed himself and tottered out anyway. Then—do you remember? The wind came up and with it the storm, and it turned cold of a sudden. I was caught in town and had to wait till the rain stopped before starting back. I never dreamt that Nick might be out in it here. I never dreamt such a thing or I—" His voice cracked. Then he went on. "Well, I don't know exactly what happened, because I wasn't here. Maybe he was too weak to pull himself up the steps alone. Maybe he tripped over his blanket and fell and was knocked unconscious. I don't know! But when I finally got back I found him lying in a pool of his own blood, soaked through and—and cold as ice."

"Has the doctor seen him since?" Alec demanded, and his stern voice held an unspoken accusation.

Nigel turned on him in sudden anger. "I resent your tone!"

"I don't care what you resent. I asked you a question. Has the doctor been here to see him since?"

Nigel faced Mary, ignoring Alec. "The doctor was here in the morning yesterday and told me he'd be starting on his circuit today. I kept hoping you'd come last night but you didn't, and I didn't dare leave him alone—" He broke off, and Mary felt his hand on hers trembling a little. "I got Nick into bed," he went on. "I took off his wet clothes. I rubbed him down good and wrapped him in blankets and gave him medicine. I couldn't find any bruise or cut on him for all that blood. I did all I could think to do. But—but he *shook* so! All night he shook. And now he's—" He stopped. "I wanted you to come," he repeated. "I kept hoping and looking—"

"If we'd only known!" Mary steadied herself. "I'll go to him now, Nigel. Is—is he conscious?"

He nodded, standing still beside her, holding her there. "Yes. I knew you ought to know. But I couldn't leave him, could I?"

"No, of course not. It was right for you to stay. I'll go to him now," she repeated. And with her hand still on his arm, she mounted the steps to the wagon. There his voice halted her for a moment.

"Mary!" he whispered hoarsely. "Do you blame me? Say you don't blame me!"

"Of course I don't blame you. How could I? I never thought of such a thing."

"I did my best."

"I know you did." She pressed his hand and then stepped through into the wagon.

Nick lay on his bunk, his face chalk white with deep dark lines carved down each nostril to the corners of his mouth. His nose was pinched and bluish as he labored for short, shallow breaths. His eyes, faded again, were open and staring upward. One hand plucked feebly at the blanket drawn to his chin.

Mary knelt beside him, more shocked by the change in him this time than she had been on her first visit.

"Nick," she said softly.

He made no answer. He might not have heard. Then he coughed and blood foamed on his lips and his eyes closed.

Mary wiped his mouth with a gentle hand.

"Nick," she repeated. "It's Mary."

Slowly his eyes opened. Slowly he turned his head. Slowly he whispered her name. Then he gave a great sigh, and his quick faint breathing stopped. "He's dead—he's dead!" Mary called to Alec and Nigel.

She found herself shaking as she rose, and Nigel put his arm around her.

"It's—too sudden," she whispered. "Oh! It's too dreadfully sudden! I—I didn't expect anything like this."

Alec spoke behind her.

"None of us did, Mary. Only Nigel was better prepared."

Nigel's arm stiffened about Mary's waist, but again he ignored the older man.

"We had best bury him right here now, hadn't we?" he asked her.

Mary nodded. "Yes. I suppose so. Unless we should call the doctor—"

"The doctor will be gone for weeks, Mary," Alec reminded her. "And it's too late for him to do anything, anyway. Nigel and I will go out now and prepare the ground. Will you wait in here? Or will you come outside with us?"

"I'll—I'll wait with Nick," she murmured.

A short while later Mary stood in the flickering lantern light beside the grave, listening to Alec's deep voice offering up a reverent prayer for her husband. And now for the first time her tears fell as she thought of the waste of all of Nick's life, of her lost love for him, and of all that might have been. A sob escaped her. At once Nigel, who was close beside her, lifted his bowed head and slipped a supporting arm about her.

"I'm—all right," she whispered.

Alec finished his prayer, and he and Nigel together filled in the grave and laid pine branches over the bare earth. Then Nigel came up to Mary again.

"Is there anything more you would like done, Mary?"

She shook her head. "It's finished." She stopped a moment and then held out her hand. "It's finished," she repeated brokenly. "But I will never forget your good care of Nick."

"I did everything I could think of, Mary."

"I know." She hesitated. What more was there to say? "Nigel, you may have the wagon if you like. And all that's in it, though there's little enough."

He nodded.

"What—what will you be doing now, do you know?" she asked.

"What will *you* be doing?" he returned.

It was hard to think. Hard to collect her thoughts. "I shall probably go north after Matt's wedding."

He said softly, "I'd like mighty much to come to that wedding."

Alec put in a brusk word. "You're not invited. Nor likely will you be. Mary, shall we be going now?"

Nigel—again—might not have heard him. He kept his look steady on Mary's face and repeated, "I'd sure like mighty much to come to that wedding."

Was he just asking, Mary wondered? Or—was there a threat to Matt beneath his request if it should not be granted? The same threat he had made once before? In the next instant she was ashamed of such a thought and wondered how it had ever happened to come to her. Nigel was much too changed a person, she told herself, and she listened as he continued.

"I have a hankering to mix once with a roomful of fine folk. I'd stay wherever you said, Mary, but I'd like to be there."

He stood before her in the uncertain light, and she saw him quiet, decently dressed, and for the moment almost humble in his manner. Even more unusual was the sudden hunger plain on his face for something beyond his reach as yet. Something she could give him.

Impulsively she answered, "Come, then, to the side entrance at Live Oaks two nights from now. If any servant stops you, send him to call Alec or me. One of us will see you get in. But you mustn't stay long. Only ten minutes or so."

Matt need never know, she thought. And Alec would remain beside Nigel and see that he left at the right time. Nigel deserved this much from her, and what harm could it do?

On their way home through the night Mary kept living

the scene over and over. Had it really occurred? Was Nick gone? But–yes–it was true. The unexpected, the unhoped for, the unbelievable had happened. Nick was gone and she–she was free again. He had truly left her this time. Forever.

She was free. Lost for a while, perhaps, in her new freedom, bruised and bewildered by its swift coming–but free. Her hand went out and reached for Alec's, and when she felt his dear clasp she spoke.

"It's incredible–and grievous–and yet wonderful, too, in a way, Alec, since not one person I know and love has been hurt by Nick's life or death–save only myself."

"And in time your hurt will pass, Mary."

"Yes."

They drove on in silence. Presently Alec broke it.

"You were generous to Nigel about Matt's wedding, Mary. Matt would not like it."

"He isn't to know. I'm counting on you to see that he doesn't."

"Why did you do it–say he could come, I mean?"

"I was sorry for him. He's so alone now. And I was grateful, too. He was kind to Nick when he had no real cause to be. He did what I should have been doing and couldn't–all the nursing. Those reasons and–I can't say, Alec, exactly! I just felt I had to."

"The lad loves you," he told her quietly. "What's more –he's no longer a lad."

She turned a shocked face toward him. "No! That's ridiculous!"

" 'Tis true, though. You're the star in his life. If you want none of him, then give him no more encouragement."

"Alec! I'm just his sister! That's all!"

She could not believe anything else and said so, and

he did not argue. Nevertheless the thought remained with her.

When they reached home again, Matt's house was completely darkened, for it was late. But Alec had a key and unlocked the door for her. Then he took her outstretched hand in both of his own.

"Thank you, Alec," she whispered. "For everything. For all your thought and care and help."

He nodded. "And now goodnight," he said gently.

There was, as always, a deep tenderness in his voice—but nothing more. And it was a moment when she would have been glad to hear more, to have some bit of comfort from him other than mere words. But he gave her none.

"It would not be fitting," she thought, as she mounted the stairs to her room. "No, I know it would not. But—but sometimes Alec bends over backward to stand up straight."

And now—again—a tiny doubt stirred in her tired heart. Did she truly love Alec as she thought she did? Or had she only turned to him in the extremity of her need because he was there and to be entirely trusted? Did he love her as she had told herself he did? Never once had he said so. No, never. It had been she who had spoken, as it had been she who had spoken at the Collect to Nick years ago.

Her cheeks burned with the realization of this. Would she never be done acting like a bold hussy? Would she never know the enfolding and protecting love of a fine and honorable man?

In weariness, in despair, in loneliness and in grief, she cast herself on her bed, fully dressed and—at long last—fell into sleep.

Chapter 19

On the morning of Matt's wedding day Mary was in her room when there came a knock at her door, and Matt walked in unceremoniously.

"I just learned from Mrs. Pinckney that she has invited you to stay with her for a while after today," he said, without preamble.

"Yes." Mary moved some of the clothes that were strewn over a chair and gestured to her brother to sit down. "I thought you wouldn't mind, Matt."

"On the contrary. It was very thoughtful of her." He frowned, his black eyes holding a sudden cold gleam. "I think it may take Myrtle and me a while to get used to living together."

"Yes," Mary said again, and added tactfully. "It does most married people."

"You think so?"

She nodded. She had been more grateful than she could say for Mrs. Pinckney's invitation. She could not bear to leave Alec not knowing, now that she was free, whether he loved her or not. Yet she had been aware that living under Matt's roof with Myrtle there too might be difficult. She—Mary—would feel in the way, she was sure. And she certainly had no desire to witness any unpleasant scenes that might take place between the spoiled and strong-willed bride and the equally spoiled and strong-willed groom. Yet scenes there would be, she did not doubt.

Matt went on now, a heavy worried note in his voice. "Sometimes I don't understand Myrtle at all."

Carefully Mary laid one of her dresses on the bed and folded it.

"I guess we're all a little hard to understand at times," she said, after a moment. "Especially around the time we're to be married."

"Did you blow hot and blow cold, too?"

Mary turned and met her brother's eyes.

"I had my moments of doubt," she answered honestly, "but I would not give them room. I—I was more eager than afraid."

"That's the way it should be." Matt sat forward in the chair, his big hands tightly clasped between his knees, his glance fixed on them. "Just last night," he went on slowly, "she wouldn't let me kiss her. And we're to be married today."

Mary continued folding her dress, seeking for words of reassurance for Matt. The past few weeks had been tempestuous ones, she knew, for him as well as for herself. Even in her own trouble she had been aware of this. For Myrtle, flitting lightly from one gay affair to another, had let herself be wholly absorbed by those who were fêting her. Only Matt was given none of her time. Only Matt must step aside for others. The decorator who was to fill the great rooms at Live Oaks with flowers and plants—the artist who was to paint her portrait—the caterer who had been imported for the occasion—the dressmaker who must put the finishing touches on her wedding gown—the bridesmaids who came chattering with questions—all these were put ahead of Matt, and, chafing under what seemed to him deliberate avoidance, he had worked hard to hold his tongue. Sensing this, Myrtle would, at the last possible moment, fling herself into his arms with an abandon that made him temporarily forget his anger. But the moment she knew it to be forgotten, she would withdraw again. It had been, for Matt, a frustrating, bewildering period. Didn't she, after all, love him? Or was such behavior normal? Uncertain, steeped in maddening doubt, he had finally come to Mary.

She said now, "I wouldn't let that trouble me, Matt. It's been a busy time for Myrtle. She's had so much to think about and plan for. So many details to remember and take care of. And then all the festivities, too. She must be tired. You know, when you're tired—when you don't feel like yourself—you only want to be let alone. I—I was that way traveling with Nick, I remember. I just—just hated him to come near me sometimes. And yet —yet I never loved him more than those first few weeks." Her voice broke suddenly.

Matt's face had lightened at her words, and he stood up. "Well, one thing is sure," he said. "After the wedding, there'll be no more nonsense. Myrtle will know she's mine. She'll know I come first." And then, becoming aware that tears were rolling down Mary's cheeks, he exclaimed, "Mary! What on earth is the matter?"

She shook her head. Then, suddenly, she flung herself into his arms and poured out all the story of the past few weeks. Matt, astounded, irate, pitying and admiring, could only stroke her shoulders as he listened.

At the end he held her from him at arm's length and said, "You're a wonderful woman, Mary. I don't know how you got through all that without my knowing a thing. But it's over now, and I'm glad. You're glad, too. You can't help but be." He searched her face, seeing for the first time the circles beneath her eyes, the look of strain about her mouth. "Are you all right? You can go through with your part in the wedding tonight?"

"I'm all right." She smiled at her brother reassuringly through her tears, wanting to tell him she was weeping as much for the uncertainty that beset her regarding Alec as for all the anxiety and tragedy she had endured. "I'm all right," he repeated.

"What about Nigel?" he demanded. "Has he cleared out?"

Mary's heart skipped a beat, and then she told Matt what she had promised Nigel about his coming to the wedding. Matt's frown was swift and fierce.

"I don't like that!"

"I—I knew you wouldn't, Matt. But I felt—indebted. And he wanted so much to come. I'm sure he'll make no trouble. Why should he? He has nothing against you or me any more. We did what he wanted back in New Bern. We gave him his start."

"Just the same, I don't trust him. But never mind. Perhaps you're right. He'd only make trouble for himself if he made it for me now." His face changed then, and he came up to Mary and took one of her hands in his. "What I really am here to ask you is this: have you written to Prue yet?"

"No. Not yet. I will soon, though. I will right after the wedding."

He nodded. Then he said, "Yes. Do that."

When he left her a moment later she rang for Belladonna to come carry her clothes over to Mrs. Pinckney's house, and then she stood alone in her room thinking. She knew why Matt had asked her about her letter. Myrtle had probably told him she wanted her new home to herself. Yes, Mary must, indeed, write at once, for she could not remain indefinitely at Mrs. Pinckney's, and if she did not feel welcome here at Matt's she had no alternative. Unless—

Her thoughts turned to Alec again. If only she knew beyond any wondering how he felt about her! Over and over she recalled every scene with him, trying to remember exactly each word, each look, and finding always that these had been controlled by his uncompromising integrity. All his kindness, all his tenderness, despite the generosity with which they had been given, had held an unmistakable reserve. Perhaps this was her own fault, she thought. Perhaps she had forfeited what she desired by her too open and too eager reach for him.

She could not bear the thought of leaving him, of going back to Stockbridge alone. But what could she do? She must, indeed, write to Prue tomorrow.

* * *

Downstairs at Live Oaks the great rooms had been turned into bowers of beauty and were now filled with the anticipatory murmur of hundreds of guests. Tall candles in all the glittering chandeliers sent out a soft but brilliant light, touching here and there the gleaming waxed floors, dancing on the tall silver vase in the center of the white-draped altar in the hall between living and drawing rooms, and resting beneficently on the calm face of the black-gowned rector. Behind the budding magnolia trees that had been transplanted to green tubs for the occasion, the musicians were tuning up their instruments while, in front of this screen, stood Matt, the impatient groom, with Alec MacDonald, his best man, beside him.

The wedding march sounded at last. And at last the wedding procession started on its slow way down the wide curved stairway. The little flower girl first, scattering blossoms as she came, then the six bridesmaids in palest green, then Mary in her apricot-colored gown, and, last of all, Myrtle on her father's arm, her dark eyes enormous in the pallid perfection of her small lovely face.

It came to Mary, keeping time to the measured beat of the music, that there was something unreal in her being here. The kaleidoscopic changes of her fortune had been too swift. Her glance sought out her brother standing below with an odd look of hard triumph on his dark, handsome face. Matt! Matt! What does this marriage mean to you? Mary asked herself in a moment of swift anxiety. You must not be ruthless. Myrtle will never be won that way. And the next moment she wondered if her sister-in-law would ever be won in any way, or if she would not always keep herself locked away, resentful of invasion, determined on the privilege of privacy and the sanctity of her own person?

A little gust of anger swept through Mary at the idea of such colossal selfishness. Matt deserved better than that! And then, with swift remembered joy, she recalled how he had made his way up the stairs to her only a little while ago to stand before her and say, "Mrs. Pinckney told me to come look at you now, because I won't have eyes for you later. She said you were as beautiful as the bride." And then he had put his great hands lightly on her shoulders, and, leaning down, had kissed her there before all the bridesmaids, murmuring as he did, so that only she could hear, "You've done me proud, Mary. All through these weeks you've done me proud. And from my heart I thank you."

She was at the foot of the stairs now, and Matt's glance was seeking Myrtle's while her own moved on to Alec's face. In it she saw for a heart-stopping second the expression she had longed many times to surprise there. Yes, the curtain was rung up on his true feeling for her, and the scope of it was not, this time, to be quickly erased. Amazed and startled and stirred beyond measure, her gaze clung as if magnetized, and then dropped—though not before her rising color had told him that she had read its meaning aright.

Turmoil filled her. For this, she sensed, was something bigger than she had dared imagine or hope for. This had a depth and a height like David's feeling for Prue. It was glorious. But it was frightening, too, as a towering wave is frightening before you give yourself up to it and are floated easily and lightly on it to a safe shore. The thought, not wholly clear but wholly disturbing, Mary put from her, for there were too many duties pending to think of Alec and herself now. There was the ceremony to be got through. She must remember to take Myrtle's bouquet while the ring was being put on the bride's hand. There was the turn-about they must all make when she —Mary—must rearrange the bride's long train. There was the line to be formed and all the guests to greet. There was Nigel to watch out for and see that he was unobtrusively ushered in and as unobtrusively ushered out.

Finally, came refreshment time and dancing. Her hopes of being alone with Alec for a moment were dashed as she saw Nigel enter the room and watched Alec move swiftly to his side. As she waltzed off with Tom Izard, her last glimpse of the two showed them in earnest, quiet conversation. Then, as the waltz ended, she felt a touch at her elbow and turned to find Nigel at her side.

"May I have the next dance?" he asked.

When the music had started up again and Nigel had skillfully maneuvered her away from the crowd, he said, "I'm leaving the party after this dance—your brother needn't worry. And tomorrow morning I'm leaving

Charles-Town. But I'll be back, Mary—I'll be back a rich man. Will you be here?"

His dark eyes burned a meaning into his question which she was too preoccupied to see.

"I don't know, Nigel. It's likely I'll leave for Stockbridge soon." She spoke almost absently, searching over Nigel's shoulder for Alec.

"I'll find you." Fiercely, he pressed her hand to his lips and was gone.

She hardly noticed. Now! she thought. Where is Alec?

But to her utter confusion and dismay Alec did not once draw near her to ask for a dance, leaving her, instead, to other partners: to Henry Laurens' son, to Mr. Lattimore, the wealthy planter, and others. Had she mistaken the look he had given her as she walked in the bridal procession? Had she—again—imagined it? A kind of sickness filled her, adding to her bewilderment and pain.

"I will not look at him. I will not expect anything of him," she told herself.

It was long after Mrs. Pinckney had slipped away, and after Matt and Myrtle had departed in their great mahogany coach amid a shower of rice, that the guests began to leave by twos and threes and fours in the early morning light. Not until then did Alec approach her. If she was ready to go, he said quietly, he would escort her to Mrs. Pinckney's. She looked at him and saw strangeness in his face.

"I'm ready," she replied, in a low voice.

The ride, holding the imminent promise of something momentous, was a curiously silent one. Alec, in black velvet with gold buckles at his knees and on his shoes, with white lace ruffles cascading over his bony wrists and a white wig concealing his rough gray-brown hair, was an unfamiliar figure. The country in the moonlight appeared unfamiliar, too, the very sounds and smells. She in her low-cut, peach-colored brocade, with curls falling over her bare shoulders, tiny peach-colored slippers on her feet, her heart beating in a tumult of emotion such as she had never felt before, was someone suddenly unknown to herself. An odd dread had fallen on her so that she was not sure—now—what she either expected or wanted. Did she, in truth, desire that towering wave to engulf her, to drown her, to carry her to a new and strange shore from which there would be no returning?

Alec's voice, tight in its restraint, measured and careful in its wording, broke in on her thoughts.

"I never meant you to know, Mary. It was my intention from the very beginning to hold my tongue and never have you guess about my feelings. You see, I could not take your own for me too seriously even if you had been free. You were overwrought, I thought, and I was the one could ease you. 'Twas for that reason you thought you cared, I said to myself. And so I held silence. But tonight—tonight you've read on my face what's in my heart, and now there's no use to blow and bubble. Perhaps it's not been right to have such a love as is in my heart for you, but there 'tis. And though I know the lass must be foolish that would take me for a husband, nonetheless that's what I'm askin' you."

The wave retreated. The surging noise in her ears died away. She was not drowning. She was not being born helplessly anywhere. She was sitting here in a jolting coach and good, kind Alec beside her was telling her, with his arms tightly folded across his chest, something she had been longing to know and which now—without warning and quite unreasonably—she did not want to hear.

Not that way, at least. Not as he was saying it. Why did she feel so? she asked herself, near to tears in the swift reversal of her emotions. Because it was so different from her remembrance of a love declared? With Nick, handsome, romantic, possessive, she had been certain—but she had been wrong. Oh, what ailed her to feel at once grievous disappointment and such an anguish of frustrated desire?

In spite of herself she shivered a little. "It's I am prideful—" she began falteringly.

But he had seen the shiver and spoke before she could finish.

"There's time aplenty for you to think on the matter, so I will not rush you. And if, in the end, you would prefer Alec for a friend, why, friend he'll be. And now here we are."

"Alec, I—I just don't know—"

"I'll not rush you. Not now or ever. I love you too much for that."

The deep, tender cadence of his voice stirred another wild tempest in her. If he withdrew again, as he had once withdrawn, she could not bear it. But she did not, could not speak until they had reached the Pinckney mansion and he was helping her out of the carriage and up the steps. There she raised her eyes to his face.

"You have honored me," she said in a whisper. "You have honored me far more than I deserve."

* * *

For the few hours that remained before daylight, Mary lay in the big four-poster in Mrs. Pinckney's guest room wondering—wondering—what answer to give Alec. And she wondered as much at her own hesitation. Which was real—the tumult she had felt or the absence of it? She fell asleep, finally, before she knew the answer.

Mrs. Pinckney, after knocking on Mary's door in the

morning, entered, walked straight to Mary's bed, and laid her fingers lightly on the dark circles under Mary's eyes.

"You have not slept."

"Not much. I—I had so much to think about."

"I know. Alec. That's why I came home early. So that you two could be alone in the coach, and he could tell you of his love."

Mary lifted an astonished glance, and Mrs. Pinckney laughed softly.

"Mary! Mary! I am not blind! I saw his look on you last night as you came down the stairs. So now you will marry him—"

"That's—what I don't know."

"Yes. You will marry him because you love him, my dear. I saw that, too."

Again Mary lifted an astonished glance.

"How can you be sure, when I am not?"

Mrs. Pinckney sat down on the edge of the bed and took Mary's hands in hers.

"Because I know it's only your reason that makes you hesitate. You are thinking how much older he is than you. Well, how much? Twelve—fourteen—years? But I tell you that doesn't matter. You will be happy. I was." She smiled and then leaned forward to kiss Mary's forehead. "One has only to listen to one's heart, Mary. Don't bother about arithmetic problems. Listen to your heart."

Mary looked up into her friend's face for a long moment, not seeing it, however—seeing, instead, Alec's lean, grave countenance and the warmth of his steady, gray eyes; hearing his voice, deep and sweet, speaking her name, making it sound like music; remembering his big hands, quick and strong and careful.

Careful. That was the keynote of Alec's character. How different from Nick and Nigel! How different from all her girlish dreams of any lover she might have. There would be nothing romantic, nothing tempestuous about living with Alec. The days with him would be placid and sweet—but uneventful.

She spoke at last, slowly.

"My heart tells me that marrying Alec would be like coming into a safe harbor after a stormy and hazardous voyage." She paused, then nodded. "Yes. That's what it will be like."

And there was relief and a lilting note of joy in her voice for a decision finally made.

* * *

April 5, 1759

Dear Prue,

The day has come when I feel I must—and want to —take my pen in hand to discover to you the events of my life since I left the kind shelter given me by Esther Burr. I scarce know how to begin, but perhaps at the beginning is best. I have been with Matt in his home in Charles-Town for many weeks, but how I came to arrive here is a long tale. I—

The cry of a gullah selling something on the street below interrupted her. The strange dialect of the African was still incomprehensible to her, but she never failed to try to understand it. This one was sing-songing what sounded like "Shri-i-bs fo' tase!" Shrimps, possibly? Shrimps for your taste? She pushed her shining brown curls back from her ears and gave the sound her full attention. But it remained unintelligible, and soon the voice died away in the distance.

She looked down at what she had written, intending to go on and say, "I was married to Nicholas Fanshaw, the pedlar whom you may remember." But suddenly she decided against it, for though she could think of Nick now without bitterness, she felt she could not be as wholly fair to him as she would like to be in a letter. Better wait until she saw Prue before trying to tell of her unhappy marriage. She wrote instead:

> I am not sure if you and Pa can forgive me for running off as I did without consulting you, and for my subsequent long silence. But my experiences were not all of the pleasantest, and I could not bring myself to trouble you with an account of them. I would like now to admit I was reckless and foolish, showing little sound judgment and only an avid desire to go beyond the confines of Princetown and see the world. I can but plead my youth for such headstrong selfishness as I have shown, and, if I erred, the Lord punished me with a mort of anxieties that turned me ill for nigh a year. To help me regain my strength, Matt, whom I came upon by the greatest good chance, took me with him on his last cruise before his wedding. We were gone more than six months, and I am now quite well again.
>
> It was on that trip that Matt told me you were expecting another baby. I was so happy for you and David. Has it been born by now? Who does it look like? Is it a boy or a girl? Could be it's there with you now, and I'll not know till you reply to this letter—if you do reply to it. Oh, I hope you do! For I have missed you, Prue, and home, and everyone there more than I have dared let myself think at times, though I must say this place is becoming like a second home to me.
>
> There is so much I would like to tell you of all that has happened here and of the life that goes on which is so different from life in Stockbridge. But I will

not take time now, for I know you are eager to learn about the girl Matt has chosen to be his wife.

She is tiny and delicate in appearance, as Matt is big and strong. You would think one good hug from him would crush the breath from her body. In that way they seem ill-mated. But she is very beautiful, and for all her gentle drawling voice and languid gestures and great appealing black eyes, she is not supine. I have seen those eyes flash fire and I have heard her voice harden, and I feel sure that the iron in Matt will occasionally strike iron in her. This may be a good thing, Prue, for Matt is overbearing, as you know, and determined on his own way. At the same time, she has been an only child and is accustomed to having her way, too. However, Matt seems to adore her. Certainly he was bound to wed her! I sometimes feel it is to him the final triumph of his life to win for a wife a girl of her social position. Which is strange, isn't it, for a man of Matt's solid unpretentiousness?

The wedding took place last night out at Live Oaks, where Myrtle has always lived. It was a beautiful affair with hundreds of guests present and the most sumptuous repast imaginable for supper. But of all this I cannot write now, either, for I am too filled with what happened to me after it was over.

Prue, I have been asked to wed. And I am going to accept. I will become the wife of Alec MacDonald. Perhaps you recall that Matt spoke of Alec the time he came home to visit. He has always been Matt's best friend and right-hand assistant. He is considerably older than I, and though big and brawny not at all handsome. He is, too, Scottish in all ways. And oh! He is good to me and always has been. He seems truly to love me, too, though he is not blind to my weaknesses and knows all my mistakes. Anyway, by the time you receive this I may perhaps be wedded to him. I wish you might be here for the occasion but I suppose your baby is too small for you either to leave or to bring.

Now one last word, Prue. I am happy as I have never been and most confident of the future. I cannot help but feel the Lord has forgiven me for my errors, else He would not have directed such a man as Alec to me and put it into his heart to care for me as he does. Should this letter and this explanation of the time I have been away satisfy you and Pa—for I can never make a fuller one—and should you want to see me again, I am sure Alec and I can come some time when one of Matt's ships sails to Boston. Please let me know if we will be welcome, for oh, Prue! I have missed you all so much! And I do so long to see you all again!

Your loving sister,
Mary.

Mary folded the letter and then sat for a moment lost in thought. If she went home with Alec she would be going as she had wanted to go—free of the past and with her head proudly up. She would not be the target for questions that she would be if she were alone. It might even be imagined that she had been on Matt's ships most of the time since leaving Esther Burr's. Yes, if she went home with Alec, she would go without misgivings.

"If—!"

Slowly she tied and sealed the letter she held. It was like sealing her fate, she thought. Yet what was it Pa had said to her when she had left home nearly four years ago? She could recall his words as if it were yesterday.

"Love built that house behind you, Mary. And love lives in it the way it always has. You kin feel it like a blessin' fallin' on you the minute you go through the door an' Prue steps out with that smile o' hers to greet you. Your sister Prue's love, Mary, is as wide as this world and as deep as the sea. And should you ever git to feelin' lonely or troubled by aught whilst you're gone, jest you stop an' remember that Prue's love is reachin' out to you from that house. Mine, too," he had finished gruffly.

There was no "if." Not really.

PART FOUR

❦

May 1759–April 1770

Chapter 20

MARY WAS MARRIED QUIETLY in Matt's home a few weeks later. It was a lovely little wedding with but a handful of guests present—Myrtle's parents, Mrs. Pinckney, the Rutledges, the Moultries, Tom Izard and his handsome sister, and a few others. Myrtle was her only attendant. Matt gave her away.

The bride and groom went immediately to Wistaria House which Alec had bought on South Bay. It was a charming place with iron grillwork edging the steps that led up to the columned portico, and an iron rail of most delicate design decorating all the balconies. Within were large airy rooms having high ceilings and long windows and gleaming parquetry floors. It was a tall house with the living room on the second floor because hurricanes often swept water in under the great front door. The bedrooms, opening out onto balconies, overlooked the colorful walled gardens and were shaded by clambering wistaria vines that reached to the roof and gave the house its name.

Here Mary settled down with Alec, her social position assured, her anxieties ended. Here she gathered her staff of black servants—Remus, Hannibal, Julius and Abraham, together with Sukey, Chloe, Columbine and Dido. Here she busied herself with the hanging of curtains, the arrangement of furniture, the ordering of china from England, and the selection of rugs and rare treasures from Matt's overflowing warehouse.

Life with her new husband was just what Mary had thought it would be—sweet, serene, and unexciting. Alec was too reverent and too gentle to kindle the fire in her that Nick had aroused. Sometimes she wished he would show her the hard strength of his arms, the full hot passion that he held in such stern check, for she knew it was there. But he did not dream that the desire to be overwhelmed and submerged by love boiled as wildly within her as within him. And Mary, fearing he might be shocked, kept her passion under a guard as rigid as his own.

Yet she was content. Sometimes she found it hard to believe she had come into such good fortune. At those times the past became a jumble of days, diffuse, without pattern, a chaos from which she had miraculously emerged. More than once she said to him, "I have the strangest feeling. As if I'd just escaped from a kind of strangling cocoon."

"Well, you've turned into a butterfly, that's for sure," he returned smilingly. "You're flitting here, there, and everywhere all the time. Tea parties, luncheon parties, dancing parties—"

"Do you mind?"

His arms drew her close, and his gray eyes warmed with the love that stood in his heart for her.

"I mind nothing so long as you're happy with me."

"I'm happy, Alec. I'm wondrous happy," she told him, her voice and eyes soft.

It was a happiness that deepened steadily as time went by and each day brought its quota of absorbing interest and activity.

First breakfast with Alec, the windows open to all the bird songs, the coffee service gleaming on the table before them, Remus tiptoeing in respectfully to offer hot crumpets. This seemed the most perfect hour of the day. Yet others followed that were, in their turn, just as full of delight.

There was the trip to market in her sedan chair borne on the shoulders of the ebony-faced Julius and Abraham. How she loved the colorfulness of the scene that met her eyes there! She watched it, as she had watched everything in her travels, eager for the unfamiliar, alert to the bizarre.

Where else but here, she asked herself, would she see such variety? Even New York had not offered so much. Seafaring men in various garbs, strutting and strolling with their accustomed unshakable confidence in themselves. Black field servants in bright cottons wandering barefoot over the hard-packed oyster-shelled streets shepherded by their swarthy, sharp-eyed factors. Feather-crowned, blanketed Indians walking silently in single file, each leading his pack horse laden with pelts and game for trading. Small ragged chimney sweeps. Fish mongers intoning their wares. The ground-nut cake woman bearing her flat basket of chewy black molasses squares atop her turbaned head. Old men carrying fishing lines and cans that held dough for bait. Britishers in their scarlet and gold, their horses prancing skittishly. Rickety goat carts, polished high phaetons, lumbering mahogany coaches, and—here and there—sedan chairs like her own. And over and through it all, the curious Gullah dialect, and the fragrance of jasmine, of honeysuckle, of wistaria, mingled with the smell of fish, salt sea, and sewers.

Yes, that was a fascinating hour, too. Yet just as pleasurable was the return to her ordered house and, in the afternoon, the friendly talk over teacups with neighboring wives and matrons when gossip of all kinds was relayed. News of Tom Izard's latest romance, of the most fashionable hair styling, of the latest book, of the return of Mrs. Pinckney's sons from England—and talk of the organization under Mrs. Avery's direction, of an exclusive group known as the "St. Cecelia Society" which was to foster concerts and other cultural evenings.

But the proudest hour was when Mary presided at her own dinner table entertaining Alec's business associates—buyers, agents, ships' masters. Or when, dressed in her finest clothes and with Alec escorting her in his, they went out to a play or a ball. On those occasions she often wondered what had happened to her New England heritage, for in her upbringing such things had been considered sinful.

"Yet I don't feel sinful," she said to Alec.

"You need not. 'Tis a different world here, and you must live in the world where you find youself."

Indeed, Mary was happy and radiant in her happiness, for this was the life she had dreamed of as a girl. Nothing was lacking, nothing was needed, those first few months of her marriage, save the madness of an emotion which, she told herself, perhaps she ought no longer to want. All she could really wish for, she thought, was a reply to her letter to Prue.

Then—at long last—it came.

My darling sister: Your letter gave me more joy than I have known in many a month. To hear you are safe was enough. I do not care about your past. It is over, and I shall never question you. Nor will anyone else. So I say for both Pa and myself that you and Alec are to come north as soon as you can. We want to see Matt, too, and would be most pleased to meet his new wife. Can you not all visit us soon?

Eagerly Mary began planning for this. But before anything definite could be arranged, she found herself pregnant. Alec, remembering her difficult experience in Cross Creek, would not hear of her traveling, and Mary was too overjoyed at her prospects to dispute him or be willing to take any risks either. Prue would understand.

"But Matt must know of our change of plans, Alec. He was going with us, you remember. He and Myrtle."

Alec nodded.

"I think I'll step over there now and tell him. He'll be home for dinner. It's near three o'clock."

"I'll go with you."

Matt's home was but a short distance from Wistaria House, and the two reached it in a few moments. They found Matt alone in his great dining room, and Mary asked in surprise where Myrtle was.

At the question Matt's dark face grew darker. "She's gone to her mother's for a few days," he answered briefly. Then he looked at Mary a moment as if he were about to say something explosive, but he changed his mind and asked instead, "Will you have something to eat? Or drink? Amos! Fetch plates!"

"We've had dinner, thank you, Matt. Don't bother, Amos. We want nothing. We came to give you a piece of news." And Mary sank into the chair Amos pulled out for her, while Alec took another. "Matt, we can't go home to Stockbridge," she said breathlessly. "Not yet. Not for quite a while."

"Why not?"

Mary waited until Amos had gone to the kitchen. Then

she leaned forward, her face alight, and answered softly, "Because I'm to have a baby."

His black eyes flashed, and he reached out a big hand to touch hers lightly. "You're pleased?"

"I'm walking on stars! Of course I'm sorry not to be able to go home yet, but if I had to choose, this is better."

At the lilt in her voice Matt sat back and pushed his plate from him in a gesture of ill-restrained violence. He was, Mary saw, in one of his moods. Oh, dear! What was the matter now?

She said, "If you don't want to wait for us—If you and Myrtle want to go, anyway—it's all right."

"We'll wait"—briefly.

"You will? But maybe Myrtle would rather not. I know she's frantic to get to New York and see the sights there."

"She is, for a fact. But she'll wait just the same. And for the same reason you're going to."

The blunt, almost angry announcement shocked Mary and puzzled her as much as it surprised her, and she looked at her brother uncertainly. She would have thought he would be eager for a child. He'd been most attached to his little Aaron and well-nigh distracted when he'd been stolen by the Indians. His next words enlightened her.

"I'm happy about it, all right, but Myrtle isn't. She acts as if I'd cheated her somehow." His hand slowly closed into a fist that he beat up and down on the table before him. "That's why she's gone home. To punish me for bringing this—this tragedy on her." And he gave a short hard laugh.

There was a silence. In it Mary saw with sudden clarity that Matt was lonely in his marriage. He had taken for a wife someone as alien to himself as she, Mary, had been alien to Nick. He had always been lonely, she suspected.

It was what made him fierce. But he had brought to his marriage an exultant hope. He had been ready to make himself an outcast, to yield to the kindness rather than the cruelty that was in him. And he was meeting rejection. If Myrtle continued as she was beginning, she would meet rejection, too, Mary thought.

She said finally, "Myrtle may just feel this way now in the early months, Matt. She may get over it. The way I got over my nausea with Nick's baby."

"She'd better get over it. I told her I'd give her a week there at Live Oaks. No more. Then she's to come back and—My God! Mary! She's going to perform a miracle! Why doesn't she see that? And rejoice as you do? But all she thinks of is losing her figure."

"She may change," Mary said again.

She said it without confidence, however, and Alec said nothing at all.

* * *

That winter twin boys were born to Mary. She named them Kim and Keith, and by the time they were a year old she began to plan once more for her trip home. She would go in the summer so as to avoid the dreadful heat in Charles-Town, she thought. But—again—she became pregnant and—again—postponed the trip. Her little girl, Phoebe, came soon after Myrtle resentfully presented Matt with a second daughter.

"He's wild for a son," Myrtle told Mary in her lazy, drawling way. "But I'm just as content havin' Lucy and Mary-Etta. I don't want any more."

It saddened Mary to see that Matt's marriage was not going well, but there didn't seem to be anything she could do to help. They were both stubborn and proud.

Poor Matt! Mary knew his love had been the rock

against which all his hopes and plans and dreams had madly eddied and swirled in tumultuous leaping waves. Now these were diminished, yet the granite—his love—remained, upthrust in a flattened sea, an object, a purpose, a demand at once caring and uncaring, a pride and a torture. Moved by the extremes of his emotional bondage, he was alternately generous and harsh, forgiving and unforgiving, lenient and exacting, indifferent and insatiable. He could neither master his wife nor leave her alone.

"He is not even sensible about her," Alec said once to Mary.

No. Matt was not sensible. Being sensible was behaving properly, not getting upset over her, not asking her for too much. Being sensible was being controlled and careful, and Matt was never one to be either. He did not care if he made others uncomfortable. Wasn't he uncomfortable, too?

What would the end be? Mary often wondered.

* * *

More than two years passed before Alec and Mary both felt their three children were old enough to be exposed to the lengthy trip north. Myrtle was not taking hers. Flatly and unequivocally she told Matt that he could choose between them and her, and he, knowing her impatience with their childish needs and demands and wanting her to appear to the best advantage in front of Prue and Pa, yielded the point.

The whole country was in a tumult of unrest and rebellion when the little party finally started out at last. It was the year 1765, and the Anti-Stamp Act Congress was to meet in New York in the fall. At this time South Carolina had shown more indignation and had exhibited a greater antagonism to the Stamp Act than any other colony had.

She it was that actually seized arms without waiting to discover if she would be supported by the other colonies. The stamps were not allowed on her shore but were stored in Fort Johnson on the west side of the harbor. Then volunteers, called for and given muskets, rowed to the Fort and took possession of it. Instead of raising the British flag, the Carolinians hoisted their own state flag —three white crescents on a blue ground—and loaded a cannon which they pointed at the vessel that had brought the stamps into the harbor. When the Commander of the vessel was ordered to come and take back the stamps or see his ship burned and sunk, he obeyed and meekly sailed away. Oh! There'd been excitement for fair—and Matt and Alec were in the thick of it.

Now they had decided to attend the anti-Stamp Act Congress in New York with Mr. Rutledge, the state representative, since their livelihood—trading—depended on the action that would be resolved upon against England's efforts to stifle all trade. The two men would go to the meeting, and Mary would show Myrtle the sights of New York, after which they would all continue their journey to Stockbridge.

It was with both delight and a lingering trepidation that Mary found herself—at last—on her homeward way.

* * *

Home! Prue, with her coronet of gold hair, her lovely smile and her deep warm love that embraced everyone.

Pa, gruff but kind. David and Johnny (both home at last from the French and Indian War), with David as courteous and sweet as ever. Johnny was still unmarried, grown from his lanky teens into a personable and charming twenty-six, with a sinewy grace and a puckish grin beneath his thick, wavy blond hair. Prue's son, Mark, whom Mary had left a small boy, was ready now for college at Princetown. And Faith, a toddler nine years ago, was approaching adolescence. A plain child, Faith, with a square, resolute face like Pa's, flying fair hair and large brown eyes—her only claim to beauty—but with a wonderful zest for living that drew Mary to her at once.

Never would Mary forget that visit. First, she herself was welcomed without question, as she had hoped but had not dared believe she might be. The past was too far past to be recalled. Esther Burr's father, Dr. Edwards, together with his family, had left town years before when he had accepted the presidency of the New Jersey college made vacant by Aaron Burr's death. No one thought to speak of the Edwardses or to inquire about Mary's visit to Esther long ago.

Then, too, Mary found an opportunity to unburden her heart to Prue about her marriage to Nick. What a relief to have nothing hidden between them any more!

All Prue said was, "Well, your experience, unhappy as it was, has made you into another person. A stronger, sweeter person. Sometimes it seems we need to use people for the furtherance of our own growth. It's a strange thing, but it's true."

It was, however, the memory of Alec's words to Mary as they were leaving that Mary cherished most, echoing, as they did, a desire that had lain dormant in her own heart, undiscovered until he spoke.

"This is a fine, clean, big, open country here, Mary. Better, to my mind, than any city was or could be. It takes me back to Scotland with its highlands and fields of purple gorse. I'd like it well could we ever arrange our lives to settle here."

"You would, really, Alec?"

He nodded, his gray eyes gleaming. "I'd raise sheep,"

he said. "Sheep and apples. 'Twould be a fair life. Could you bear it, Mary, to leave Charles-Town with all its gay balls and theaters and parties and such?"

Mary's face grew sober. "If war comes, as Matt seems to think it will after what happened at the Anti-Stamp Act Congress, there'll be no balls or theaters or parties, Alec. Then—yes—I'd rather be here near Prue and Pa." She paused. "I think, in many ways, I'd rather live here, anyway," she finished. "It's—home."

Alec nodded again. "We must wait and see. 'Tis something to think on, anyway."

Chapter 21

IT WAS AFTER Mary's visit to Stockbridge that Nigel Fanshaw came back to Charles-Town.

"He's bought the tavern," Alec informed her one day in January. "I'd heard it was to be sold, but I didn't know—" He broke off. "He said he'd come back here," he went on slowly. "He said to me at Matt's wedding that was his intention."

"Yes. I know."

Alec hesitated. Then he said, "You never mentioned to me that you knew. Didn't it worry you?"

"Oh, Alec! Why would it worry me?"

"Worry your conscience, thinking out ways you might help him when he appeared." He smiled upon her, all of his gentle love for her warm and bright in his eyes, as he withheld from her his own worry. "You've a big heart, Mary. Generous and tender. A man like Nigel could presume upon it."

She said, "It's you that's been worrying. Over nothing, too! Well, are you still worried now that he's here?"

Again he hesitated. "Nay," he said, at last.

"You are—a little, I think. Why, Alec?"

"Well, he's changed. It's hard to guess what that foretells."

"Changed?" she repeated, with quick interest. "How?"

She had thought about Nigel many times since her marriage to Alec, wondering where he was and what he was doing. Hoping she would see him, too, because she still had his welfare at heart. Occasionally she had thought, also, of Alec's words to her long ago—that Nigel loved her. Not that that ever had or ever would have the least importance, she told herself.

"How has he changed?" she repeated.

He deliberated, choosing his words. "For the better, I would guess. Leastways, he appears to be in little need of help from anyone. In one hop he's a wealthy-appearing man and proprietor of a tavern that brings in a fair and steady profit."

"You've seen him, then! You've talked to him, I mean!"

He nodded. "Aye. I met him in Zigzag Alley. He remembered me, and he'd heard you were my wife." He paused. "He asked permission to call on you," he finished.

"I'd love to see him again, Alec! I'd love to see how he's changed! You gave it, I hope?"

"Aye." There was a note of reluctance in his voice which she thought his next words explained. "Knowing you and your curiosity I gave it, though it's not customary here in Charles-Town for an innkeeper to call on ladies of quality, and it will make folks talk."

Mary gestured impatiently. "Remember that I'm from the north. From a Mission where Indians and whites stand on an equal footing."

"That came to my mind," he agreed. "Also your—relationship. Besides—" Again he seemed reluctant to speak, but his own sense of justice impelled him to add, "Besides, I see no reason, myself, for not giving a man, whoever he is, a welcome in your home so long as he behaves himself in it."

Mary came to him, perched on his knee and put her

arms about his neck, at the same time laying her soft cheek against his leathery one.

"I do love you so, Alec!" she murmured. "You make me terribly proud of you!"

"Now why all this blarney?"

"It's not blarney. It's the truth. You really don't like Nigel, I know, but you told him he might come here because—well—because you're not a real Charlestonian in your thinking. You're too perfectly fair."

"Also because—perhaps—I knew 'twould please you. Does it?"

She nodded. "Very much. Do you mind? I feel a kind of—of proprietory interest in him. I know what he wants in life. And if he's getting it, I'd like to tell him how glad I am." She fell silent a moment while he stroked her hair with his big hand. "Where did he get all the money to buy the inn, Alec?"

"There's all sorts of rumors, but no one knows for sure —and he's not telling."

"Well, I suppose it's really none of our business. I wonder—" she added musingly, "—when he'll come?"

* * *

Nigel appeared two days later. Mary saw him from the upstairs living-room window as he turned in through the garden gate, and her brown eyes widened in surprise at the sight of him, despite Alec's forewarning.

He was clad in a well-fitted riding suit of bottle green and buff, his black hair neatly clubbed and tied, his leather boots glinting. But it was his bearing more than his clothes that marked the change in him, for he moved with perfect assurance, and his face, lifted for a moment to scan the house before him, no longer carried any expression of aggressive belligerence. It was quick and alive and intent with interest.

Seeing her, he waved and sprang up the steps, a darkly handsome, powerfully built figure of a man, and a few moments later Remus ushered him to the upper living room where Mary was waiting with her little daughter, Phoebe—the replica of Alec with her long, solemn face, grave, gray eyes and sandy hair. The twins were outdoors in Columbine's care.

"Mary!" he exclaimed, and moved forward to take her outstretched hand, his composed, confident, smiling manner concealing well the turmoil she stirred in him.

"Success becomes you," she said, her look upon him warm with her usual friendliness. "I'm so happy for you, Nigel."

He bowed his thanks with grace. "And marriage becomes you, though it nigh broke my heart to learn of it."

Mary caught her breath. Why, this bold and easy flattery made him more like Nick than ever! And the way he returned her to her chair had in it all the charm and ease Nick had once shown. Flusterment held her silent a moment, and before she could find words he was speaking again.

"Yes, I had my dreams," he was saying lightly. "Built, after all, on a not unreasonable foundation." And at her startled look, he explained, his tone still light but his black eyes telling her she could take him seriously if she chose. "Sometimes one who has been burned at the altar of love steers shy of approaching the flames a second time." He paused. "It was my hope that you would take your time," he finished gravely.

Mary knew a brief confusion. Alec had been right, then. Clearly now his words came back to her. "The lad loves you. You're the star in his life. If you want none of him, give him no more encouragement."

Evidently she really had seemed to be encouraging him. She had let him come to Matt's wedding, and apparently around that small kindness he had erected his aircastle.

Nigel was watching her silently. "Don't be sorry," he said softly. "Thinking of you in that way has helped me in my climb. Indeed, you have been my inspiration."

"Nigel, I never meant—"

"I know."

There was a little silence. In it Mary gathered herself together and spoke with a firm dignity.

"What you really felt, Nigel, I am sure, was gratitude. But you were young and confused, and so your feeling was wrongly translated into another emotion. You forgot —you did not stop to think—that I am years older than you."

"Not so many. And Alec is years older than you, for that matter." His dark eyes burned upon her as he went on, still lightly and smilingly persisting. "Love knows no barriers, Mary. You, of all people, surely must admit that. But what you don't realize—" he continued, before she could interrupt, "—is that you were the first to believe in me. The very first. And that I can never forget. If I am anything today—anything better than I was—I have you to thank for it. Can you blame me for caring?"

Suddenly Mary knew a tremor of alarm. Why was Nigel talking this way to her? Why was he pushing so vigorously against the defense her marriage to Alec had erected around her? It was flattering—yet it was disturbing, too. And it must not be allowed. She meant to—she wanted to—speak sternly, with a show of anger, but in the face of his humble gratitude her reproof held but a small measure of sharpness.

"I can only blame you if you continue to make such remarks."

His glance never left her face as she spoke, nor in the moment's silence that followed. Even as she rebuked him there was a grace, a softness, a warmth about her that stirred his blood. She was so exactly what he wanted! Why should he abandon his dream of her? Many things could happen that might make it still possible. For one thing, Alec's age was against him. For another—a war threatened. If it should come, Alec would take part in it and share in its dangers and risks. There was no reason, Nigel told himself, to give up hope. Time and his own youth were definitely on his side.

But he bent his head with a show of contrition.

"Forgive me. I thought you knew—or guessed—what my feeling for you was. Though I think I would have had to tell you, anyway, because I came back here to ask you to be my wife. It was a blow to find I had arrived too late." He gestured his unhappy resignation. "Should I be blamed, then, for something over which I had no control? Can we not at least be friends?" He paused. "I'm—lonely here, Mary. I'm a stranger. And I need a friend," he finished, on a low suppliant note.

He needed a friend, indeed. For already he had learned that, as owner of the tavern, even though he himself did not operate it, he had not acquired the standing he had anticipated. Though he knew everyone and everyone knew him and he was accorded respectability, no one's doors had been opened to him socially. Until today, when he entered here, he had not passed the threshold of any of the fine homes in Charles-Town. But what other business could he have entered? Inns were all he knew anything about. He had been in enough of them! As a matter of fact, it was at various inns about the countryside, over their card tables, that he had made his first real money. Then his months of piracy had given him enough to get him into the business of buying and selling slaves—much more lucrative and less hazardous.

But now Mary was answering him, a slight tremor in her voice born of his unexpected assault upon her emotions.

"We can be friends," she was saying, "on one condition only."

"And that is?"

"That you never lose sight of the fact that I am happy in my home and in my life with Alec."

"You have my word," Nigel promised. It was an easy thing to give, for he had heard the tremor which he took as a sure indication of her inner uncertainty about her marriage. Yes, he could promise easily enough. "And now—" with a gesture of dismissal of the whole matter, "—suppose you introduce me to your small daughter?"

* * *

"And how did Nigel seem to you today, Mary?" Alec asked.

It was evening and the two of them were alone in their upstairs living room. The three children were in bed, Keith sprawled in abandon across his tumbled sheets, Kim curled in a tight ball on his, arms doubled, fists clenched, Phoebe tucked neatly beneath hers and lying straight as a ramrod. Their sleeping habits, Mary often thought, were symptomatic of the differences in their natures. She looked up at Alec's question now, her face alight.

"Oh! So changed! So improved! I was proud of him, Alec. I was glad he came back here so I could see how well he'd done."

Yes, he thought, she would be glad. She had always felt

a sense of responsibility toward him because he was Nick's brother and an injustice had been done him by Nick. She had always felt he had a rightful claim on her interest for that reason. But how far should this feeling be carried? Now that Nigel had achieved a measure of success for himself—now that he had established himself here in an enterprise of his own choosing—

"But he's lonely," she went on. "I think we will have to be kind to him."

Slowly he took his pipe from his mouth. "What do you mean—be kind to him?"

"He has no friends, Alec. He knows a great many people here. They come and go in and out of his tavern. They speak to him on the street. But he has never been invited into anyone's home. And that's what he wants."

"Is it? Depends on what you mean by 'anyone.' Plenty of people would be glad to make friends with a decent, honest innkeeper."

He was watching her closely. Did she know—as he did—that what Nigel wanted was Mary herself? To be sure the man was well aware that Mary was not to be had because she was already married. But how much would that fact matter to Nigel? He was unprincipled. He had always been unprincipled. There was nothing in his background to make him respect any laws or conventions if they ran counter to his plans and purposes.

Mary was saying, "I wish you could have seen him with Phoebe. He was very sweet."

I never should have told him he could come here, Alec thought. I knew it would be the beginning. Yet how could I not? Mary is so loyal. It's what makes her vulnerable. It's both her strength and her weakness. Well, I shall have to trust her loyalty to me. There's no other way. And of course I can.

He said, "So you told him to come again."

She lifted her brown eyes to his. "Yes. Naturally."

"Naturally," he repeated, and relit his pipe and went on smoking, trying not to remember that though Nigel might be unprincipled, he was handsome, attractive, bold —and young. And Mary was young, too, while he himself was over the threshold of middle age.

Yet what difference did that make, after all? Mary loved him. She had come to him of her own free will without any urging from him. And now she belonged to him. Everything began and ended with that certainty. Mary was his wife.

And Mary was thinking that she would not tell Alec of Nigel's dream of her. It would only be upsetting. And Nigel knew now it was useless. She had told him so. She had drawn a line across which he had promised not to go. She had drawn it firmly, too, she told herself.

Chapter 22

MARY HAD NEVER KNOWN greater happiness than she knew in the next few years. To be sure, threatening clouds continued to boil up on the horizon, and South Carolina continued to show herself sympathetically responsive to the rebellious spirit being incited in the north. But war, as yet, was still far distant. In Charles-Town life went on as usual with its round of gay social events. Though incipient rebels had quietly organized a group called the Sons of Liberty, and, indeed, had begun drilling on the edge of town, these signs of determined action were ignored by the King's party.

And they were ignored by Mary. She was simply too busy with her family to give them thought. The twins, Kim and Keith, both blue-eyed and fair-haired, were normal, active boys although quite different in temperament. Kim was slow of speech and thoughtful, like his father, while Keith had all of Mary's quick, impulsive eagerness. Yet their differences offset each other well and lent a balance to their youthful activities and escapades. Kim restrained Keith, and Keith spurred Kim. And the two were inseparable.

The twins required vigilant attention. There was nothing they did not think of doing. For Keith, no daring was too great. As for Kim, once a project was planned, organized, and given his seal of approval, no fear and no argument could hold him from a persistent, stubborn attempt to complete it. By contrast to the firm rein Mary had to hold over her boys, Phoebe was easy to handle. She was reasonable, conservative, obliging. She had neither Keith's volatile explosiveness, nor Kim's relentlessness. She moved and spoke with a quiet care, an aloof, self-containment that made her seem sometimes more like a grown-up than a child. To Mary, who was so outgoing, she was an enigma—and very soon a source of worry. For, solemn and quiet as she was, how would she ever fit into the pattern of life that Charles-Town offered its young ladies? Oh, it was early, Mary knew, to be thinking of such things! Yet already Phoebe was definitely an outsider at children's parties. From the edge of the circle of prattling little girls and well-mannered little boys, she surveyed their activities without interest and with a kind of proud, remote dignity that made Mary's heart ache for the loneliness she knew it hid.

Only Nigel could penetrate her reserve. Only Nigel had managed to break down her sober resistance to friendly overtures. How he had done it Mary never knew, but, soon after his first visit, she had returned from market one day bringing Mrs. Pinckney with her, to find him there, and Phoebe, bright-eyed and flushed, riding on his shoulders as he raced around the garden.

Breathless, he had stopped before the two women.

"As you can see, I am a captive in your daughter's hands," he told them smilingly.

Mary looked from his face to Phoebe's.

"I'm not sure whether it is you or she that is captive," she returned. "Mrs. Pinckney, this is Mr. Fanshaw. Phoebe, darling, don't kick Mr. Fanshaw!"

"I want him to giddap again."

"But he's tired. He's all out of wind. Wait a moment."

Phoebe only shook her head and beat her small heels imperiously against Nigel's chest. "Giddap, Nye! Giddap!"

"You see?" he said. "I think I'll have to teach her to ride—with your permission. It will be easier than this. Once more, then, Phoebe, and that's all."

Mary watched them with a sense of happy relief hearing Phoebe's laughter ring out. Now the child was being natural. Now she was being like Kim and Keith—normally boisterous and gay.

That night she said to Alec, "Do you know something? Nigel is good for Phoebe. He is bringing her out of her shell."

Alec looked at Mary and shook his head. "Out of her shell? What makes you think she's in one? You worry about her too much, Mary. You must not forget she's not like you nor ever will be. You must not expect her to change with or without Nigel. She's a quiet one by nature. Leave be."

* * *

The days fled by. Nigel had become a regular visitor at Wistaria House, accepted by Alec who could find no valid reason for not accepting him, welcomed by Phoebe if Mary was not there, welcomed by Mary when she was.

For he was keeping his promise. His behavior was completely circumspect. And as she saw him established in the town in the position he had chosen and making a place for himself by—oddly enough—a show of Nick's remembered charm, she was delighted that her faith in him had born fruit. Sometimes it was hard for her to believe he had so completely changed, but success could, she knew, work wonders.

Yet his success was a measured thing. It was not enough for him that his tavern operated at an increasing profit to him, that he was on easy terms with various men of position throughout the area, that plenty of young girls were put into a flutter at his appearance on the street, that he had friends among the King's party who saw to it that he received invitations to large public functions, that Phoebe, who was showing herself an apt little horsewoman, was allowed to go on long rides with him. Success was not complete in his estimation as long as certain homes were closed to him.

Mary knew this, but she was helpless before the fixed conventions of this southern city. She, herself, was enduring a degree of adverse criticism because of her friendliness to "that pushing innkeeper." However, democracy was too well ingrained in her for her to mind. And her own social position was too well assured for it to matter. It was, nevertheless, beyond her power to persuade others, even Mrs. Pinckney, to offer him the same friendliness. As for Myrtle, she would not even recognize him on the street.

"No one really knows anything about him," she said to Mary one day. "Where he comes from or where he disappears to fo' weeks at a time. Or who his folks were. Even though you say you knew him up no'th, you can't tell us any of those things. I don't see myself how you dare let him be so free in your house and with your little girl. Givin' her ridin' lessons, indeed!"

Mary tried to explain. "We both—Nigel and I—knew someone who was very dear to me at one time. Besides, I was brought up differently from you, Myrtle. Where I come from everyone is on the same level."

Myrtle shrugged. "Well, you-all can do as you please. But I shall never have anything to do with him. And I'll never allow Lucy or Mary-Etta to come to your house when he's there. So don't expect it."

Matt's attitude was no more generous. His objection to Nigel, however, was not based on any snobbery. He simply did not like the fellow and never had liked him since Nigel had forced him to pay over the sum of money Nick had owed him. That had always stuck in his craw. A curt nod if they met face to face was the most Matt would ever give him. No one could make Matt do a thing against his will and manage to remain in his good graces. Neither was Matt pleased that Mary saw so much of Nigel.

"A leopard doesn't change his spots, remember," he warned her.

All this snubbing pricked Nigel where it hurt, and Mary knew it. She was not, therefore, surprised to have him appear one spring day with the announcement that he had turned over his tavern to Jack Murray. Ostensibly Jack was the new owner. Actually Nigel had a big mortgage on it.

"I'm clearing out of that picture," he said to Mary. "I'm washing my hands of it."

His voice, hard and even and cold, as she had not heard it in months, told her why, and he did not need to explain, though he did, his black eyes blazing with mutiny.

"Gad! Mary! Am I poison that I'm not made to feel welcome in this town? What's wrong with me? Am I a hunchback? Ill-mannered? A bore? How long must I wait? Do I have to die—and be born again?"

"It's difficult, I know, Nigel."

He cut his whip suddenly across the leather of his boot, and the sharp crack of it startled Phoebe. Quickly he reached out and patted her on the head.

"Sorry, Phoebe. I didn't mean to scare you." He looked across to Mary. "Forget what I said. I don't give a damn."

"Of course you do. And I care, too. I wish I could help more."

"You've done your best. And I'm grateful. The point is, your attitude hasn't the weight that Mrs. Matthew Martin's has."

She nodded. A silence fell. He broke it by rising and moving to the window where he stood with his back to her, his hands clenched by his sides.

"She goes by me as if I were a hitching post." Suddenly he spun about. "Well, I'm not licked yet! I'll beat your sister-in-law and your brother at their own game before I'm through."

Startled at the venom in his tone, Mary said, "What do you mean?"

His eyes gleamed, and he showed his teeth in a sudden brilliant smile.

"I mean I've bought land. It's way out along Back River. But it's a good piece. And there's a house on it. It's been neglected and needs a lot of doing over. Still—it's a fine house."

"You will live there?"

"I will live there. I will raise indigo. And tobacco. And rice. I—" He laughed harshly. "I will be one of the landed gentry myself. It's the planters and the merchants that run this town! 'Merchant princes,' they call themselves. Well, I mean to be one, too. Didn't I tell you so once? I'll be someone they can't ignore. Wait and see! Will you help me fix up my house?" he finished abruptly. "It'll need a woman's hand."

"Yes"—slowly. "I'll help you, Nigel."

He looked at her. Why the reluctance? Did she doubt his ability to reach the goal he had set for himself?

As if guessing his thought, she added quickly, "Of course I'll help you."

He continued to look at her, fire smoldering in his eyes. "Of course," she had said. "Of course!" She would help him as she had always helped him. But what did that mean? Exactly nothing. Time was slipping by and what was he gaining? Again—exactly nothing. All his circumspection and care had brought no results whatever.

He cut his whip across his boot a second time and came close to her, so close that she could feel the heat emanating from him, could smell the mixture of soap and leather from his clothes, could sense the hardness and virility of his body beneath his clothes. And when he spoke it was with a measured metallic force.

"The world is made up of people who want a whole lot and of other people who'll settle for anything. I'm one of the former, Mary. I've never mixed with the second kind, and I don't intend to. Remember that!"

He flashed her another dark look, disturbing in its vague challenge, and went out.

For a long moment she sat there as if he had cast a spell on her. It was an odd feeling that stirred her to a strange faint fear. Once before she had felt it, when she had lain, an invalid in a chair on Mrs. MacDonald's lawn, and the strength of his determination then had set her world a-tremble. But now—now she was safe in another world. What could he do now?

What she was remembering was less his words than his power and grace as he had stood before her, and she was aware that danger had brushed by her on swift, silent wings and that if it came too close she would—sometime and inevitably—have to meet it.

Chapter 23

The summer of 1769 was a busy one for Mary. Not that helping Nigel with his plans for his house occupied her as he was not ready for that yet.

"There's a lot of reconstruction work to be done first," he had told her. "I'll let you know when I need you. I'll come for you. But I don't want you to see the place the way it looks now. It's a shambles. Wait."

Mary was glad to wait for two reasons: it would give Alec an opportunity to forget his early objections to the idea of her lending Nigel any further personal assistance and interest, and it would leave her free to entertain her niece, Faith, whom Prue was permitting to come make a visit at Mary's home.

Alec's opposition to Nigel's request for help had surprised her.

"I do not hold it against a man to keep trying to better his condition," he had said. "If he can really become what he's set his sights on, so much the more credit to him. But in this instance, he can't."

Mary's eyes flashed in unexpected indignation. "Why do you say that? You don't know!"

"I do know. I know Charles-Town. And I know Nigel's limitations. He'd be better off to admit them himself and stay in his tavern. 'Tis where he belongs. There's no disgrace in settling down as a respectable and respected innkeeper."

"Alec! I don't think you're being fair!"

"I'm being honest."

Mary looked at her husband in a flurry of anger. Why was he talking like this? He never had done so before. She said, "I think he should at least have his chance to try."

"Oh! He'll have that. I can't stop him from buying his land and moving onto it. But I can stop my wife from giving him the help he's asking her for."

Her flurry of anger settled into something solid and cold and resolute. She was astonished at the strength of her feeling. What Alec was trying to do (she told herself) was to break off a special and unusual relationship to which she felt morally bound and in the result of which she took pride.

"Why should you stop me?" she asked, forcing her voice to quiet.

His eyes, glinting gray, met hers, and, as always in emotion, his Scottish accent grew more pronounced.

"I dinna approve of him. That's why. I never ha'e approved of him and well ye know it. And I consider ye've done enough for him already. Now let him mak' his own way."

Really he was tired of having Nigel come to his house; of finding him there in the upstairs living room, laughing and talking with Mary as if he belonged there; of seeing him in the garden, carrying Phoebe on his shoulders in a wild gallop about the paths; of hearing him call out—"Let your father ride you now, Phoebe! It's his turn!" Yet his manners were impeccable. His deference, his courtesy, though a shade too emphasized, could not be quarreled with. It was inevitable that, failing to find any fault he could hang on Nigel with justification, the time came when the older man could no longer tolerate the other. And when Mary had told him of Nigel's plan to buy himself a plantation, he had thought, with relief, Let this be the end.

But it was not the end, for what was it Mary was so carefully saying?

"What you are trying to do, Alec, is be my conscience for me. And—I'm sorry—but that is impossible."

Her quiet tone now held a note that he did not miss. It spelled anger, and Alec did not want to develop opposition in her.

He said slowly, "Nay. I can't be your conscience. But I'm askin' you to consult yours further. Then, later, we'll discuss the question more."

"Let's discuss it now—and settle it."

Alec was silent a moment. He was telling himself that he had erred in once believing that Mary's experience with Nick had matured her greatly. It had not. She was still naive, still remarkably innocent of the evil that lived in men. And of course she was both moved and flattered by Nigel's insistence on his need of her. So long as that was his appeal, what was there Alec could do? Little but stand by, keeping a close watch on her and waiting for the moment when her better judgment would give her a clearer vision. Thinking this, he sighed faintly. It was a sigh of defeat.

"Perhaps it will do you no harm to give Nigel the advice he wants about his house," he conceded presently, "although I do not like it. But when you go there, Mary, promise me you'll always take the children with you, the children and Columbine. For you know well how Charles-Town talks."

She said slowly, "It's only talk you've been fearing, Alec?"

"Chiefly—aye."

"Not Nigel?"

Her brown eyes, wide and questioning, met his, and in them he thought he saw a shrinking look. Of hurt for his possible suspicion? He would not hurt her for worlds. He spoke quickly.

"Not Nigel," he assured her. "Though I know full well he loves you. Indeed, 'twas because of that I gave him permission to come to the house in the first place."

Astonishment caught her. "Because of—*that!*"

"Aye. I wanted the hope I could see he still bore in his heart settled once and for all. And only you could settle it."

There was a tiny silence. Then Mary spoke softly. "I did, Alec. I did settle it. The first time he came."

He nodded. He had been foolish to worry, he told himself. A foolish, jealous creature. Come! Have done with it!

"You did not need to tell me," he said. "I knew. No, Mary, I do not fear Nigel, because I know and trust you."

Tears sprang suddenly and inexplicably into Mary's eyes, and she came into his arms with a little rush. "Oh, Alec!" she whispered. "You're so good! So *good.* Hold me! Hold me—tight!"

* * *

Faith arrived early in the summer, expecting to stay for a month and remaining for nearly six, having captured the heart of young James Humphrey and needing (as Mary wrote Prue) more than a period of four short weeks in which to make up her mind about him.

Her visit was, for Mary, an unmitigated pleasure. Her

niece was more like herself than Phoebe would ever be, with the same eager, outgoing spirit, the same friendliness, the same zest for life. It gave Mary the greatest possible delight to plan for Faith's social life, to oversee her wardrobe and to watch with satisfaction the way the hospitable but fastidious town took the young girl to its heart.

Mary was glad she was free from Nigel's demands so as to be able to meet Faith's needs. The twins, too, required less of her since they were coming more and more under their father's jurisdiction, both being drawn to the ships and wharves as flies to honey, and being allowed, now, to spend several hours daily at the water front under Alec's watchful eye. Phoebe was Mary's greatest concern for, though she had her cousins, Lucy and Mary-Etta, to play with she did not like them. However, she seemed content to bask in Faith's reflected light, even taking some of it from her cousin's presence. Yet Mary knew the child missed Nigel's companionship and his almost daily visits. This she told him once when he stopped at Wistaria House on one of his trips to the city for supplies.

"You have really won her affections," she concluded. "What is your wizardry? Is it because you get down to her level? Or have you some secret spell you weave about her?"

"The answer is really simple."

"Tell me."

He came close, his black eyes holding hers as he replied.

"What you fail to realize, Mary, is how you and Alec and the twins appear to her. She adores you because you are everything she would like to be—and isn't. Beautiful, full of grace, gay. Really perfect."

He was speaking with complete objectivity. Even so, she felt the rush of those wings of danger fanning her cheeks to a rising blush.

He went on: "But you are too perfect. She can only worship from afar in a kind of dumb anguish—a feeling I can well appreciate. Alec is too stern," he continued quickly, "too silent, so she stands in awe of him. And the twins alarm her with their rough, bold ways. But I—" He shrugged deprecatingly. "I am not too perfect or too stern or too rough or too bold or too anything. I'm just—well—like her."

Mary forced herself to speak casually. "Lonely?" she suggested.

"Yes. Exactly. We—comfort each other."

She had not meant to give him such an opening. And he was close. Too close. Her throat felt dry as she replied, "It seems a reasonable explanation."

"Sometimes there's reason in unreason," he replied.

* * *

Matt was away when Faith arrived. Indeed, despairing more and more of finding happiness in his marriage, he had returned to the sea and was gone much of the time. Myrtle, reveling in her freedom, immediately began putting herself out to be agreeable to Faith, planning luncheons, taking her to a St. Cecelia ball and entertaining her and a dozen other young people for a long weekend at her parents' plantation, Live Oaks. Why? It was unlike Myrtle, and Mary wondered.

The answer was given her one day when she inadvertently overheard a conversation between Myrtle and Faith.

"If you do decide to marry James, Faith, you ought to have the wedding at your aunt's house. I'm sure she would love to give it. She has so often said she doesn't know how she will ever get your mother to come down to visit her, and that would be a reason. Of course Mary would have space for you and your parents, and at my place there would be room for anyone else that might come. Your uncle John, for instance. Will you tell him?"

Mary was stunned. Myrtle—interested in Johnny? Why, she had hardly seen him on that visit to Stockbridge! Then Mary remembered little things to which she had then attached no importance: a look—a few low-spoken words—their long walks together. But most of all she remembered Myrtle's inadvertent discovery that Matt had a son who was part Indian. In her humiliation and shame and wild fury Myrtle had turned from Matt to Johnny for comfort and understanding. Was it persistent thoughts of Johnny—a man her own age, a man as different from Matt as day from night, as storm from sunshine—was it thoughts of him which were making her so cruel to her husband?

"Myrtle is a law unto herself," Mary thought helplessly.

Should she then (she asked herself) aid and abet Faith if she wished to have her wedding here?

But Faith did not intend to accept young James so quickly. She was enjoying her popularity, and she was enjoying being courted. She became, in the months she was there, a much more sophisticated young person than when she had arrived, and she managed to keep James dangling while she kept her own heart free.

* * *

And now Christopher Gadsen more than ever inflamed the rabble element of Charles-Town with his patriotic harangues beneath what was known as Liberty Oak outside his own residence. Now the Tory rector of St. Michael's church found his flock more and more openly disapproving of his expressed loyalty to the crown and his exhortations to them to declare the same sentiments. And now more and more blue uniforms with scarlet facings, worn by the South Carolina militia, could be seen parading on the streets.

The whole colony was seething again, for though the Stamp Act had been repealed, taxes had been declared on other articles, and the slogan "The cause of Boston is the cause of all!" was heard with increasing frequency. It all filled Mary's heart with deep anxiety. She wrote to Prue,

> I hate to let Faith return to you, but in view of the excitement here, it seems wise to end her visit soon. We are, I feel, living on the top of a volcano. There are cool heads on both sides, but I often wonder if there are enough of them? One incident in Charles-Town could start a conflagration that would sweep the entire country. Alec has joined the Sons of Liberty, as, of course, has Matt, though he is here seldom to drill. And now my boys, who are not yet ten, speak of wanting to join, too. I am glad I shall have Nigel's house to divert my mind from thoughts of war, for he has finished the reconstruction work and is ready for advice on the decorating. I will write you how we progress. I can understand his ambition to improve his standing here, but I must confess I have moments of doubting the success he envisages for himself. The whole town is smiling and smirking in a hateful way. It puts me more staunchly then ever beside him. Well, we shall see.

* * *

Came the day, not long after Mary had sent her letter to Prue and Faith had departed, that Nigel appeared in his new coach to pick up Mary and drive her out to Back River for her first look at his estate.

A little to his surprise he found that she had the twins and Phoebe gathered about her ready to go.

"The boys love to get into the country," she explained.

"They can all play around outside while I go over the house with you. Columbine will watch out for them."

"Columbine, also," he murmured. "We shall be well chaperoned. Did Alec think we needed it? If so, I am flattered."

The color came up to her face. "Alec thought it would be best this way," she told him quietly, "since he cannot join us himself and since the town is such a gossip pot."

He made no answer beyond the lifting of an eyebrow.

It took over an hour to reach his property, and long before that the twins were squirming with impatience. When at last the coach rolled up to the front door, they tumbled to the ground with whoops of joy.

"Tell them not to go out to the barns," Nigel warned Mary. "The floors are unsafe there. They'd best play in the open close to the house."

"And don't let them get near the river, either Columbine," Mary added, "or next to fallen trees, because that's where rattlers hide."

"Columbine know how tek care her mis't'ess chillen," the woman replied, a bit testily, for she did not wholly approve of this jaunt. Mist' Fanshaw not quality. She—Columbine—know quality when she see it. How come Mist' Alec lettin' his wife hab any truck wid such as he? Mist'ess Mary best worry 'bout herseff, not her chillen, 'cose her chillen safe as could be.

With her turbaned head high, Columbine and her three charges went wandering out onto the unkempt grass while Mary stepped from the coach to the low verandah that ran the full width of the house before her. There she turned to look about. As yet the grounds had not been touched. The lawns were littered with fallen branches. The bushes had grown wild. The drive over which they had come was filled with weeds. But the view of the glittering river beneath the arch of immense spreading trees was lovely, and Mary impulsively threw her arms wide to the scene.

"When this is clipped and trimmed and terraced to the water front, it will be perfect, Nigel!" she exclaimed.

"You really like it?"

"Oh, I do, indeed! You've chosen well. I'm glad you bought it. I think you did the right thing."

He was filled with exultation, for now, at last, the dream he had always had of himself was beginning to take shape. "There's a lot of work to be done outside, I grant you," he said. "But come see what I've accomplished inside."

He was like a boy, a young, eager boy, as he flung open the wide white door for Mary. The house was one of those five-part mansions she had seen on the Eastern Shore in her long journey southward with Nick. Though it had been empty and neglected for a number of years, Nigel had restored the main central portion and the immense double stairway that curved up from both sides of the big hall presented an imposing appearance in its fresh white paint with the mahogany hand rail gleaming and the parquetry floor below shining under its many coats of wax.

But it was empty. There was not a rug or a chair or a mirror or a hanging in it. And the great rooms on either side were as barren. However, the noble proportions, the carved wooden valances above the windows, the simple mantels, and the clear, cool blue-gray paint held an authentic promise of beauty to come.

Nigel watched her face, seeing it kindle with pleasure.

"I'm leaving everything to you the way I said I would," he told her. "I haven't bought a stick of anything."

She nodded. The self-consciousness he had put upon her once or twice before was gone now, vanished before the interest of the house. She was glad. This was the way they should be when together. With rising pleasure and confidence she followed him to the library wing where two Negroes were finishing up the last of the painting, and then to the pantries and kitchen which had not as yet been touched.

"You've still plenty to do," she observed critically.

"Yes. But the main house is ready. And I'm impatient to see it in its finished state. I want you to go ahead right away, if you will, and buy what I should have. Spare no expense. It must be right."

He spoke forcefully, with an undercurrent of excitement that Mary's ears did not miss.

"As soon as I can," he told her, "I mean to give a housewarming. It will be—by gad!—the most sumptuous housewarming ever given in these parts. It will be something no one will ever forget. I've got it all thought out. Listen, Mary! I mean to import musicians, I mean to import caterers, I mean to import entertainers. Nothing will be left to chance. Not a thing!" He stopped, a bit breathless.

Mary heard him with a sinking feeling of dismay. She wanted to cry out, "Not so fast, Nigel!" But he would not have heard her. He would not believe that what he planned could possibly fail of its purpose, that he could fail, by lavish expenditure, to stun the oligarchy that ruled Charles-Town into accepting him as one of them.

Nick, she remembered, had astounded himself with the success of his duplicity until he had acquired an overwhelming confidence in it. Did Nigel have an equal confidence, equally false? Money was not enough, not for Charlestonians.

She said, "It will take time, Nigel, to make this place as I know you want it. You shouldn't be in too much of a hurry. I wish—"

"You wish what?"

"I wish you wouldn't rush things. I know you want to impress people, and I understand why. But, Nigel! Really, you should prove yourself first."

"What do you mean—prove myself?"

"I mean"—earnestly "—I think you should get your whole plantation into good working order. Get your stables and barns fixed as well as your house. Get your crops in and your slaves bought and your factor engaged. You will need a factor, you know. Let everyone around realize that you're in earnest about this way of life. Let them get used to you in your new status. Truly, Nigel! That's the wisest way. It may take several years, but—"

"Several years!" He stared at her. "I told you I was impatient. No, it won't take several years. Why should it? If I wait that long the house will no longer be new and it won't be a proper housewarming. No! I'll have it long before that. By late next spring, I should think." He swept aside her words with a gesture. "Now, tell me! What do you advise for a rug here? I don't know the names of any, but I guess it ought to be of French make. For the hall I fancy red. And for the library—Mary, where can I buy books? Hundreds of them?"

He was both laughable and pitiable. But he was not to be swerved, that was clear, and Mary was appalled at her discovery that he was not so changed as she had believed him to be. Scratch the veneer of gentility and below lay an abyss of ignorance. She should have known.

Well, she knew now, and what could she do to save him from himself? Her old protective instinct! Sometimes it was a weight on her. But in connection with Nigel, she had always asked herself what Prue would do? Prue would defend him, she thought. Prue would not let him give his housewarming. Somehow, then, she—Mary—must prevent it. Thinking—wondering—and feeling more and more depressed, she followed him about, only half of herself replying to his questions.

Presently he led her upstairs.

The same grandeur here—and the same emptiness, save that in the bedchamber Nigel had chosen for himself there was a narrow cot, a cheap chest of drawers, a single straight chair, and a small frayed cotton rug. Looking at the meager furnishing, Mary was visited by an idea.

"Your bride should select what is to go in here," she said.

"My bride!"

"Yes." She went on quietly. "You should have a bride before you have a housewarming. This place calls for a mistress. And how proud she would be of it! For it is truly beautiful, Nigel." She regarded his face for a moment, puzzled by its look of outrage, but giving it no importance before the rush of her own thoughts. Yes! This was the solution! She went on. "There are a number of girls, you know, who would look on you with favor."

She stopped before his sudden furious gesture. Then he folded his arms across his chest, leaned against the doorjamb and looked at her with his eyes holding a strange black fire.

"I'm not contemplating matrimony—yet."

"You should, though." Disturbed by his look and faintly alarmed, she pushed on. "You should," she repeated. "You're lonely, Nigel. You told me so yourself."

"Yes. I'm lonely. I've always been lonely. But until I can bring across my threshold the woman I want, I'll stay lonely." He paused, his gaze holding hers, riveting it, as he added meaningly, "I don't let go of an idea easily. I told you that once."

He had not moved. He was still leaning against the doorjamb, his arms folded across his chest, but his words and his look wrapped her in hot flames. What was this? What was happening? Had he dared to cross the line she had drawn? Her limbs felt heavy as though they would not hold her up, and she had the wildest desire to let herself sink against his strength while at the same time she wanted to run. It was then that a memory came to her. Once again she was on Jean MacDonald's lawn and Nigel was standing before her saying, "You were too good for Nick, and he had to let you go. But if you belonged to me, I'd never let you go." He never *had* let her go. Even though she did not belong to him, he had held her. Even though she was now Alec's wife, she was, in Nigel's thoughts, his.

She said finally—uncertainly, "You are breaking your promise to me, Nigel."

He could have reached her, then, and caught her in his arms and bent her body to his in a fierce and silent demanding. But caution withheld him. She must not be frightened. Not yet. He might only bring about a strong revulsion of feeling that would end everything before it was begun. He would be satisfied this time with having seen the chink in her armor and with having pierced it.

He said, "I'm sorry." And he turned from her to stride to the window that overlooked the lawn. There he stood staring out at Columbine and her three charges.

He saw the boys playing Indian, stealing up behind their unsuspecting Maumau with sticks in their fists and wide grins on their young faces. Phoebe was a few paces distant in the sunlight, her small hands reaching for wild flowers.

He looked at her idly, not thinking of her, thinking still of Mary as her silence behind him grew more and more forbidding. If she once withdrew from him it would be final, he knew. So it had been with Nick—until his illness—and so it would be with him. He would have to make her believe she had not been in his mind at all a moment ago.

He turned slowly, his face clear of all the dark passion it had recently held.

"I'm sorry," he repeated. "I only meant to say that the ideal you gave me long ago is hard to duplicate."

Mary bent her head. She felt a little foolish. Nigel had not, really, been threatening her personally, at all. Perhaps, he had not even been thinking of her. Her too ready suspicion—or was it her vanity?—had precipitated an embarrassing moment for them both.

"It—it was my fault, perhaps," she murmured. "Let's—forget it."

But her hand trembled in his as he led her down the stairs, and she knew that a new element, as yet unadmitted, had entered into their relationship.

Chapter 24

MARY'S PREOCCUPATION with Nigel's house did not end until winter ended. The time had passed as a dream passes, in an atmosphere not quite real yet with each moment vivid. By spring there was nothing left for her to do. Everything that had been ordered had arrived and been put in place. Even the hangings at the windows, the candles in their sconces, the hundreds of books on their shelves (books that Nigel never before heard of and never would read). House slaves spent their days keeping the rooms in a state of shining perfection. All that remained now was to put the grounds and gardens in proper shape, and for that, Mary said, Nigel could, perhaps, rely on himself, his new factor (whom Alec had procured for him) and the field hands.

She said it slowly, reluctantly, not wanting these visits with their odd fascination to end and hoping for a denial of her words.

He replied, "You—and Mrs. Pinckney—have been most generous with your time. I can hardly expect more from you. Indeed, I can hardly thank you adequately for this much. But at least I can promise you, Mary, one thing. You will open the ball with me at my housewarming. Will Alec object?"

"No. Of course not."

What were his black eyes telling her? Was he agreeing

that he no longer needed her help because he had had enough of Mrs. Pinckney's presence? She was lovely, but she had been consistently and persistently too gracious, too—superior. And this had rankled. Still, Alec had been willing to let his wife come without Columbine and the children only because the older woman had accompanied her. And well Nigel knew that it was Mrs. Pinckney's cooperation that had added not only decorum to Mary's visits but a measure of dignity to his enterprise. Because of her, the lifted eyebrows and the amused smiles at mention of the innkeeper's purchase were diminishing. The two women together had helped to stop caustic wagging tongues. It did not matter that Mrs. Pinckney had not really wanted to lend herself, that she had said frankly she did not approve of either Nigel or his ambition; she came with Mary because she did not wish any harmful gossip to besmirch her young friend.

Mary had always brought another companion, too—Phoebe. The child had been of no trouble. She had followed the grown-ups around in quiet, unobtrusive contentment, and, when she tired, she rode on Nigel's shoulders. Then, after consultations were over, measurements taken, lists made, and plans completed, Nigel would invite her to join him in a short gallop. Or, hand in hand, if the day were warm enough, they two would wander to the summer house by the river where Phoebe's rare light laughter would come echoing back to Mary and Mrs. Pinckney resting on the verandah. Phoebe, Mary told herself, was Nigel's escape valve. She was his excuse for leaving her and Mrs. Pinckney when the latter's smooth, impenetrable remoteness became more than he could endure. Those were the moments for which Phoebe waited eagerly and those were the moments when Mary discovered within herself a strange, angry ache of unfulfillment.

For Nigel was giving Phoebe all of his gay companionship when it was she—Mary—who found herself wanting it, who, indeed, needed it. She had become lonely because the pressure of Alec's affairs with Matt's business, with the Sons of Liberty, and with secret committee meetings planning against the event of an outbreak of hostilities, left her so many empty hours. Nigel—young, broad-shouldered, handsome, intense—provoked, antagonized, and lured her. Nigel, his eyes, his smile, always half promising something he never offered.

These thoughts and feelings were a tide within her, rising steadily, carrying her—she did not know where. She did not try to find out. She lived in a curious lethargy of waiting while she floated on this full, strong tide. Somewhere on the shore, faithfully following along it, steadily watching her with a mixture of anxiety and love, was Alec. It was good to know he was there. But ahead of Alec, in the water with her, was Nigel, his dark head lifting above the waves, his smile flashing back at her and saying silently, "A little further! Only a little further!"

There were rapids ahead. She could almost hear them. What would happen when she reached those rapids? Would Alec save her? Or Nigel? Or would Nigel carry her down into turbulent depths from which there would be no returning?

His voice, now, brought her back to the present.

"It won't be until April, I guess—my housewarming," Nigel was saying. "The grounds will take a couple of months. But it will be warmer then, so perhaps it is just as well."

Mary nodded.

Mrs. Pinckney said, "April is usually a perfect month in the country. Will you summon the coach for us, Nigel, please?"

But not even Mrs. Pinckney's presence—or Phoebe's—prevented Mary's dwelling in two worlds—the world of her thoughts and fancy where she was a girl desired and desiring and free, and the world of reality where she was Alec's wife and the mother of his three children.

* * *

Came the day at last when the invitations to Nigel's housewarming were sent out. A black servant, resplendent in yellow and white livery, riding in Nigel's new white-and-gold coach, delivered all of them except Mary's. This Nigel brought to her himself.

"Everything is arranged for. Everything is ready," he told her, standing tall and straight and exultant before her. "It will be in three weeks. I may count on you, of course?"

"Of course, Nigel."

He began pacing back and forth in ill-restrained excitement, striking his riding whip smartly against his boot as he walked. "I tell you, Mary! My shindig is going to make this town sit up! It's going to give people something to talk about that will put all the scare over the Boston Massacre in complete eclipse!"

"That will be a welcome respite," she told him soberly. Then, in a sudden curiosity, she asked on which side he stood in the controversy. "You've never said," she finished.

He laughed easily. "I stand on the winning side, of course."

"But each side feels sure of winning—if war really comes."

"Well, only one can win in the end—and I'll be on that side." His eyes narrowed speculatively. Then he gestured impatiently. "But forget it. Gadsden's just a windbag.

Pinckney's General Committee of the new Provincial Congress has no real power. And the Royal Government doesn't recognize either that or the Committee of Safety. Let's talk about my affair, instead." His face went dark for a moment. "I should tell you, I suppose, that I've not invited your estimable brother and his wife. Or her parents, either. The Averys."

Mary looked startled. "Oh, Nigel! You shouldn't have left them out!"

"Shouldn't I? And why not?" His tone, his expression hardened. "Myrtle has never seen me as long as I've been in Charles-Town. Her folks are the same. As for Matt—he used words to me in Cross Creek years ago I've not forgotten and never will forget."

Here was the old vindictive Nigel Mary remembered. It had been so long since she had seen this side of him that she had almost forgotten it existed. It was probably useless to argue with him in this mood, yet she must try. For now, more than ever, because of her own confused feeling about him, she wanted his party to be a success. She wanted to be able to say to the townsfolk, "See? He is all right! I told you so. I wasn't wrong to take him under my wing. He has made no mistakes, so give him the welcome he deserves!"

She spoke with care. "Nigel, I really think you should reconsider. It's not too late. You may not like Matt or Myrtle, but they have it in their power to hurt you."

"How can they hurt me?"

"They are influential. Myrtle's mother is the social leader here. And Matt—"

He flung back his head. "They can't hurt me! Let them try! No. It's *my* turn to be particular. Do you imagine I'm going to give them a chance to turn me down?" He laughed suddenly. "I'd like to see your sister-in-law's face when she learns that practically everyone is invited except her!"

He was too defiant. It made her tremble for his success which was uncertain enough at best. She put out a hand in blind pleading.

"Nigel—please—"

She did not realize how her eyes—her whole face—pleaded, too, telling him more than she guessed or was even sure of. He looked at her. Then he caught her outflung hand and pulled her close to him.

"You care!" he exclaimed.

Her answer came in a jerky fluttering. "Of course. I—I don't want you—hurt."

"I mean you care as I do! You can't deny it!"

She closed her eyes before the bright, wild triumph that she read in his, and all her senses whirled. What happened next was wrong, she knew, but she could not help herself. She could not stop the rain of his kisses on her face. It was not until his mouth closed on hers in a brutal bruising that her head cleared somewhat. Then she pushed desperately against him and fought free.

"Oh! No—no—!"

But her softly sobbed denial did not deceive him, though he let her go and, himself, stepped back a pace.

"Yes. You care!" he repeated.

And he laughed. The sound of it echoed in her ears long after her pointing finger and whispered command had sent him from her.

"Let me think—I must think—," she said.

* * *

Nigel was right. His invitations did, indeed, put talk of war into the background. There were, of course, those who laughed at his brashness and tore up the carefully worded notes, and announced in no uncertain terms that no one would ever catch them accepting hospitality from an innkeeper. There were others, however, the mammas with homely but marriageable daughters and the papas who wanted to stay on the right side of a man of money, who took a different view. After all, Nigel was settled here amongst them, wasn't he? He had given up the tavern and become a planter, hadn't he? He was personable—handsome—rich. Why not accept him? There were still others who said they might go just to see what the inside of his house looked like.

To all these varying comments Myrtle listened quietly, divulging to no one the fact that neither she and Matt nor her parents had been invited. Actually, Mrs. Avery gave the matter little thought beyond a contemptuous laugh, but Myrtle felt differently, and a few days after the invitations were out she called on Mary.

"I understand your protegé is launchin' himself into society here—or tryin' to," she observed, after greetings had been exchanged.

Mary nodded. She had trained herself to a casual manner when Nigel was mentioned, though thought of him since the time he had taken her in his arms filled her with turmoil and uncertainty. But no one knew that save herself. Except Nigel himself!

"I'm sorry he didn't include you and Matt," she said now, feeling certain this was what Myrtle had come about.

"You knew, then."

"He told me."

Myrtle shrugged. "It doesn't matter. We wouldn't have gone, anyway, of co'se. But since you and he are such good friends, I'd advise you to tell him to call off his party."

"Why?"—sharply.

"Beco'se I'm goin' to give one the same night. And when folks have to choose between his and mine, they'll choose mine." And she raised a hand to stifle a yawn as if the whole subject was boring to her.

Mary was aghast. "Myrtle! You wouldn't!"

"I certainly would."

Mary looked at her sister-in-law, seeing her curled up childishly in a big wing chair. How fragile she looked, and soft—like a bird. Everything about her was soft. Her small, boneless hands, her great shining black eyes, her drawling voice. But she was not soft. She was as hard as a nail. And unforgiving. Had Johnny fallen in love with her softness and her helplessness, as Matt had? If so, both men had been fooled. Myrtle could and always would take care of herself. There was nothing helpless about her at all.

"So you'd best tell him to forget his plans," Myrtle concluded.

Mary felt a black anger rising in her, but she would not let it show.

"It wouldn't do any good to tell him," she said, and then, with her voice trembling in spite of herself, she went on. "Why should you do a thing like that, Myrtle, if it doesn't matter, as you say, and you wouldn't have gone, anyway? Why do such a thing?"

Myrtle's eyes flashed. "It was an insult! That's why. And no innkeeper insults an Avery and gets away with it!"

* * *

The time for Nigel's big affair drew near. Ten days before it was to take place, Myrtle issued her invitations, and the town went wild with excitement.

Everyone was aware what it meant. And everyone who had accepted—or contemplated accepting—Nigel's hospitality quickly reshaped their plans. Mary, taking the pulse of Charles-Town, grew more and more troubled, and at last hesitatingly turned to Alec.

"Shall I warn Nigel?" she asked him. "I really don't know what to do! Shall I warn him?"

"Do you think it would do any good?"

Reluctantly Mary shook her head. "He's bent on this thing, I'm afraid."

"Aye. He's bent on it."

"I don't think he'd believe me, either. Oh, he knows there'll be refusals. But he's counting on curiosity to get a lot of people there."

"Curiosity might—if Myrtle hadn't turned de'ilish."

"Alec, *we're* going."

"Aye. We're going," he agreed slowly.

"You promise?"

"I promise. And I'll add this. If ever I plan to cut a man's throat, I'll face him when I do it."

Mary's eyes rested on him with warm affection, seeing him just as he was—a man with graying hair and sober face and broad shoulders stooped a little. Seeing the whole, gaunt, dour, steady, strong, kind look of him—and loving him for it all. Could she possibly love him and Nigel, too?

The unexpected question, shooting through her like electricity, startled her. Was she mad? What was she thinking of? She was married to Alec! How could she possibly love anyone else? Or—was it love she felt for her husband? Had it ever been love? Wasn't love more like the breath-taking excitement and fear that Nigel stirred in her?

"What are you thinking about, Mary?"

She gave a tiny gasp. "Oh! Why—I was wondering how

—how Matt feels about this whole business. He's home now. Has he said?"

He had heard the gasp, and it was a moment before he replied.

"He doesn't care. To him 'tis a woman's tempest in a teapot. Besides, more and more Myrtle can do as she pleases about things." He sighed. "She was never the one for him, Mary, and that I knew well." He added, "I doubt he'll even be in town. He's taken to the sea again for his love, and a ship's to sail next week."

There was a silence.

"Myrtle will cut us off her calling list," Mary said presently.

"No. That she will not do, you bein' Matt's sister and Matt havin' the money he has on which she is dependent." He paused. "Mary, Nigel's party means a good deal to you, doesn't it?"

"Oh? Why—yes. Naturally! We've—I've worked so hard to help him get ready, and he's counting on it so much—" She stopped, faintly frightened by Alec's penetrating look.

But he only nodded and said, "Of course."

* * *

Slowly and with an air of defiant confidence that he was far from feeling, Nigel came down the grand stairway in his great hall. He was wearing a suit of pink taffeta with silver-laced buttonholes and the sheerest Machlin lace at wrist and throat. On his legs were white silk stockings and on his feet silver-buckled shoes, while his black hair was covered tonight with an elaborately clubbed white tie-wig that made his face and eyes seem darker than ever.

Below him his house servants in their white-and-yellow

livery stood at their designated posts, their ebony faces solemn with their importance. They fitted into the picture well, Nigel thought, and his glance swept from the hall with its scarlet silken rug and scarlet hangings to the drawing room where he could see gold drapes and a delicate Aubusson carpet of beige and pastel blue and pale rose, and furniture covered in gold satin striped with thin lines of the same blue and rose.

He reached the bottom step just as a horseman clattered up to the verandah, and he waited tensely while Scipio stepped forward to receive on a silver salver the missive handed to him at the open door.

"Bring it here!"

"Yassuh."

Nigel tore it apart and read the first few words.

"Mr. and Mrs. William Henry Drayton regret that a previous engagement—"

Smothering an exclamation, he tossed it back onto the silver plate and then strode past the servant into the night.

The April air was cool and sweet. In the soft darkness of the sky hung a slender silver crescent of moon, while around it a few stars pricked out. It was light enough for him to see the white curve of his hard-packed oyster-shelled driveway, and the clipped even lawns stretching down to the river. On the lawn halfway to the little summer house a great wooden platform had been built beneath a group of trees festooned with hundreds of glimmering paper lanterns. Here musicians had already taken their places and could be heard tuning up their instruments.

Nigel raised his hands, cupping them about his mouth, and shouted an order to them from the verandah. "Play!"

The fiddles responded at once. Presently the entire band was heard—bugles, fifes and drums, sounding a martial air. It was to this accompaniment that the first coach appeared far down the drive, bringing the first guests. Who would they be? Eagerly Nigel went forward to greet them and could hardly suppress his surprise when Mary, wrapped in a white velvet cape, stepped out—alone.

She faced him and spoke breathlessly, her eyes dark with excitement and at the same time wide with her secret fear. For him—and for herself, too, because of her temerity in thus venturing here unescorted.

"Alec was delayed. I waited—but he didn't come and I didn't know how long—and I was afraid—I mean I knew—"

She was floundering badly before his bold, bright gaze and her own dreadful certainty of what lay ahead for him. It was that, really, which had impelled her. Nigel must not be left to face his failure alone. He must not think that she, too, had deserted him. Pulling herself together, she turned to her coachman.

"Julius! You are to go straight back to the wharves and find Mr. MacDonald. Find him! Tell him you have already brought me here and that I'm expecting him to follow me at once."

"Yes, ma'am."

Julius cracked his whip. The coach lumbered about and went back down the avenue. Out on the lawn the musicians continued playing, but it seemed to Mary that Nigel must hear, above the instruments, the sound of her own loudly beating heart.

"I don't know what can have kept Alec so long. He knew I wanted to come early so we could show him the house before the others arrived. I suppose a ship came in."

She moved forward ahead of Nigel, away from his black eyes that had never once left her face, to the edge of the verandah.

"Oh, Nigel! What a beauty spot this is! You've done—marvelously."

He came up behind her and put his hands on her shoulders. The hands were possessive, and quickly she slipped from them.

"That's exactly what you mustn't do," she told him quietly.

His voice held a slight roughness of emotion boiling up. "What else am I to do when you are so lovely—and come here alone?"

"But Alec *is* coming! He promised!"

She stood there in her turquoise-brocaded silk gown bathed in moonlight and mystery. Was it true what she was saying, Nigel wondered? Had Alec really been detained at his office? Or had he, too, like so many others, been unwilling to appear here and she had dared to defy him? The thought was a heady one, yet not unbelievable. She had never punished him for his kisses that time. Still he must not lose his head until he was certain. He held out an arm to her.

"Shall we walk a bit?" he asked.

They moved along slowly in time to the music wafted over the lawn. Through moonlight and shadow they paced, slowly, decorously, both striving to hide the wild turmoil within them.

"Why are you trembling?" he asked abruptly.

"I'm not."

"You are. I can feel you. What are you frightened of? Me? Or Alec?"

She stopped and faced him, her hand dropping from his arm. "Nigel, tell me truly. Have—have you heard from many people? About coming, I mean."

"Too many."

"You—I don't understand."

"It seems a good many have a previous engagement."

She nodded. His next words were a bitter explosion.

"But my invitations were out long before Myrtle's! Blast her soul! Blast it, I say!"

"I know. It's—I'll never forgive her for this, Nigel."

He said, through his teeth, "Nor will I." Then, recovering, he shrugged. "Well, it's early still."

"Yes. It's early."

"No doubt many aren't bothering to reply. They'll just—appear."

"No doubt." Mary tried to sound casual and convincing. "Is there anything I can do before they come? Anything you want me to check on?"

"Well, you might just take a look around."

They went inside. In the great hall Scipio bowed low before her.

"Ladies upstairs, please, Mis't'ess. De rose room on de right."

"Thank you." Mary smiled at Nigel. "I'll just take my cape up. I won't be a moment."

But she lingered up there, fussing with her hair, making talk with the two young black servant girls who hovered about her in yellow dresses and white aprons, listening for the sound of the coach bringing Alec, her hands growing colder and colder as the minutes passed and no coach came—and no other guests. Suddenly the door was flung open and Nigel stood there, his black brows frowning.

"Come!" he said peremptorily. His voice a trifle thick, his face flushed. He has been drinking, Mary thought. All this waiting—and nobody coming—he has been drinking. And the fear that had been in her heart ever since she had so boldly set out by herself now filled all of her. If only Alec would come! Whatever was keeping him?

But she went forward smilingly, crushing down her fear, making bright talk so that Nigel would not guess how she felt. And she slipped her arm through his and led him out of the room toward the stairs. Down they went, past the little group of silent musicians on the landing where the two stairways met, and on down to the Great Hall. There the sight of all that waiting splendor and the vast, empty rooms stretching out on either side, and the servants like statues in their places—all waiting—waiting—turned her almost sick with nervousness.

"I can't think why Alec isn't here by now," she was saying, when Nigel pulled her through the front door and out into the deep shadows of the porch.

"Don't pretend any longer! You're through with Alec. Else why did you come here without him? You're mine. Mine!" And he drew her roughly close against him.

In his arms she felt the April night whirling, the stars spinning, the moon vanishing, and there was only blackness where there had been beauty a moment before.

Blackness—and madness. Not the kind of madness she had known with Nick ages ago. This was different. There had been a sweetness in delirium then, a wonder on his part that checked greed, but in this there was only a savage, ruthless hunger that filled her with terror. And the thought pierced through her that Nigel had always filled her with terror ever since she had known him. Even before she heard the sound of a coach approaching she struggled to break away. Nigel turned toward the driveway with a muttered curse while Mary, shivering, flattened herself against a shutter trying to regain her composure.

It was Alec. Alec, out of the coach before it halted. He was still in his street clothes, his gray hair rumpled, and his eyes went past Nigel as if he had not seen him.

"Mary?" he called.

She stepped from the shadows, pale but radiant in her relief. He strode to her and laid his hands heavily on her shoulders.

"Why did you do this?"

She raised her eyes to meet his. They held an apology, an entreaty, and a humble, joyous welcome.

"You were late. But you had promised, and I knew you would come."

His glance searched hers. Then he drew a deep breath and turned to Nigel.

"I'm sorry, Nigel. A ship was to sail tonight, and there was a delay getting the cargo loaded. There was a brawl, and several men were knocked up. Matt was hurt, too. Not badly," he added quickly to Mary. "But I couldn't get away. Everything was in confusion. Yet Matt was bound to sail anyway—"

He broke off, aware suddenly that the musicians were playing to an empty lawn, that the verandah held no one but themselves, that there was no movement in the rooms within the house.

"I seem not to be too late, after all," he finished.

Nigel's laugh was not good to hear. "No. Not too late," he said. Not late enough, he was thinking, and so thinking, he spoke the words aloud.

"Just what do you mean by that?" Alec demanded.

Mary stepped between the two men and put a hand on the arm of each. "Let us show Alec your house, Nigel, now that he's here."

The three went inside where Mary somehow managed to keep up a casual chatter as Nigel led them around. It was she who called up to the musicians on the landing to play some soft music. It was she who pointed out to Alec the long plank tables set up in the dining room and spread with white cloths on which—now—was a staggering array of food.

"Boned turkeys!" she murmured. "And game pies! And jellied terrapin! And just look at those sculptured sweetmeats, Alec! Did you ever see such an outlay? It's all too beautiful to touch." She smiled and shook her head at the dusky servants who hovered ready and eager to pass crystal glasses and vintage wines, while Nigel's countenance grew ever darker as the minutes slipped away.

Never in her life would Mary forget that hour: the Negroes, their eyes beginning to roll in startled wonder and uneasiness as no other guests appeared; the musicians, whipped on to unremitting efforts by Nigel's fierce gesture of command or his angry shout whenever they paused; Alec, stalking stiffly by her side, a growing pity together with a wary concern holding him quiet; Nigel's eyes flashing dangerously now as he felt the imminence of his social defeat crashing down and everything on which he had staked all he had about to fall in ruins—and her own small voice going desperately on and on and on, while she and Alec sipped the sillery that Nigel had begun to take in great draughts.

"Shall—shall we dance?" she asked at last, without thinking.

"There are only three of us," Alec reminded her quietly. "Not enough for a set, Mary."

It was a situation that was bound to crack sooner or later, and the moment came when the imported caterer approached Nigel and asked in a low voice, "Shall I serve now, sir?"

Nigel whirled on him, hurling his empty glass at the man's feet, where it broke into glittering splinters.

"No! Blast your impudence! We'll not serve until the guests arrive!"

And then he went suddenly stiff and still. The music on the landing stopped, and he did not notice. The slaves in their white and yellow stirred in fright, but still he did not notice. He simply stood there staring into space for a long moment before he came to life with a strange-sounding laugh.

"Guests! Yes! We'll have guests! Scipio! Find Digby! At once!"

Scipio hurried away. Nigel turned to Mary who had fallen silent at last.

"This is what you knew would happen."

"I was afraid—"

"You should have made it clearer."

Alec's arm came about Mary's waist as he answered for her. "And would you have listened, Nigel?"

Before he could reply, Digby, in his riding clothes, arrived. He was a red-bearded, red-headed man of piratical appearance from a Georgia plantation, never meant to be the sailor he had tried to be on one of Matt's ships. Fortunately Alec had rescued him from that life when he had heard of Nigel's need. Now his master gave him a swift look.

"Good. You're ready." And his next words, falling into the tense stillness, came with shocking clarity to Mary's ears. "Ride at once and as fast as you can to the tavern! Tell Jack Murray that he and everyone there is invited to come here! Tell them to come afoot or on horseback or in wagons! I'll pay for their hire! And tell them to bring their women! But above all, tell them to *hurry!*" He turned to Mary again as Digby went off at a lumbering run. "I said I'd have a housewarming, and a housewarming I'll have." He looked up at the musicians on the landing. "Play! Damn you!" He strode out to the verandah and cupped his hands again and roared into the night to the musicians on the wooden platform. "Play! Play! Play!"

Alec said quietly, "We'll go now, Mary."

But Nigel heard and strode back in again and faced them both, his face livid, a little pulse beating high on his forehead.

"No, you'll not go," he said. "You'll stay and meet my friends and eat and drink and be merry with me. I couldn't possibly let you go before that, since you were good enough to honor me with your presence. Besides, you'll not have anything to tell of this party unless you see it through to the end." He laughed harshly. "Shall we wait in the dining room? Don't be afraid," he added. "Myrtle and Matt are the only ones who need be afraid." And there was venom in his voice.

"Nigel—" Mary began. But he took her elbow in a vise-like grip and said only, "Come!"

Clearly, he was not to be refused or trifled with. They went with him, accepted chairs, accepted plates heaped with food, and sat beside him in a terrible silence, watching him as he stared into space with a frightening smile curling his mouth, as he emptied with a steady hand goblet after goblet. All the time their ears were strained to hear distant sounds above the music—and presently they heard them. Galloping hoofbeats, rattling wagons, wild cries, and drunken shouts. Closer and closer these came until, finally, the rabble of Charles-Town, the squalid riff-raff, as well as some of the more respected elements who did not hold themselves too high—the shopkeepers and tanners, the tinkers and tailors—burst in through Nigel's front door under the bewildered and uncertain leadership of a thoroughly frightened Jack Murray.

"Ye sent f'r us to come!" he called defensively.

Nigel nodded and stood up. He waved an arm in a grandiloquent gesture.

"Loose the balloons!" he shouted to his slaves, and immediately dozens that had been tied in the corner of each room bobbed upward to the high ceilings.

For a second the mob hesitated at sight of Alec and Mary who stood behind Nigel at the far end of the room. But their own numbers pushing from the rear and Nigel's forward lurch to welcome them gave them confidence. In they swept, jigging to the music, reaching for the balloons, uproarious and exultant over this totally unexpected event that would last a lifetime in the telling.

Almost at once the scene became bedlam. They swooped upon the food, they snatched at the filled glasses, they pushed and crowded, beating each other on the backs, spilling, throwing discarded bones into the air in an attempt to puncture the floating balloons. Someone started a lusty tuneless singing. Someone else jeered at the sound. An arm came out and a blow was struck. In a trice there was a melée in one corner of the room.

"Now!" said Alec to Mary. "Through the pantries. Do you know the way?"

Mary nodded, and they edged quickly to the door where Digby stood watchfully, his whip in his hand.

"Y'r coach is by the platform outside," he said to Alec from the corner of his mouth. "I told y'r man to wait there f'r ye."

They slipped past him and away. The last thing they saw through a long window at the front was Nigel, his dark face twisted in rage, seizing an end of a tablecloth and jerking it to dump all it held onto the heads of the struggling combatants.

"You'll behave or you'll be thrown out!" he bellowed above the tumult.

He had, indeed, as he had promised he would, given a housewarming such as Charles-Town would never forget.

Chapter 25

THAT RIDE HOME with Alec was one Mary would remember all her life. She sat in her corner of the swaying coach, listening to the sounds of revelry grow fainter and fainter behind her, trying to conceal her shivering as shame of herself, dread of Alec's so-far-unvoiced anger, and remembered horror of Nigel held her in a trembling turmoil.

He spoke at last. "You are cold. Where's your cloak?"

"It—I left it upstairs there."

He took off his own coat and drew her to him and wrapped her in it.

"Thank you," she murmured, and would have retreated to her corner again, but he held her fast. So they rode for another mile or so in silence while she, taut with the conflict within her, sought for words with which to ease the tension.

It was he who found them. "I think, Mary, we need not put ourselves out for Nigel any more in the future."

"We" not *"You."* Bracketing himself with her in this mild censure against the catastrophic error she had made. For it had been hers—all hers—and only she could be blamed. She cried out, then, in a humility that could no longer be born.

"It was my fault, Alec. All of it! I've been a fool. Oh!

I've been such a fool! I—I thought he could be different."

No. She had thought more than that. She had thought she could play two roles. She had tried to escape from the bondage that matrimony and motherhood had put on her into the freedom that had once been hers as a girl. She had let herself imagine she could do it safely. She had persuaded herself that duty and friendship governed her, when these had really been but words to conceal the restless, vain seeking that had held her in its grip. How right Alec had been once, years ago, when he had accused her of liking to play with fire!

Well, now, in the space of one short evening she had discovered her folly. She had been scorched but not burned. And, riding home wrapped in Alec's coat, held close in Alec's arms, the metamorphosis that had been stirring within her throughout the evening took its final form. Without further speech, save for his two short words—"I understand"—she became a woman who had learned, at long last, the difference between gold and dross in a man's heart—and in life. A woman who, clear-eyed and repentant, accepted with gratitude and an unspoken prayer of thanks the hope of happiness that was still hers to take.

"Forgive me—don't despise me," she whispered, at last.

"How could I despise you when I love you, lass?"

"Call me *Mary,* Alec."

"Mary. My beloved. My wife."

Home again at last. Mary came into it as if she were seeing it for the first time, feeling its peace and beauty with a new poignancy. She went about moving a chair here, adjusting a draped curtain there, touching a favorite small figurine. How nearly she had lost all this! she was thinking. What madness had been in her blood? What blindness had nearly closed her eyes? Suddenly she turned to Alec, who had been watching her, and went into his arms with a quick rush.

"Oh, Alec!"

He stroked her hair, waiting.

"Do you really forgive me?"

"What is there to forgive?"

"I've been so—so *stupid!*"

"You've been more young than stupid."

She drew back and looked at him, her face gravely beautiful. "Yes. I've been young. I know that. And yet—"

"Yet what?"

She said softly, "I'm not as young in one way as you think, Alec. In my heart—in my love for you—I'm—I'm fully a woman."

His look searched hers. Did she mean this as it sounded to him?

"I was never quite sure, Mary."

"You can be sure—now."

They went up the stairs together slowly, arms entwined, and that night Mary discovered in Alec's embrace that it held more than a kind and sheltering strength. It held a towering passion, too. And she gave herself up to it recklessly, joyfully, feeling fully absolved, feeling—treasured, as for the first time she both lost herself and found herself in the love of her husband.

* * *

Hours later, after she had heard some of the returning revelers go straggling or galloping by, she was just sinking into sleep when she was startled to wakefulness again by a hoarse shout outside.

"Fire! The town's afire!"

Both she and Alec sprang from bed and went to the

window. Already the sky was lurid with a wicked red light, as tall and terrible flames went leaping across it. Where was it? What was burning? It seemed to be in more than one place, but the worst conflagration was down at the East Battery.

"Matt's ships!" Alec exclaimed, and he hurried into his clothes. Slipping on a dressing gown, Mary went with him down to the front door where, as Alec opened it and stepped out, he tripped over something. It was Mary's cloak which had been left at Nigel's, and now flung up here as if in mad haste by someone—Nigel, of course. In repudiation of her? Or—just prior to a final act of defiance and revenge?

For it was, indeed, as a passerby yelled to them, the East Battery that was burning—all the wharves and the docks and the warehouses and ships, Matt's ships, Matt's warehouses, Matt's docks—and Matt's house, too.

Yes. Matt's house. For now Myrtle and her two girls, followed by a couple of whimpering house servants, came staggering down the street, all of them wrapped in scorched blankets over their night clothes. Myrtle came with only a handful of jewels she had managed to save. She said, in a voice shrill with the terror she had lived through—"Gone! Everythin' gone! Everythin'! This is the doin' of Nigel Fanshaw! I know it! And if I ever lay eyes on him again I'll shoot him dead on sight! I swear I will! But he won't give me that satisfaction. He'll nevah come 'round here again. He'll never dare."

No, he wouldn't dare, Mary thought, as she and Alec tenderly helped them all into the house.

"Take care of them," Alec said then. "Call Columbine to help you, Mary. I must go."

"Go?" Mary looked at him in quick alarm. "Alec! Must you?"

He nodded. "I must see what I can salvage for Matt."

She put a hand on his arm. "Be careful, my darling. Oh, please, promise me to be very careful!"

He nodded again. Then he was gone.

* * *

To Mary the hours that remained before daylight were endless. Myrtle, alternately crying and raging, together with her two frightened, bewildered children, kept her occupied for a while. She helped them to bed, had Columbine bring bowls of hot soup, calmed the little girls with quiet talk, and finally left them all to sleep. But now the twins were awake, and, scrambling into their clothes, insisted upon rushing out to view the excitement.

Alone, Mary paced from window to window, following the path of destruction made by the fire. Somewhere in that awful vivid brightness was Alec. What was he doing? What did he think he could do? And her boys! She hadn't been able to stop them, but they were too young, too irresponsible to judge danger. What if they should be hurt? Oh, God! If anything should happen to them or to Alec!

Suddenly she could endure the waiting no longer and, calling Columbine, she ordered her to sit at the top of the stairs and listen for any sound from Phoebe or from Myrtle and her two children.

"I'll be back soon," she said, and, tossing a cloak about her shoulders, she, too, went out into the street.

Hurrying along to the scene of destruction, she could plainly hear the crash of falling buildings, the rush and roar of flame and wind, the shouts and cries of men and women and their running footsteps as they fled in terror. But she pushed on until the great heat forced her to a stop behind a knot of people who were standing transfixed before a blazing inferno. What were they staring at? What were they waiting for? She edged closer to hear their words and in so doing saw Kim far forward in the front. He was trying to wrench free from a man who was holding him back.

"Lemme go! Lemme go!" the boy was shrieking.

Frantically Mary pushed through and reached his side. "Kim! Stop! What is it? What's the matter? Where's Keith?"

The man answered her. "If Keith's his brother, ma'am, he's in there." And he nodded toward the flames. "His pa saw him go in and he went after him. This un would ha' gone, too, only I caught a holt of him."

Keith—and Alec—in that furnace? Mary's heart stopped, and a low moan burst from her. Then she caught Kim's other hand and held it tight.

"Why did Keith go in?" she asked, not knowing she had spoken, hardly hearing his sobbed reply.

"There was a dog in there, Ma. It was caught under a beam. He went to help it get out."

She made no answer. What answer was there to make? A dog. And Keith had gone to rescue it, acting—as usual—on impulse and without thought. And Alec had gone to rescue Keith. She gripped Kim's hand and waited, her eyes straining into the red glare and billowing smoke, her lips moving in silent prayer.

And then—then—she saw a figure staggering through the enveloping flames: a tall familiar figure bearing a limp, small burden. With a cry she flung herself forward, but before she could reach him Alec collapsed on the ground, his unconscious son in his arms.

* * *

Alec, swathed in bandages and fighting for his life. Keith, bearing burns with an adult fortitude. Myrtle, weeping over the loss of her home and the financial ruin that had come to Matt. Myrtle's two girls—and Phoebe—yes, and Kim, too—nervous and uncertain before the catastrophe of sudden change.

All this Mary met daily for an interminable time, the burdens of pain and loss and anxiety suffered by her household weighty enough on her heart, her own burden of guilt almost unbearable. For was she not the cause of everyone's agony? If she had not been irresponsible and selfish—if she had had a true understanding of integrity—none of this could have happened. She had thought herself absolved in Alec's arms that night, just before the fire. But it had turned out to be not so simple and easy as that. How could she ever atone for her part in bringing on the catastrophe by her encouragement of Nigel? For now she recognized and admitted the truth—about him and about herself.

* * *

Alec and Keith were not the only ones hurt by the fire. Several others were burned and the lives of two elderly watchmen at the warehouses had been lost. Moreover, there was enormous property damage, mostly Matt's property.

"My fault! All my fault!" Mary kept thinking. How could she ever face Matt again? Her brother, who had rescued her from a desperate and hopeless plight years ago, now faced an irreparable financial loss because of her. What a return for his generosity and kindness! What would he say to her? How could he forgive her? With Myrtle's love lost, what had he except his ships and his trade? Alec exonerated her, but would Matt be able to do the same? If he would only come home! If she could only see him, tell him how sorry she was, and win his forgiveness!

* * *

Several weeks later the devastated warehouses and wharves were rubble, and the ruins still smoked. But Keith was almost himself again and Alec, his legs bandaged and one arm in a sling, was moving about with caution. It was then that Matt returned.

Bearded, unkempt from long days at sea and with his black eyes burning in his wind-darkened face, he strode into the house and up to the living room where Alec lay on a couch with Mary close beside him. Myrtle and the children were out in the garden.

Alec got to his feet with difficulty and went to meet him, speaking his name, but Mary could not move. She could only wait in a trembling silence for his wrath to burst about her head.

"So!" Matt exclaimed, and his quick glance ran over Alec's face, gaunt from suffering, and over the arm that hung in a sling. "So! We have to thank our friend Nigel for a great deal, I understand!"

Mary caught at her courage. "Not Nigel more than me, Matt. If I hadn't—Oh, Matt! I feel terrible! *Terrible.* If only there were something I could say or do to make you know! To—to make amends—"

"What are you talking about?"—roughly.

"You. All you've lost. Your docks—your ships—your house. Matt, I can never forgive myself, so how can I ask you to forgive me? But—but I do! I must! You must not hate me! My own brother! I couldn't bear it—"

She stopped, both hands flying to her face to cover her eyes from the look in his. But even as she did so, the blaze she had seen died and in the next moment Matt stooped to her and pulled her hands down and spoke to her with unexpected gentleness.

"You are blaming yourself for everything?"

She nodded. "I insisted on thinking Nigel was changed. If I hadn't—"

"There's no proof 'twas he did it."

"No definite proof—no. But it's certain just the same—from what he said to Alec and me at his party—from the hate he bore you—from his disappearance—and from the fact that it was *your* house and *your* warehouses where the fire started. Oh! If I hadn't tried to build him up into something—"

"Something he never was and never could be," Matt interpolated.

She nodded again. "I was foolish, Matt!"

He dropped her hands, and now there was thunder and lightning in his face again and Mary shrank inwardly. But what was he saying?

"You were foolish? Aye. Perhaps. But Myrtle was, too. She *knew* what Nigel was like. She was never deceived! Yet she risked his fury. I told her not to give that party!"

"You mean you—you blame Myrtle?"

He turned from her abruptly and stepped to a window where he remained with his back to all of them for a long moment.

"No," he said finally, in a strangely low voice. "No. I don't blame Myrtle, either. She was—herself. As you were, Mary. And as Nigel was. And—and as I am."

Mary went to him and put a hand lightly on his shoulder. She did not understand what he was saying or what he meant, but she was troubled. And a little afraid.

"Matt?" she said.

He faced her, an odd expression on his countenance that she had never seen there before. A look of mingled humility and defiance, of fury and frustration, of defeat and relief.

"I wanted certain things in life," he said. "I was bound to have them no matter at what cost. I–I was arrogant. And hard. And proud. Well, I've had them." He paused. "Though it could be," he continued, "that I went after them the wrong way and this is my come-uppance." He paused again. "So be it!"–harshly. "So be it," he repeated. "I've had what I wanted! If I've lost it all now–" He shrugged. "I'm going back to the sea. It's where I belong," he finished.

He started past Mary but stopped beside her and touched her cheek lightly with one finger.

"What I'm saying is–I've brought my troubles on myself, Mary. So keep no more woe in your heart for me."

A wave of comfort swept over Mary. He didn't despise her!

"But Matt!" she exclaimed. "You aren't going *now*. Why! You've just come!"

"I'm going now."

Alec said, "Myrtle's here, Matt."

Matt's laugh was bitter.

"You've–no message for her?" Alec asked.

"I've nothing for her now, not even money. I'm for the sea. And if war comes, that's where I'll do my part. You can tell her that. And tell her I'll be back–some day. Now, good-by."

He clapped Alec's shoulder gently, turned to look at Mary once more, and then moved on to the door.

Mary cried out, "Matt! Don't go, Matt!"

But he was gone.

A few nights later, when Alec and Mary were alone in

their bedroom, Mary spoke Alec's name with such slow thoughtfulness that he turned toward her at once.

"What is it, beloved?"

"Alec, I want to leave Charles-Town. I want to leave it now. At once! Just as soon as you feel fit to travel, I want to go—before any war breaks out, I mean, because then we couldn't."

He came to where she sat before the mirror with her brush in her hand, and they saw each other clearly in the glass. His gray eyes were keen and searching, her brown ones full of love and pleading.

"Mary?" he said questioningly.

She turned, then, and looked directly up at him, speaking fast as she poured out the thoughts that had been in her mind of late.

"Don't you understand? There are so many reasons! Phoebe is one. She—she doesn't belong in this city, Alec. She never has belonged here. She never will. She is like you in her reticence and shyness. She just—she just won't be happy here, especially with Mary-Etta and Lucy. But I can see her at Stockbridge—"

"Stockbridge!"

"Yes. Don't you remember? You said once you'd like to live there. Well, let's go, Alec! Let's go right away. What's to keep us? There's nothing of Matt's for you to care for any more, not even his ledgers. You're free."

"What about Myrtle?" he asked gently.

"Myrtle can stay on here in our house. Why not? Already she's taken it over. Already she's giving orders to my servants. Oh! I don't mind. But—don't you see? We can't go on forever living under the same roof. It just won't work. Besides, this house is the one thing we can give her to make up for what she's lost. It—it would make me feel *good* to know we had given her back a home, Alec."

He nodded slowly.

Mary went on: "She won't feel deserted. I'm sure of that. She will be looked after. She has hosts of friends who will look after her. She has her parents, too. This—Charles-Town—is home to her, Alec. But it's not to me. It has really never been." And her voice shook a little.

He put out a big hand and laid it on her head.

"You have not liked it here? I never guessed. I'm sorry."

"You've made it bearable. But only you. Think, Alec! I came here under false pretenses, and for weeks and months I had to live a lie as Matt's unmarried sister. Then there was Nick and all the agony of that time. And then—Nigel." Her glance never wavered as she went on. "Nigel—and the fire and all that it did to you and Keith and Matt. Nigel was my own mistake," she finished. "All my own. But he so nearly brought ruin to my happiness with you—so nearly brought death itself to my door—that I find it hard to forget him. Yet I must! I *want* to!" Her eyes filled suddenly, and, reaching up, she pulled Alec's good hand down to her face to hold it close against her lips for a moment. "I want to go where he has never been."

"I see."

"Alec," she continued presently. "You and I have a new life to live together if we leave here. It isn't given to everyone to be able to end one chapter and start another as happily as I have done—twice now. But let us live our new life in a new place! A place where no memories will bind us to the past. Oh! Can't we do that? *Can't* we? I have the feeling that if we can—if we do—the best still lies before us."

Alec was silent a moment, his hands on both her shoulders as he looked over her head out of the window to the star-studded sky.

" 'To everything there is a season and a time to every purpose under the heavens,' " he said. "Yes, Mary, I think you may be right. I think 'tis time for us to go."